W9-BDC-508

INDIAN RIVER CO. MAIN LIBRARY
3 2901 00647 8276

THE PILLAGERS

THE PILLAGERS

Max von Kreisler

GUNSMOKE

This hardback edition 2010
by BBC Audiobooks Ltd
by arrangement with
Golden West Literary Agency

ISBN 978 1 408 46244 7

All of the characters in this book are fictitious, and any resemblance to actual persons, living or dead, is purely coincidental.

British Library Cataloguing in Publication Data available.

Printed and bound in Great Britain by
CPI Antony Rowe, Chippenham and Eastbourne

With a rushing click the last of the scattered houses slid past the coach window, leaving the small town of Brainerd behind. In open country now, the sun's light was muffled only slightly by the brown grass rolling gently away from the railroad tracks.

Craig Morgan breathed deeply, feeling a sudden inner expansion as he stared through the cinder-specked window at the forested land ablaze now with autumn color—white pine, birch, maple, Norway pine—and wondered just what drove men like Hugh Stark and his Pine Ring to want to reduce all this to an ugly, stump-littered wasteland. He knew the answer, of course; he simply did not want to accept it.

Greed.

Leaning back, he watched the trees draw slowly up to his view, then zip past, the land rotating in the distance and rudely popping up and out the window. Only the sky remained unchanged, blue with puffy white clouds and a wedge of high-flying geese moving southward across it.

In the luggage rack overhead his suitcase slid noisily back and forth as the once-a-day train from St. Paul to Walker whipped around curves, bucking and rocking over the uneven roadbed, its axles heating up by the minute.

The single coach was nearly empty, most of the passengers having gotten off at Brainerd. A man, visible only by a dark collar and a black Homburg, sat six seats up the same aisle, quietly reading a newspaper. On the other side, farther up, two kids kept changing seats and wrestling over candy bars as they punched and tickled one another, while their exhausted mother dozed fitfully beside them.

That was it.

A tall, deceptively lean man wearing boots, whipcord pants and a brown flannel shirt, Morgan sat with the sun over his shoulder, thinking.

With his business in Washington, D.C., completed, he had looked forward to returning to his logging headquarters in Oregon's Rogue River country where there was still room to breathe and, at night, to stare up at the stars until the swift rush of the Rogue lulled him to sleep.

But at the last minute, Senator Leland, vacationing at Leech Lake on the Chippewa reservation in north central Minnesota, had wired asking him to stop off to discuss "a matter of the greatest importance to both of us." With Leland, a powerful figure in the Senate, able to tie up bills in committee, he had deemed it wise if inconvenient to accept.

Now nearing Walker, a small town on the south shore of Leech Lake, he had already begun to regret his decision. For one thing, he did not trust the senior senator from Minnesota. From his brief contacts with the man, limited to timber legislation, Leland had struck him as an opportunist. So whatever Leland wanted to discuss—he had hinted that it concerned a complaint made by a Chippewa chief named Bog-o-nay-ge-shig against Hugh Stark's Pine Ring—one could almost be certain that the Senator himself stood to gain from the situation. There had to be a profit angle; there always was whenever Indians were involved.

At thirty-five, Craig Morgan had come to recognize, if not to accept, the fact that the Indian everywhere was being victimized by greedy, unscrupulous whites—from reservation traders to the very agents assigned to protect their interests. Even the inspectors, whose job it was to police the agents, frequently were a part of the conspiracy, whitewashing those suspected of cheating their wards.

Timber men, logging contractors like himself, were often as bad as the rest. Many of them, cooperating with the railroads and land-hungry settlers, had slash cut their way through Indian lands across the nation, cheating the tribes out of millions of dollars.

Although the Indians sent delegations to Washington with their complaints, seldom did anything ever come of it. Neither a disinterested Congress nor the Bureau of Indian Affairs, riddled by incompetent political appointees, did more than listen with one ear, make empty promises, and then send the chiefs back to their reservations with a pat on the back.

Nobody really gave a damn, Morgan thought, including the senior senator from Minnesota, James Leland. Whatever Leland's motive, it was not altruism; and he, Morgan, wanted no part in any shady political maneuvering. He would listen to the Senator as a matter of courtesy; but then tomorrow he would be on his way home.

Relaxing, he closed his eyes as the train halted at a small town to take on and discharge freight. And then they were moving again with the weathered depot sliding past his window and out of sight.

Pine City . . . Backus . . . Lothrop . . .

"Ticket!" Dimly, in his mind. "Ticket!" He started, came awake.

A stocky man, wearing a blue conductor's uniform, was bent over the armrest.

Morgan stared at him blankly a moment. "I'm sorry; I guess I must have dozed." He handed the conductor his ticket stub. "How far are we from Walker?"

"We're due there in about five minutes." The conductor waved with two fingers from the bill of his cap and walked on down the aisle.

Craig Morgan straightened, feeling his stiff muscles bend and stretch from their joints, listening to the *click-click* of the wheels over the steel rails and not fooling himself any longer about why he had come.

He knew.

It had been the first time he had ever seen reservation Indians, robbed of their lands and reduced to the status of beggars waiting in line for their monthly handout. A ration which by the time it reached them had already been dipped into by a dozen greedy hands.

They had been Nez Percé, Chief Joseph's people, once proud, brave warriors. They had stared at him with black, unblinking eyes, and he had sensed their apathy, the hopelessness which had slumped their shoulders and darkened their hearts. Even their resentment had been diluted by their unwilling dependence upon the white man.

He had turned away, not wanting them to read the pity in his eyes nor to sense the shame, which flushed his face, that so-called civilized people had done this to them.

It had been a traumatic experience, this sudden awakening to the fact that Indians were people, *human beings,* not savage animals, and it had left its mark upon his conscience. True, he had not been responsible for what had happened to the Nez Percé; he had been only a boy. But he was a man now; and a man stood for something only so long as he was willing to fight for it.

If, as Senator Leland had hinted, Chief Bog-o-nay-ge-shig's people were being cheated by crooked logging contractors—men in his own business—then he could not stay out of it, even though he knew that to side with Indians in a dispute involving white men could mean his own financial ruin.

He had always been a fool when it came to the underdog, he thought ruefully. A weakness which someday just might destroy him. Sitting there, quietly watching the forested landscape flash past his window, he experienced a strong premonition that perhaps that day was already here.

He was standing in the coach's vestibule, suitcase in hand, when the train slowly rolled to a halt beside the Walker depot.

A motley crowd of curious onlookers milled around on the station platform waiting to catch their first glimpse of the descending passengers.

Loggers, with heavily muscled chests and arms, in waist overalls and caulked boots . . . fishermen carrying stringers of walleyed pike for the local markets . . . Chippewas, fine, well-built men in whites' clothing, their hair plaited in thick black braids, holding a brace of fat ducks or balancing a quarter of venison on their shoulders . . . merchants in double-breasted vests and gold watch chains . . . bookkeepers, identifiable by their black sleeve guards and green eye shades . . . a couple of flashily dressed gamblers . . . and women and children of every age and description. All turned out for this high point of their day—the arrival of the once-a-day M & I passenger train from St. Paul.

Quickly, the lone woman passenger and her brood were surrounded by a group of laughing, chattering relatives.

The man in the black Homburg threw Morgan an inquiring glance, then started to move away.

Morgan stood quietly, suitcase in hand, looking about him. There wasn't much to see. Following the shoreline of Leech Lake, a single block of business establishments, along with a few first-class homes. A block inland, a second street with the railroad tracks running between them and the depot, the roundhouse and the turntable in the center. Scattered along the shore of Walker Bay, the whole town probably numbered no more than eight hundred people.

By now, the crowd had begun to disperse. He looked about for Leland but saw no sign of the Senator. Frowning, he shifted the suitcase to his other hand and started walking.

Fifty feet ahead, the man in the black Homburg halted and waited for him to catch up. He wondered why. They had not exchanged a word during the journey from St. Paul.

For the first time, he took a good look at his fellow passenger. Forty, probably, with shrewd, miss-nothing eyes, a wide mouth crooked by a weary cynicism, and a lightweight's body whose off-the-rack suit fit him exactly as an off-the-rack suit could be expected to fit—poorly. A man who obviously cared little for externals and who, from the confident set of his head and shoulders, had no need of them.

As Morgan approached, he smiled, the fine wrinkles at the corners of his eyes deepening and spreading outward like tiny nets.

"Jason Bradshaw," he said. "St. Paul *Globe*. Noticed you aboard the train, but you looked like you had a lot on your mind so I didn't bother you. Anyway, if you don't know the town, the Pameda Hotel's nice and clean and the rates are very reasonable. You're welcome to come along."

"Craig Morgan." Shaking hands. "Timber. Grants Pass, Oregon. And you're right; I don't know the town. So, thanks."

They started walking, heading toward the bay. "Lake Street,"

Bradshaw volunteered, turning west. "The Pameda Hotel's further down."

Lake Street was well graded, Morgan noted, with a boardwalk in good repair and—studying the store signs in passing—with a diversified business section.

Gardner's Drug . . . Bank of Walker . . . Day Light Store . . . Croff's, Meats and Groceries . . . Wright Bros., Dry Goods, Hardware, Boots, Shoes, Flour & Feed . . . City Dray Lines, Jos. Lane, Prop. . . . Brummond's, Clothing, Genl. Merchandise . . . Delury & Felts, Law Offices . . . Quam & Drysdale, Photography . . . Quam's, Gent's Furnishings . . . Pioneer Press . . . Walker Saloon, J. J. Frost, Prop. . . .

"Quite a little town," Morgan said. "It looks prosperous. Is it?"

"For the merchants, yes," Bradshaw replied. "They draw their business from the fishermen—there are a lot of them here—from the logging contractors and their crews, and from the reservation Indians. For the Indians, it's another story. But then it's always another story when your skin is red, black or yellow." He slanted Morgan a humorless smile, his words heavy with irony. "Or haven't you noticed?"

"I've noticed," Morgan said. "And I don't like it."

"Have you ever done anything to try and change it?" Hard, challenging.

"Whenever and wherever I could," Morgan replied. "Starting with my own logging operations. Same wages for the same job; same food and bunkhouse accommodations. A fair price for their own timber. I don't hire Indians, Mr. Bradshaw; I hire people."

In front of the Pameda Hotel, Jason Bradshaw stopped and surveyed Morgan with shrewd, sharp eyes. "Is that why you're here?" he asked. "Because of the trouble brewing between Hugh Stark and the Chippewas?"

"No." The question took Morgan by surprise. "Whatever gave you that idea?"

Sidestepping an answer, Bradshaw pressed the matter. "But you *have* heard about Chief Bog-o-nay-ge-shig's charges against Stark, Meir, the Indian Agent, and O'Connor, the U. S. Marshal who's been raising hell with the Chippewas?"

Bradshaw's bloodhound-who's-picked-up-the-scent eagerness

put Morgan on guard. "I've heard rumors," he admitted, "but that's all."

For a moment, Bradshaw studied him with a narrow-eyed skepticism. Then, shrugging, he led the way into the hotel.

A friendly desk clerk carried on a running conversation with them while they registered.

"Didn't figure to see you again, Mr. Bradshaw," he said. "You back to try and dig up a story on the feud between Marshal O'Connor and Chief Bog-o-nay-ge-shig?"

Bradshaw frowned. "There's a lot more there than shows on the surface. I think someone's using the Marshal to keep the Chippewas stirred up. I intend to find out how and why."

"Heck, Mr. Bradshaw," the clerk replied. "Like I told you the last time you were here, the Marshal's an Indian hater from away back. His parents were killed by Sioux during the New Ulm massacre in 'sixty-two. Now Sioux, Chippewa—don't make no difference to him—he hates them all. Far as he's concerned Bog-o-nay-ge-shig and his Pillagers are a pack of mangy wild dogs that ought to be exterminated."

"And does the town feel the same way?" Morgan asked, looking up from the register.

"Why"—the clerk flushed, his Adam's apple bobbing up and down nervously—"we've got nothing against them. They don't cause any trouble; and Bog—that's what we call him—is a mission-educated family man respected by everyone, Indians and whites alike."

Spinning the register, he glanced at Morgan's signature, looked up quickly and exclaimed, "Why, Senator Leland's been expecting you, Mr. Morgan! As a matter of fact, he reserved the best room in the hotel for you." He lifted a brass key from the rack on the wall and handed it to Morgan.

"Up front, the second floor with a fine view of the bay and Leech Lake. I think you'll find it comfortable. If there's anything else you need just let us know."

"Thank you," Morgan said. "Now where can I find the Senator? I understand he has a vacation cabin around here."

"Yes, sir. A couple of miles southwest of Lake May. But you'll not find him there now. He was in this morning and ordered dinner for the two of you for seven o'clock. By the time you unpack your things, he'll be here. The Senator's a stickler for punctuality."

"Good." Picking up his suitcase, Morgan turned to Jason Bradshaw. "Since I'll be returning to Oregon tomorrow I probably won't see you again. Thanks for your help and good luck with your story."

As he started up the stairs, Bradshaw called, "Wait!" and hurried after him. He turned, one foot on the step, and said, "Yes?"

"Tell me, Mr. Morgan"—the reporter gave him a crooked smile—"why would an Oregon timber man meet with an opportunist like Leland on a Chippewa Indian reservation? Would it have anything to do with Chief Bog-o-nay-ge-shig's charges against Hugh Stark and his Pine Ring? Or Frank Meir, the Indian Agent? Or Mike Davitt, who's peddling whiskey to the Pillagers? What's behind Marshal O'Connor's harassment of Bog-o-nay-ge-shig? And just what is your connection with Senator Leland?"

Under the barrage of questions, Morgan stiffened, the smile going out of his eyes. "Whatever you're trying to prove, Mr. Bradshaw, is no concern of mine," he said coldly. "Nor is my meeting with Senator Leland, for whatever reason, any business of yours. Good day, sir."

"Come off it, Morgan," Bradshaw retorted. "When a U.S. senator meets with an obscure Oregon timber man on a remote Indian reservation where trouble is known to be brewing between the Chippewas and powerful logging interests, the public has the right to know why." His mouth settled into a stubborn line and his voice sharpened with quick resentment. "Something's going on in these woods, Morgan. I spent three days here last week and came up with nothing except rumors. But I can smell a story a country mile. Trouble's brewing out there on Bear Island, Ottertail Point and Sugar Point, where Bog-o-nay-ge-shig lives. Now you can tell me what it's all about, or I can find out the hard way. But one way or the other"—he grinned at Morgan without resentment—"I *will* find out."

Some of Morgan's hostility faded. Confidently aggressive but not offensive, Jason Bradshaw was simply a good reporter trying to come up with a story.

"Do me a favor," he said. "When you find out tell me, and then we'll both know."

He left Bradshaw standing there, red-faced and frustrated, and went upstairs.

His room, comfortably furnished, faced on Lake Street and overlooked Walker Bay. For some moments, he stood at the window, staring thoughtfully out across the blue waters of Leech Lake, thinking about what Jason Bradshaw had said. Why *had* Senator Leland chosen to meet with him on a remote Indian reservation rather than in the nation's capital where they had both been the previous week? Why was the U. S. Marshal harassing a band of apparently peaceful Indians? What was the nature of this trouble between Hugh Stark's Pine Ring and the Pillagers? Knowing men like Stark, he could guess; but then he could be wrong.

A growing unease gripped him. More than ever, he regretted having accepted Leland's invitation. However, there was nothing he could do about it now. He was stuck here until tomorrow morning when the M & I's once-a-day passenger train returned to St. Paul. He might as well make the best of it. Resigned, he turned away from the window and began to unpack his suitcase.

Promptly at seven o'clock, wearing a Western-style whipcord suit and dress boots, he entered the Pameda's dining room.

The Senator was waiting for him.

"Cigar?" the Senator asked.

They had finished dinner and now sat sipping their brandy, while they evaluated one another with the professional expertise of men well versed in human nature.

"Thanks." Craig Morgan selected a panatella from the silver case which Leland offered. Leaning forward, he touched the cigar's tip to the extended match flame. When it was burning evenly, he sat back and studied Leland with a faint frown.

Six feet, just beginning to thicken at the waistline, Leland, with his cloud-white hair and pink-cheeked face, could have passed for an actor or a New Orleans gambler. The outer warmth, the quick-flashing smile, and the never-touched-by-life features suggested the first; the cold, expressionless eyes and the well groomed figure, the second. Few would ever have guessed him to be one of the most powerful men in Congress, although it was rumored that his popularity at home had declined and that he might be voted out of office in the next election.

Drawing gently on his cigar, Morgan watched the blue-gray smoke curl upward toward the ceiling. Then he said, "All right, Senator, suppose we get down to business. You stated in your telegram that a Chippewa chief named Bog-o-nay-ge-shig had made serious charges to the Commissioner of Indian Affairs against Hugh Stark, head of a so-called Pine Ring, and Frank Meir, the Indian Agent. You also indicated that the matter was of great importance to me, as well as to yourself. Now suppose you fill me in on the details, and then explain just how all this affects me."

Leland swished his brandy around the sides of the snifter glass, sipped it and nodded his approval. Then he set the glass down and appraised Morgan with his gambler's eyes.

"Have you ever met Hugh Stark?"

"No," Morgan said, "but I've heard of him. He's involved in logging operations in half a dozen states. He's a slash cutter. You know. Young, green trees, and trees so far from water or a railroad spur he'll never get them out, everything. Unless you people in Congress do something to check him and his kind, we'll have no forests left within another century."

Carefully, the Senator tapped the ash from his cigar; then, hooking one arm over the back of his chair, he said, "Suppose I told you that Stark's ultimate goal is control of the timber industry throughout the nation."

Morgan froze, brandy glass poised in midair. Every business had its ambitious men, and that was all right. But for a man like Hugh Stark, a slash cutter who left nothing behind but ugly, stump-littered wasteland, to gain control of . . .

"How?" he asked sharply, and sensed immediately that Leland had read his thoughts.

"*How?*" The Senator echoed the question, speaking around the cigar in his mouth. "By, as a member of Congress, introducing legislation favoring unrestricted logging operations. By seeking to ease current federal regulations covering dealings with Indians. And by entering into alliances with the railroads to gain control of Indian lands and open them up to settlement."

"As a member of Congress?" Morgan raised a questioning eyebrow. "I didn't even know Stark was in politics."

"I didn't say he was," the Senator countered. "I said that, *as* a member of Congress, he hopes to gain control of both the timber industry and Indian timber lands. His operations here—cheating the Chippewas in a dozen different ways—are only the beginning. He's building up a strong political organization and funding it at the Chippewas' expense."

Inwardly, Morgan relaxed. He had expected something of a more immediate urgency instead of this dramatic, unsubstantiated accusation. He disliked histrionics, and he disliked the way Leland was beating around the bush.

"Frankly, Senator"—his voice was just short of open cynicism —"I can't recall you ever having allied yourself with conservation groups before. Nor, at any time, of having spoken out for Indians' rights. Why this sudden concern now for a small band of Chippewas?"

Under the mane of cloud-white hair, Leland's old man's face lost some of its boyish look. Obviously, he did not like being flushed into the open. He hesitated, surveying Morgan with a measured calculation.

"As I told you, Hugh Stark is a powerful man with political ambitions. It's"—his pink cheeks reddened with anger—"well, it's being rumored that he plans to run against me in the upcoming elections."

"And you could lose?" Morgan prompted.

"I could lose."

"I see." Morgan, thin-lipped, smiled his understanding. "So you figure that if you can link Stark to a scheme to cheat and defraud a bunch of poor, ignorant Indians, you can force his withdrawal from the race. Is that it?"

The Senator shrugged. "I'm a pragmatist, Morgan. If a man goes for my jugular, I'll cut his first, one way or the other. If the truth will serve, so much the better."

"Can you prove that Bog-o-nay-ge-shig's charges against Stark have any basis in fact?"

"No," Leland admitted candidly. "All I know is what the Commissioner of Indian Affairs told me last week in Washington when he asked me to come up here and look into the matter."

"And just what did the Commissioner tell you?"

"That he had received a complaint from Chief Bog-o-nay-ge-shig, leader of a small band of Chippewas called the Pillagers, along with a warning that his people's tempers are beginning to run short. That they're tired of being cheated—at least they say they're being cheated—by Hugh Stark, an organization known as the Pine Ring, which he heads, and by the reservation Agent, a man named Frank Meir."

"You mentioned that in your wire," Morgan said impatiently. "But cheated how?"

"Hell, I'm no timber man," Leland retorted. "I don't know. Something about false scaling, cutting of young timber, the 'dead and down' timber law, arson, unfair wages in the sawmills, and the Agent stealing most of their annuity. You understand all that a lot better than I do."

"Have you talked to Bog-o-nay-ge-shig about this?" Morgan asked.

"No."

"What about Meir, the Indian Agent?"

"No." Leland cleared his throat. "Not yet."

"Well, then"—irritation sharpened Morgan's voice—"just who *have* you talked to?"

The Senator shifted uncomfortably in his chair, a faint frown cutting thin furrows across his unlined face.

"Actually, no one," he admitted. "I thought I'd wait until you arrived and let you talk to them. As I told the Commissioner, Stark and the Indian Agent could be robbing the Chippewas blind and I wouldn't know it. But with your experience and strong stand on conservation and Indians' rights, I was sure you'd be willing to take on the investigation."

For a moment, Morgan looked at Leland, sitting across from him, smugly sure of himself, and thought, *You bastard! You deliberately brought me all the way up here just to help you cut Hugh Stark's political throat.*

It was a galling experience made even more humiliating by the knowledge that the Senator had outmaneuvered him. For as he had sought to use Leland's powerful influence in the Senate to press for conservation and Indians' rights legislation, so had the Senator schemed to use his, Morgan's, knowledge of timber to destroy a threat to his own political career.

"Now, look, Senator," he said, his anger rising. "I've no intention of becoming involved in a matter clearly within the jurisdiction of the Bureau of Indian Affairs. Nor"—he looked Leland straight in the eyes—"to act as your political hatchet man. You've got a hell of a nerve, tricking me all the way up here for that."

"Tricking you!" The barb drew blood and erased Leland's smile. "For the past ten years, you've been hounding every man in Congress, including me, to legislate for conservation and Indians' rights." He pointed the cigar in his hand at Morgan like an accusing finger. "Now when you have a chance to advance the cause of both, you sit there and accuse me of trickery. Mr. Morgan, I call *that* a hell of a nerve!"

It was a case of the pot calling the kettle black, yet there was enough truth in what Leland said to put Morgan on the defensive.

"What do you expect me to do?" he demanded. "Hell, I'm a timber man, not a Pinkerton detective."

"That's exactly why I recommended you to the Commissioner," Leland countered quickly. "Because you *do* know timber. The political appointees sent to check on Bog-o-nay-geshig's complaints in the past didn't know a pine from a maple, much less anything about logging. Stark either bought them off or made fools of them. Now the Pillagers are demanding action." Little furrows of simulated concern appeared around the Senator's eyes and deepened as they ran down his cheeks.

"Personally, I don't believe even the Commissioner realizes the danger inherent in this situation. He seems to have forgotten the Sioux massacre at New Ulm in 'sixty-two. My God, how could anyone ever forget what happened there?"

You hypocritical bastard! Morgan thought. *You just can't help but play the actor, can you?*

"Save the Indian 'scare' for your constituents, Senator," he said coldly. "Your only interest in this situation is to destroy Hugh Stark politically in order to save your own career. And you're trying to play upon my known sympathy for Indians to accomplish it." His high-cheekboned face took on a bitter cast. "If I refuse to go along with you, you will, of course, twist facts and feed the story to the newspapers. The press would make a Roman holiday of it. '*Champion of Indians' Rights All Big Talk, No Fight!*' Do you realize what that would do to me?"

"Offhand"—Leland spoke smugly around the cigar in his mouth—"I'd say that it would cost you whatever support you have in Congress for Indians' rights legislation. Or, for that matter, for any kind of legislation. But then there's no need for that. Go after Stark, the Pine Ring, and the Indian Agent, Meir. That should win you the support of Indians, conservationists, and legitimate timber men throughout the nation."

The seconds ticked away while Morgan sat motionless, eye-impaling the Senator, resenting being backed into a corner, resenting even more the ruthless, smug-faced opportunist who had maneuvered him there.

True, he could tell Leland to go to hell and walk out. But by doing so, he would betray everything in which he believed, as well as those who believed in him.

Or he could compromise. He could agree to investigate Bog-o-nay-ge-shig's charges; then, when he had completed his investigation, he could turn his findings over to the Commissioner for whatever legal action the government might decide to take . . . and *then* walk out.

Professional suicide.

If the evidence proved Hugh Stark guilty of conspiring to cheat and defraud the Chippewas, and his political dreams were smashed, the Pine Ring leader would never stop until he had destroyed the man responsible. And yet . . .

Morgan looked at Leland, sensing the cool, smug confidence behind those bland features, and knew that he would go through with it regardless of the cost. Not because Leland had forced him into it; not out of fear of what the newspapers might do to him; but for the simple reason that he could not forget those once proud Nez Percé warriors staring at him with dull, hopeless eyes while they waited in line for their monthly handout.

Damn fool, he thought. *A ridiculous Don Quixote stupidly tilting with windmills!*

Small comfort to stand among the ruins of the timber business it had taken him fifteen years of hard work to build up, knowing that he was a hero to a small band of Chippewas and a handful of idealists who believed in justice and human dignity. Stupid, yes; but he would do it because he was what he was, and he was damned glad that it was so.

"Well?" Leland asked, a little impatiently. "What do you say?"

Morgan told him, mincing no words. "If you want to capitalize on the situation to strike at Hugh Stark politically, that's your business. But I'll have no part of it. No joint investigation, no advance release of any evidence I may come up with, nothing. You'll get your information from the Commissioner, not from me. One more thing"—his voice was cold, uncompromising—"when you leave for Washington tomorrow, that will be the end of it. I don't want to see or hear from you again. Do we understand one another?"

The Senator's shoulders lost their hostile set. An easy smile spread his lips, showing his fine, white teeth. Used to hard bargaining in smoke-filled caucus rooms, he had anticipated some such compromise and was satisfied. With the Commissioner a good friend of his, he could count on any damning evidence against Stark being leaked to the press as a favor to him. Once the news hit the streets, Hugh Stark's political dream would end in a nightmare.

"Perfectly," he said without rancor. "And since I was sure you wouldn't disappoint me . . ." He drew a couple of letters from his pocket and handed them to Morgan. "Your appointment as a Bureau of Indian Affairs inspector, approved, signed by the Commissioner, and effective as of this date. Also a letter to Frank Meir, the Indian Agent at Onigum, informing him that you have been assigned to investigate Bog-o-nay-ge-shig's charges against him. Incidentally"—a faint irony tinged his words—"should you ever decide to quit the timber business, you could apply for the job on a permanent basis."

Morgan viewed him with open distaste. "That, Senator, is not funny. But then politicians are seldom amusing people; they only think they are. Now since you'll be leaving early in the morning, I suggest you get a good night's sleep. And, Leland, keep away from me in the future."

The half-smoked cigar shredded between Leland's fine white teeth. Shoving back his chair, he rose, gray ash spilling on his fancy vest. For a moment, he stood staring down at Morgan without change of expression.

"You can be a damned difficult man, Mr. Morgan," he said in a flat voice. "I can overlook that. But if you back away from this Chippewa investigation, I'll table every legislative bill that comes before my committee favorable to Oregon timber interests; and I'll make it known to Oregonians that you're responsible. You'll do well to remember that."

He left Morgan sitting there and made his way across the well-filled dining room. Near the door, he paused, spoke briefly to a strikingly vivid, olive-skinned young woman of twenty-seven or twenty-eight and nodded toward the Oregonian. She turned slightly, her startling blue eyes meeting Morgan's with frank interest. A moment later, she rose and left the dining room with Leland.

If nothing else, Morgan thought, the Senator had good taste in women. He wondered what Leland had told her to so obviously arouse her interest. Certainly nothing bad or her smile would not have been so warm.

Now *his* interest was aroused. Who was she? What was her connection with the Senator? Mistress? Political ally? Simply a secretary? Or was she, like him, Morgan, being somehow used to strike back at Stark? If this were true, then she must be a good friend of Bog-o-nay-ge-shig and, hence, no friend of Hugh Stark. A point to remember if he had trouble communicating with the chief.

Trouble? This entire situation suggested nothing but trouble. Ruthless logging contractors . . . a crooked Indian agent . . . an unscrupulous politician . . . an Indian-hating U.S. marshal . . . a small band of Chippewas whose tempers were running short . . . a vivid, strikingly attractive young woman who might be anything . . . and a damned fool named Craig Morgan.

Finishing his drink, he went out into the lobby.

At the desk, Pollock, the clerk, smiled and handed him his key with open curiosity.

"Senator Leland said you'd be staying with us for a week or two, sir. Not that it's any of my business, but surely you and the Senator don't place any stock in Mr. Bradshaw's suspicions.

After all, he's a reporter; it's his job to write sensational stuff. But that doesn't mean it's true."

"No." Morgan eyed him steadily. "But can you prove that it isn't?" Then as the clerk flushed, he asked in a more friendly tone, "Tell me, who was the young woman who just left with the Senator?"

Magically, the clerk's face cleared. "Why, that was Gail Saunders," he said. "She runs a general store her father left her a couple of years ago. She's a very good friend of Bog's. Sells a lot of the Pillagers' handcrafted work for them. Woven flexible wallets, bags, mats, wampum belts, birchbark baskets and blankets. She's even talked some of the big stores in St. Paul into handling a good deal of it, including birchbark canoes by special order."

"Sounds like quite a woman," Morgan replied, smiling. "How long have she and Senator Leland been good friends?"

"They're not." Pollock frowned. "As a matter of fact, she was speaking out openly against his reelection until he suddenly took an interest in Bog and his Pillagers a couple of months ago. Kind of funny about that. The Senator never paid any attention to the Chippewas' complaints before. Could be that Stark plans to run against him in the upcoming elections."

So Leland *was* using Gail Saunders to strike at Stark, Morgan thought. First, Bog-o-nay-ge-shig, then her, and now him, Morgan. How many others had the Senator drawn into his little net?

He looked at Pollock, nodding his understanding. "Then I gather she's no friend of Hugh Stark."

The clerk grinned slyly. "Not so's you could tell it, although Stark's been courting her for almost a year now. She doesn't like the way Stark treats the Pillagers, especially those who work for him. They're always fighting over his double standard. Fifty cents a day for Indians, two dollars a day for whites, and separate bunkhouses and dining halls. The Pillagers claim they're being short-rationed and that the food is not even the same quality." Looking about the lobby to make certain no one was listening, Pollock rested his arms on the counter, his expression furtive, conspiratorial.

"And I hear, too, that Gail and Stark's daughter, Elaine, don't get along very well. Not hard to understand. Elaine's like her father; she's got her sights set high. She knows what she wants and she's not above using any means to get it."

At the moment, Morgan considered it unwise to ask any further questions. Pollock, although a pleasant man, was a natural gossip. Within twenty-four hours, the whole town would be speculating upon his, Morgan's, connection with Senator Leland, and upon his purpose in Walker. Before that happened, he wanted to talk to the Indian Agent, Frank Meir, and, if possible, with Chief Bog-o-nay-ge-shig. With the authority to conduct an investigation now in his pocket, he was eager to get on with it. His own logging operations in Oregon needed his personal attention.

"Well, I think I'd better turn in." He had laid down his key; now he picked it up and nodded to Pollock. "I've got a busy day ahead of me tomorrow. Good night."

As he turned toward the stairs, he bumped into Jason Bradshaw, leaning against the counter just behind him.

"So the Senator talked you into staying." The *Globe* reporter smiled amiably. "Want to tell me about it?"

Keeping a tight rein on his temper, Morgan said evenly, "Mr. Bradshaw, where I come from a man's business is his own affair; and anyone who meddles in it is likely to get his head blown off. Newspaper reporters are no exception."

Still smiling, Jason Bradshaw pushed away from the counter. "If you're threatening me," he retorted, "you're wasting your time. I'll not be frightened by you, nor Leland, nor whatever it is that's going on out there on the lake. If you're here to help the Pillagers, I'm with you all the way. But if you're mixed up with Leland in some scheme to further cheat them then watch out for your scalp because I'll be after it. And, Morgan, never underestimate the power of the press."

Studying the lightweight figure, confidently aggressive despite the shapeless suit and the out-of-character Homburg, Morgan could not help but respect the man. Whatever else he might be, Jason Bradshaw was a fighter, a hard-nosed reporter totally dedicated to his profession. You couldn't buy him off; you couldn't scare him off; the only way you could get rid of him would be to kill him. A step which Hugh Stark might not hesitate to take if Bradshaw started digging too deeply into his affairs.

Bradshaw? Hell, the same thing could happen to him, Craig Morgan. If what Senator Leland told him was true, he was up against a ruthless, powerful man with political ambitions and influential friends. Assuming Bog-o-nay-ge-shig's charges were true, Hugh Stark wasn't going to permit a temporary Bureau of Indian Affairs inspector to dig up the evidence that could destroy him.

In addition, there was the Indian Agent, Meir, and Mike Davitt, the reservation whiskey peddler, to contend with. Meir, he knew nothing about. As for Mike Davitt, he knew all he needed to know. Moonshiners began spilling lawmen's blood by the time they were fifteen.

Only a fool would have taken on such an assignment alone; yet both he and Bradshaw, for different reasons, had done just that.

Thoughtfully, he regarded the reporter with an altered interest. Smart, determined, a no-back-down fighter with an intuitive nose for chicanery, and with the power of the press behind him. Add to that his, Morgan's, own knowledge of logging and of Indians and . . . *Why not?*

"All right." He threw a quick glance toward the clerk, busy now at the other end of the counter, then continued in a low voice. "I'll lay it on the line. Not because of your damned cock-of-the-walk arrogance, but because the two of us, working together, may have a chance to get at the bottom of this mess without being killed."

Bradshaw's face took on its bloodhound-who's-just-picked-up-a-scent expression. "That dangerous, huh?" he said. "Go on."

"Leland's after Stark's political scalp," Morgan informed him. "It seems that Stark's planning to run against him in the upcoming election; and that the Senator's not sure he can beat him at the polls. He'd hoped to use me to prove that Stark is acting in collusion with Frank Meir, the Indian Agent, to cheat and defraud the Indians in a dozen different ways, including . . ."

". . . Green timber, false scaling, arson, defrauding them of a part of their annuity, moonshiners keeping the young men drunk and troublesome, the U. S. Marshal harassing the whole band . . ." Bradshaw gestured impatiently with one hand. "I know all about that. What I want to know is what you told Leland."

"That I'd do what I could to help Bog-o-nay-ge-shig," Morgan replied. "But that I'd have no part in his political fight with Stark. That whatever evidence I might turn up against Stark, he would have to get from the Commissioner of Indian Affairs, not from me."

"What did he say to that?"

For the first time, Morgan smiled—a smile that deepened the weather lines of his face and accentuated its underlying humanness.

"He said that it was all right with him. And then he handed me a political appointment as a Bureau of Indian Affairs inspector, signed by the Commissioner, authorizing me to look into Bog-o-nay-ge-shig's charges."

"Sly bastard!" The way Bradshaw said it colored the word with added insult. "He knows the Commissioner has no more use for Stark than he does—and that given the chance, the Commissioner will be happy to barbecue Stark."

A troubled look darkened Morgan's face. "Do you think there's anything to Bog-o-nay-ge-shig's charges?"

Bradshaw's shoulders lifted in a wordless shrug. "Bog-o-nay-ge-shig's a smart man. If he says his people are being cheated, then they're being cheated." He shot Morgan an inquiring glance. "Where do you intend to start?"

"I'm going over to the Agency tomorrow," Morgan said, "and talk with Frank Meir. After that, I want to see Bog-o-nay-ge-shig if I can find him. From there, I'll play it by ear. Keep in contact. If anything comes up, I'll let you know."

For a moment, Jason Bradshaw stood observing him with cool, still suspicious eyes. Then, apparently satisfied, Bradshaw nodded agreement and started up the stairs. Morgan paused, smiled good night to Pollock, the desk clerk, then followed the reporter.

On the upper landing, Bradshaw stopped, his face suddenly grave. "You're going up against a dangerous man, Morgan," he said quietly. "Don't make mistakes. They could get you killed." Turning away, he walked down the hall, the Homburg tipped aggressively over one eye, the shapeless suit giving him the impression of extra pounds which he did not have.

Sobered by Bradshaw's words, Morgan let himself into his room, undressed, and stood at the window overlooking Leech Lake, thinking. What, he wondered, would happen out there on those islands if Chief Bog-o-nay-ge-shig's charges against Stark, the Pine Ring, and the Indian Agent, Meir, could not be proved?

Only a couple of hours ago, he had accused Senator Leland of trying to raise an "Indian scare." Now, staring out across the moonlit lake, he was no longer sure of that. Even though it had been almost thirty-six years since the New Ulm massacre, and twenty-one years since Crazy Horse—accompanied by Red Cloud, Little-Big Man, Little Hawk, He Dog, Old Hawk, and Big Road—had led his people out of the Black Hills near Camp Robinson and offered his left hand to Lieutenant W. P. Clark, sent out to escort him into camp, saying, "Friend, I shake with this hand because my heart is on this side; I want this peace to last forever." Then He Dog had put his scalp shirt on the Lieutenant to show that the war was over.

Craig Morgan had been fourteen years old at the time. Yet closing his eyes now, he could still hear his father, Sergeant Jim Morgan, U. S. Cavalry, who had served under General Crook during the Yellowstone and Big Horn expeditions against the Sioux, talking about it with a cold, savage ferocity.

"The damn red bastards came windin' out of the hills, eleven hundred of 'em, *singing*, by God, tryin' to make it look like a victory march 'stead of the surrender it was! We oughta given 'em a taste of the same medicine Custer gave Black Kettle at the Washita. And what Colonel Chivington—you know I served with Chivington?—gave to the bastards at Sand Creek. Old men, women, children. Didn't make no difference.

"See that hooped scalp on the wall with the long hair? Squaw. Twenty, maybe. Eight, eight an' a half months pregnant. She tried to run. I shot her in the chest an' lifted her hair while she was still screamin'. Then I shot her again, sliced open her belly, yanked out the kid and bashed its brains out against a rock. Like the Colonel said, a nit grows up to be a louse. Damned pretty hair for a squaw, ain't it?"

Twenty-one years, Craig Morgan thought, *and it still made him sick.* Yet remembering brought it all out in the open—the real reason he had been fighting for Indians' rights ever since he had become a man. Not just because of those Nez Percé on the reservation. No, it went much deeper than that.

Damned pretty hair for a squaw, ain't it?

He was wearing a hair shirt of repentance for his father's crimes. Even though Apaches, not Cheyennes, had exacted from Sergeant Jim Morgan, serving with General Crook in Arizona Territory in '83, fitting justice for those crimes. Capturing him on patrol, they had spread-eagled the Sergeant naked on the sand, cut off his eyelids, tied a piece of wet rawhide around his neck, slit open his belly and filled it with *cholla* cactus, and then sat in a circle around him, laughing and drinking *tiswin* while he screamed his life away.

Holed up in the rocks three hundred yards distant, the rest of the patrol later reported that he had taken a long time to die. Not until just before sunset did the screaming stop. An hour later, under cover of darkness, the patrol had slipped away and made it back to camp.

Bucking timber in Oregon, Craig Morgan had heard about it six months later. For a trooper whom he had never met, he would have felt compassion. But for the man who had been his father, he felt nothing. Within a day, the man was forgotten, but not his crimes.

Now, moving away from the window, Morgan could not help but wonder if the sins of the father were not, indeed, visited upon the son. Certainly his own conscience had driven him into a situation which might well cost him his own life.

Yet as he slipped under the covers and let sleep take over, his last thought was not of the Pillagers, nor of Hugh Stark and his Pine Ring, nor even of the danger into which he was walking, but of Gail Saunders' startling blue eyes smiling at him across the Pameda's crowded dining room.

A light, chill wind blew in off the lake as Morgan walked down the deserted street through the pre-dawn silence. Here and there a light shone weakly through a frosted windowpane, and the smell of stove wood rose above the town. In another half hour, Walker would be bustling with morning activity. Already fishing boats were putting out from the dock, heading for open water.

By the time Morgan reached the floating dock further down, the two birchbark canoes he had seen there the previous evening were already tiny specks in the distance.

Retracing his steps, he halted beside a boat at the west end of the dock. A man wearing a sweater and a watch cap was just getting ready to cast off his mooring line. Spotting Morgan, he paused, balancing to the gentle rock of the boat.

"Morning," he said. "You looking for someone?"

"I just missed them." Morgan nodded toward the distant canoes. "I was hoping to hire one of them to take me over to the Agency." He hesitated, then said, "I don't suppose you'd be willing to. I'd pay, of course."

In the faint light, he could feel the man's eyes resting on him in a quick-building judgment. "You're Morgan, the timber man from Oregon, aren't you?"

"Yes." Surprised. "How did you know?"

"Everybody knows," the fisherman said. "All right. Come aboard. It's only about three miles. I'll take you over and then head out through the Narrows."

"Thanks." Morgan waited until the boat swung against the dock, then jumped onto the deck.

Casting off his line, the fisherman hoisted sail and, as the wind caught the canvas, set a course across the bay. Morgan remained silent, listening to the faint swish of the bow cutting through the water and to the creak of the boat's rigging. Not until the heavily forested shoreline fell behind them did the fisherman speak again.

"I'm Jean Baptiste Chardin," he said. "I was born in these woods, and my father before me. My great-grandfather, Louis Pierre Chardin, was a *voyageur*, a boatman and trapper with the Mackenzie Company. My great-grandmother was a full-blood Cree; my maternal grandmother was a Yellow Knife; and my mother was half English. I figure that makes me a part of this land."

He turned a dark-skinned, aquiline face toward Morgan with an inquiring glance. "So you're here to help Bog-o-nay-ge-shig and his Pillagers. It's time someone listened to him."

"Did Pollock at the Pameda Hotel tell you that?" Quick irritation sharpened Morgan's voice. "Or was it that *Globe* reporter, Jason Bradshaw?"

"Neither one." Chardin smiled. "I figured it out for myself. Saw you having supper with Senator Leland last night. Now everyone knows that with elections coming up, the Senator's taken a sudden interest in Bog-o-nay-ge-shig's charges against Hugh Stark. So when he spoke to Gail Saunders, and I saw her smile at you . . . Well, I just put two and two together."

"And whose idea was it for you to hang around the dock this morning and take me over to the Agency?" Morgan asked. "Yours or hers?"

"Gail seemed pretty sure you'd want to go there."

"Why should she want to help me?"

Chardin shrugged. "She's Bog's friend, a good friend to all the Chippewas."

"And you?"

The fisherman looked him straight in the eyes. "Does a man betray a part of his heritage just to satisfy the whole? Bog-o-nay-ge-shig is a chief; he is also my friend. Besides, as I said, I am a part of this land, and this land is a part of me."

For a moment, Morgan lapsed into a thoughtful silence. Clearly, Bog-o-nay-ge-shig had staunch allies in Jason Bradshaw, Gail Saunders and Jean Chardin. But could they be counted on to help in his, Morgan's, investigation? Bradshaw, yes; he had already made his mind up to that. As for the others, he could only wait and see.

By now, they were running before a stiff breeze, the boat heeling until the starboard gunnel was almost awash. For Morgan, it was a relaxing experience. He stared out across the blue waters of the lake and, without turning his head, said, "We have lakes in Oregon, too, but not so many as here. How big is Leech Lake?"

Chardin lifted his shoulders. "Around six hundred and forty miles of shoreline. Almost thirty miles across to Sugar Point where Bog lives. A mile less to Bear Island. From Ottertail Point to the furthest point in Sucker Bay twenty-five miles. Average depth is about twenty feet. Bear Island's three and a half miles long, about a mile wide. There's several other islands but none of them as big. Pelican, Goose and Submarine, only Submarine's actually nothing but submerged rocks just below the surface."

"Where do most of the Chippewas live?" Morgan asked.

"Around the east and north shores, on Ottertail Point, Sugar Point, and on the islands. Bog's people mostly live on Bear Island."

"Tell me about Bog-o-nay-ge-shig," Morgan said. "What is he like? I mean, what kind of man is he?"

Altering course to bring the boat to a new heading, Chardin eased off on the wheel and turned a steady glance on Morgan. "If you mean is he a liar, a troublemaker, forget it. Bog's a family man, a hard worker with a lot of pride and self-respect. Except for Stark, Meir, and that bastard, Marshal O'Connor, I can't think of anyone who doesn't like and respect him." Chardin spun the wheel to take advantage of a quartering breeze. "I can tell you something else. He's also a fighter. If the government doesn't do something about their grievances this time . . ." He shook his head, a somber expression clouding his sharply planed face.

"You think there could be trouble?" Morgan questioned. "Senator Leland hinted at that possibility."

"I've got no use for Leland," Chardin said bluntly, "but, for once, I think he's right. The Pillagers are a peaceful people, yet there's a limit to what they will put up with. Yes, I think there could be trouble." His eyes rested on Morgan with a sudden cool challenge.

"Now, Mr. Morgan, I think it's time you answered a few questions. Gail Saunders says she's heard of you and of how you've stood up for Indians' rights all your life. She's ready to back your investigation all the way. I'd like to think she's right. Is she, Mr. Morgan? Are you really here to help Bog, or just to make headlines for Leland?"

An ingrained caution slowed Morgan's reply. Could Chardin have been planted at the dock by Hugh Stark or Frank Meir to try and pump him for information? Quickly, he rejected the idea. He felt an instinctive warmth for Jean Chardin that, so far, he did not share with Jason Bradshaw. In a crisis, Bradshaw's first concern would be for his story; whereas in Chardin he sensed a deeper loyalty, a genuine concern for Bog-o-nay-ge-shig and his people. A blood tie which was stronger than the white man's blood in his veins.

"She's right." He drew a deep breath, exhaled slowly. "I'm not here to gather headlines for Leland, although that's what Leland had in mind when he asked me to come to Walker. I'm a temporary Bureau of Indian Affairs inspector, assigned to investigate Bog-o-nay-ge-shig's charges against Hugh Stark, the Pine Ring, Meir, the Indian Agent, and U. S. Marshal Richard O'Connor. Also, to check out the activities of a whiskey peddler named Mike Davitt. If you are a friend of Gail Saunders and the chief, you'll say nothing of this to anyone. Not even them. Let me do that."

Without taking his eyes off the lake, Chardin offered his hand. "Then do it soon," he said, "because I have a feeling that time's running out."

They did not speak again until they rounded the point and Chardin brought the boat alongside the Agency dock. Then as Morgan reached for his wallet, Chardin shook his head impatiently. "You help; I help." He waited until Morgan had stepped ashore then called after him, "I'll wait and take you back."

"What about your fishing?" Morgan asked.

Chardin shrugged. "The pike can wait. There are bigger fish to catch right now."

A faint frown wrinkled Morgan's forehead. "What is your interest in the catch, aside from helping the Pillagers? There is one, you know."

Imperceptibly, Chardin's aquiline features altered, hardening until the bone structure stood forth in bold, sharp planes and the lips thinned to an invisible line.

"It's a personal matter," he said shortly. "I don't want to talk about it." Then as suddenly as it had come, his dark mood was gone, and he was smiling at Morgan with a good-natured ease. "Like I told you, I'm a friend of Gail Saunders; and Gail is a friend of Bog's; and I'm half Indian, and, well, that sort of makes their enemies my enemies."

Morgan measured him with a long, steady look, nodded, and walked toward the Onigum Agency.

Set back in a clearing a hundred yards from shore, the Agency differed but little from other agencies Morgan had visited over the years in Oregon, Washington, Arizona Territory, the Dakotas and Colorado. A large frame building, obviously administrative headquarters, flying the colors from a white pine flag staff. A small two-room cabin, identified by a hanging sign as the U. S. Land Office. Next to it, the trading post where the Indians could buy, sell and barter for shoddy, overpriced merchandise. Some seventy-five yards behind and to the left, a very large structure that would be the warehouse.

Further back, at the eastern edge of the clearing, a schoolhouse. And not far away, a steepled, white frame church topped with a gilded cross that gleamed brightly in the early morning light. A hospital, and, scattered here and there, several dozen small houses for those who lived and worked at the Agency.

Not until he stepped off the dock and headed for the Agent's office did Morgan notice the two birchbark canoes drawn up on the shore. He frowned, wondering what the Chippewas were doing here instead of out on the lake, fishing. Or if they were sawmill hands, why they weren't on the job. Irritated, he thrust the thought aside.

Just outside the Agent's office, he paused, hearing the sound of angry voices within. Quietly, he opened the door and stepped into the plainly furnished room. Unnoticed, he swept the group with a quick glance. The black-moustached man seated at the battered desk, his face dark with anger . . . the two Chippewas, drunk, dirty, and shouting vociferously . . . the crumpled bills on the floor.

Suddenly, the man behind the desk looked up and saw him standing there, and his eyes, black as the heavy moustache and the short, coarse hair, flashed with a quick aggressiveness. Without turning, the Agent spoke sharply to the Indians in Ojibway and jerked a thumb toward the door.

One of them, a short, powerful man with a broken nose and a V-shaped scar on his right cheek, slammed his fist on the desk and cried in broken English, "No more, Meir! No more!"

Followed by his companion, he brushed past Morgan and staggered across the clearing. Launching their canoes, the pair paddled an erratic course eastward.

"Damned drunken bastards!" Angrily, Meir jammed a stubby bulldog pipe between his teeth, struck a match and cold-eyed Morgan over the flame. "Do you make a habit of eavesdropping?"

"The door was open," Morgan replied evenly. "And I don't speak Ojibway."

Flicking out the match, Meir tossed it into the wastebasket beside the desk. He drew gently on the pipe, measuring Morgan in silence, probing, testing, seeking to force the Oregonian to speak first.

And in that moment, Morgan realized just how badly every one—Senator Leland, Bradshaw, the desk clerk, Pollock—had underestimated Frank Meir. Six feet, one hundred ninety pounds, wearing khaki shirt and pants and a Colt .45 in a plain holster at his hip, Meir was no weak political appointee, as he had half expected, but one of the old breed of Indian agents who had served on reservations all over the West before ending up here. Still untamed by eastern law and order, Frank Meir was a dangerous man to cross. *A damned dangerous man.*

It was Meir who finally broke the silence. Evidently sensing Morgan's thought, he removed the pipe from his mouth, showed good but faintly yellowed teeth in a humorless smile, and said, "Well, what did you expect, Morgan . . . a flat-chested, pasty-faced clerk?"

"More or less," Morgan admitted. "How did you learn my name? From those Chippewas who just left?"

"I knew who you were before you reached Walker."

"Do you mind telling me how?"

"I mind," Meir retorted. "Maybe people in Oregon go for that Indian rights talk of yours, but this isn't Oregon. We don't like people like you coming up here to cause trouble for us. If you start poking your nose into my business, or Hugh Stark's, you're likely to get yourself killed."

"Are you threatening me?" Softly.

"No." Meir jerked the pipe from his mouth and aimed the stem at Morgan like a gun barrel. "I'm *telling* you. And if you are smart, you'll listen. Leland's not interested in Bog and his Pillagers. He's after Stark's political scalp. And mine because he figures it's the way to get at Stark."

"Is it?" Morgan asked calmly.

The Agent's eyes met his in open challenge. "Isn't that what Leland brought you here to find out?"

"Leland is a cheap opportunist," Morgan said. "I turned him down. Told him to use his own political hatchet."

"You turned him . . ." Quick suspicion sharpened Meir's tone. "Then why are you here?"

Morgan hooked up a chair and sat down. Tossing the Commissioner's letter on the desk, he leaned back and watched the Agent's jaw ridge putty white as he scanned it.

"That mission-educated bastard's a born troublemaker." Anger twisted Meir's face into an ugly mask. "If he's not complaining about one thing, he's complaining about another. All this talk about false scaling, arson, dead and down timber, cutting of young trees, unequal pay in the sawmills, and *me* stealing part of their annuity—a pack of lies!"

Morgan stared at him. "Why would Bog-o-nay-ge-shig lie about you and Hugh Stark?"

"That's Leland's doing." Meir shifted the pipe to the corner of his mouth. "He's got Bog stirred up just to embarrass Stark during the elections. Well, that's between him and Stark. But when that damned Indian starts to make trouble for me, that is a horse of a different color. By God, I'm fed up with him and his lies!"

Close to fifty, Meir displayed the undisciplined arrogance of a man with but little use for the new breed that was inexorably replacing him. Yet beneath that hot blanket of emotion, Morgan sensed a calculating mind that knew exactly what it was doing at all times.

"Lies?" He stared steadily at the Agent. "Then you deny Bog-o-nay-ge-shig's charges against you?"

"Hell, yes, I deny them!" Meir snapped. "I've never robbed the Pillagers of a single dollar. Or conspired with Hugh Stark to cheat them in any way, form, or fashion."

"What about this whiskey peddler, Mike Davitt?" Morgan asked. "From what I've heard you haven't done a very good job of keeping him off the reservation."

"Put the blame for that where it belongs—on Bog!" Meir shot back, his temper mounting. "I warned Davitt half a dozen times to keep his moonshiners away from the reservation. When he didn't, I notified O'Connor, the U. S. Marshal for the area. In the past year, O'Connor, his chief deputy, 'Colonel' Sheehan, and several deputies have made more than fifty arrests, including three of Davitt, himself. But when the cases come up for trial not one damned Pillager will testify for the prosecution. *Not one!* And whenever O'Connor arrests a Pillager as a material witness, Bog screams that they are being harassed. Harassed, hell!" A vicious note thickened his voice.

"You remember what happened to Tatanka Yotanka, Sitting Bull, six or seven years ago, when that Paiute Wovoka got the tribes all worked up with that Ghost Dance nonsense of his? The government was scared that Sitting Bull might leave the Red Cloud Agency reservation and join the movement. So they sent a detail of Indian police under Lieutenant Bull to arrest him. When Tatanka Yotanka and some of his people decided he wasn't going to go, the shooting started. It ended with Sitting Bull dead, killed by Red Tomahawk, one of the Indian police. Well, now, Bog's asking for the same thing. And if he's not careful, he's going to get it. O'Connor's just hunting an excuse to kill him."

"If O'Connor doesn't stop harassing the Chippewas," Morgan replied grimly, "*he* may be the one to get it. I gather Bog-o-nay-ge-shig hates him as much as he hates Bog."

"O'Connor won't stop." Meir spoke through his teeth, pipe anchored firmly between them. That pipe was as much a part of him, Morgan thought, as the heavy black moustache and the plain, walnut grips Colt at his hip. "Either they'll start cooperating or he'll make them wish they had."

"A real Indian-hater, huh?"

"He's got reason to be. Parents murdered and scalped by Sioux at New Ulm in 'sixty-two, leaving him a three-year-old orphan to be passed from one relative to another until he was fourteen. Then kicked out on his own."

"That was thirty-six years ago," Morgan pointed out. "And by Sioux, not Chippewas."

A dull flush rose to the Agent's cheeks. "An Indian's an Indian," he said. "Thirty years, three hundred years, he's not going to change. He's a savage who'll always walk with his toes turned in."

"You'd be out of a job without him."

"I may be out of a job *because* of him." Suddenly, the pipe turned into a gun barrel again. "Look, Morgan, I've got work to do. Take my advice and go back to Oregon where you belong and let Minnesota take care of its own Indian troubles. Otherwise, you could end up in a pine box."

"Maybe." Rising, Morgan moved toward the door. "And then again, *you* could end up in prison." In the doorway, he paused and said coldly, "I'll be in touch. The next time, I'll want to see your books. Have them ready."

"You go to hell!" Tobacco spilled from Meir's pipe, burning tiny holes in his shirt as he came to his feet, sending his chair crashing over backward. "If the Commissioner wants to come up here, I'll talk to him. But I'll have nothing to do with an Indian-loving bastard like you. Now, get out!"

Not bothering to answer, Morgan stepped outside, almost colliding with a big, handsome man about to enter. With a curt nod, he kept going.

Chardin already had the boat's bow swung around and the sail up. He gave Morgan a questioning glance. "Sugar Point?"

Undecided, Morgan hesitated. So far, save for Meir, all his information had been secondhand. It was time he talked to those others actively involved—Bog-o-nay-ge-shig, Stark, O'Connor, Mike Davitt, and perhaps Elaine Stark. But first he wanted to meet Gail Saunders. Being Bog-o-nay-ge-shig's friend, she should be able to brief him on the overall situation.

"You want to go to Sugar Point?" Chardin's voice interrupted his thoughts.

"No, not today." He jumped aboard. "I'd like to talk to your friend Gail Saunders first."

Using an oar, Chardin shoved away from the dock; then, as the wind caught the canvas, he stowed the oar and took over the wheel.

"She was hoping you'd do that," he said, "before jumping to the wrong conclusions."

Seated on the tiny hatch cover, Morgan laid his elbows on his knees and relaxed as the small craft headed back across the bay. He felt a certain relief now that he had committed himself to an all-out investigation. It was something he had not wanted to do, but which conscience had dictated. Meir's open threats had only strengthened his decision.

"Well," Chardin turned a curious face toward him, "what did Meir have to say?"

"He warned me that if I started poking around, I could get killed. As a matter of fact, he practically guaranteed it."

The fisherman's eyes rested on him in shrewd appraisal. "What do you intend to do?"

"Do?" Morgan sat up, frowning. "Why, what I agreed to do when I accepted this assignment. Check out Bog-o-nay-ge-shig's charges and then go home."

A silence settled over them with the only sound the swish of the water and the creak of the rigging. Suddenly, Morgan remembered the big, handsome man he had almost bumped into outside Meir's office. He had intended to ask Chardin about that but had forgotten. He asked him now.

"Why, that was Hugh Stark." Chardin stared at him blankly. "I thought you knew. You can bet he knew who you were. Two to one, he was there to warn Meir to be on guard. And if he knows, you can be pretty sure that O'Connor and Mike Davitt will know by dark. The Marshal's over at Stark's place every evening courting his daughter, Elaine. And Davitt's got spies in town all the time to keep track of the Marshal. That's why it's hard for O'Connor to make arrests; Davitt always knows when a raid's coming. Anyway, they'll learn about you before the night's out."

"Probably," Morgan agreed, and lapsed into silence. The need for secrecy was past. Even before he had a chance to talk to Bog-o-nay-ge-shig the battle line was clearly drawn. It remained to see how and from where the first move would come.

Despite Meir's threats, he doubted that Stark would resort to open violence at this stage. He would remain in the background as long as possible. Only if things got out of hand would he openly assume command. If tact, diplomacy and no doubt bribery failed, then he would bring the full force of the Pine Ring's prestige, money and political influence to bear upon Craig Morgan and the small logging kingdom it had taken him fifteen years to build up.

Some of the bright sunshine went out of the morning for Morgan. He knew of other men who, for one reason or another, had chosen to stand up and fight Hugh Stark. Men of courage, character and intelligence. Stark had destroyed them all. If the Pine Ring leader, threatened with exposure, should decide to strike at him . . .

Suddenly, the incongruity of his reasoning drove home to him. Here he was, sitting in a small boat sailing peacefully across a beautiful lake, and foreseeing his own destruction at the hands of a man whom he had never met—and had only seen for a single brief moment at the Agency headquarters! A man whom, with no other evidence than the unsubstantiated charges of a Chippewa chief and an election-scared U.S. senator, he had already condemned as guilty.

Watching the timbered shoreline of Walker Bay loom up ahead, he realized the need to talk to Gail Saunders as soon as possible. At this stage, he was like a man walking in the dark, not knowing exactly what he was fighting, what to watch out for, nor from what direction danger might come. Hopefully, Gail Saunders might be able to supply some of the answers.

As Chardin brought the boat alongside the dock, Morgan stuffed a ten-dollar bill in the fisherman's pocket. "Look, you have to live," he said. "Besides, I'll be needing you again tomorrow, and I'll not use you without pay."

Before Chardin could protest, he was gone, walking toward the center of town with long, easy strides.

"Hey!" Chardin shouted. "You want me to introduce you to Gail Saunders?"

"No, thanks," Morgan called over his shoulder. "I'll introduce myself."

Unconsciously, he quickened his pace. Ever since that moment in the Pameda Hotel's dining room, he had looked forward to meeting the woman behind those startling blue eyes.

He had just come abreast of Quam's Photography when he heard the first shot, dull, muffled, followed almost immediately by a second, from down the street.

An Indian burst out of Saunders' Mercantile, his dark face twisted with pain. Blood flowed down his leg and filled his moccasin, so that when he ran he left crimson footprints on the boardwalk.

Ten feet from Quam's, he stumbled and fell heavily on his side. He lay there, staring up at Morgan without expression, making no sound save for the broken rush of air through his clenched teeth. As Morgan bent over him, a bullet splintered the boardwalk a foot away.

"Keep away from there!"

Slowly, Morgan straightened. A big man, so big that his shoulders all but filled the doorway, stepped out of Saunders' Mercantile, a pistol in his hand. Sun bounced off the U. S. Marshal's badge on his shirt front. He scowled at Morgan, the corners of his mouth pulled down in an ugly, arrogant expression.

"Get out of the way."

Morgan looked at the gun in the Marshal's hand, down at the wounded Chippewa, then at Gail Saunders standing behind and to one side of O'Connor, and, finally, around him at the people filling store doorways and gathered in small groups up and down the street. His mouth thinned. He set his feet firmly on the boardwalk.

"That badge, Marshal, doesn't give you the right to go around shooting unarmed Indians just because you hate them."

"Unarmed, hell!" O'Connor's eyes shone like quicksilver. "The bastard tried to knife me in the store."

"That's a lie!" Gail Saunders circled until she faced him. "Shab-on-day-sh-king was talking to me when you came in and began cursing him and knocking him around. When he drew his knife in self-defense, you tried to kill him. You would have, too, if I hadn't knocked your gun aside."

"He ought to be killed," O'Connor retorted angrily. "He's a troublemaker, just like Bog. Always complaining about not being paid the same wages as white sawmill hands, when he's not even worth the fifty cents a day Stark pays him. The lazy dog!"

"And, of course"—Gail Saunders' voice was laced with sarcasm—"there's no such thing as a lazy white man!"

"The laziest white man in the world could work that Indian into the ground," O'Connor shot back. "Now shut your mouth and get back into that store where you belong." Stepping from beneath the wooden awning, he walked toward Morgan. The sound of his breathing carried clearly in the silence.

"And you—" he said. "I'm taking this man into custody. Interfere and I'll kill you for obstructing justice."

"Don't try and bluff me, O'Connor," Morgan retorted. "Maybe you can get away with harassing peaceful Indians; but you're not fool enough to kill an unarmed white man." He stepped away from the wounded Chippewa.

"Go ahead and make your arrest. Since he's a ward of the federal government you have that authority. But before you take him anywhere, you'd better have his leg looked after." Then as O'Connor hesitated, he pressed his advantage. "If that Indian comes to trial, I'll testify that you tried to kill him when he was wounded and unarmed. And I'm sure that Miss Saunders will be willing to swear under oath that you, not he, attempted premeditated murder in her store. You'd be wise to drop the matter, Marshal, before it gets out of hand."

"Sir"—Gail Saunders' voice reached out, clear and firm—"nothing would give me more pleasure than to help put that . . . that *animal* behind bars!"

The blood rushed from O'Connor's face. "You bitch!" he said softly. "You damned Indian-loving bitch! You ought to be run out of town." He glared around him like a bull being tormented by picadors. "You and this . . ." His quicksilver eyes flicked back to Morgan. "Who the hell are you anyway?"

Cautiously, Morgan relaxed. He had been in very real danger and knew it. But behind the Marshal's angry outburst, he sensed a frustrated retreat.

"My name"—he leveled a cold look upon O'Connor—"is Craig Morgan."

A guarded expression replaced the rage on O'Connor's face. "So you're the man Leland brought up here to cause us trouble. It seems you're not wasting any time."

"I've no connection with Senator Leland," Morgan countered. "And I'm not here to cause trouble. I'm here as a Bureau of Indian Affairs inspector to investigate charges brought against you, Hugh Stark, and the Indian Agent, Frank Meir, by Chief Bog-o-nay-ge-shig. You seem determined to convict yourself. Now make your arrest. Or get out of the way so we can take this man to a doctor before he bleeds to death."

He felt O'Connor's hate reach out for him, so intense that it was almost a physical thing. Then with a savage motion, the Marshal holstered his gun and, showing Morgan his back, strode past the little groups of men and women in the street, looking neither to right nor left; and sensing the dark passion in him, no one dared speak or laugh. Not until he turned into the Walker Saloon at the end of the street did the tension break. Then, like puppets brought to life, people burst into an excited buzz of conversation.

Several men moved forward to help Gail Saunders, on her knees now beside the wounded Chippewa. By the time Morgan reached her, she had already applied a borrowed belt tourniquet around Shab-on-day-sh-king's thigh and stopped the bleeding.

"Do you have a doctor in town?" Morgan asked.

She lifted her head, her long blue-black hair sweeping down her back; and at close range the impact of those startling blue eyes left Morgan strangely shaken.

"Dr. E. C. Lindley," she said. "He has an office in his home on the outskirts of town. We can take Shab-on-day-sh-king there in the back of my delivery wagon. It will save time and also be easier on him." She motioned to a bespectacled, middle-aged man wearing a white shirt and dark tie.

"Mr. Allison, will you bring a blanket from the store, please. Spread it on the wagon bed. Then you and Tom"—she nodded to a husky youth, evidently the delivery boy—"can put Shab-on-day-sh-king in the back. When you're ready, call me. I'll take Tom with me. You stay here and tend the store."

Rising, she stood smiling at Morgan, so close that he could smell the clean, natural fragrance of her hair and sense the vitality that seemed to permeate her entire being. She was much taller than he had first thought, five feet eight, maybe, with a full, generous mouth and an excellent figure.

A lot of woman, he thought. *Attractive, financially secure, independent, too much so for most men. But not for . . .*

"Would you like for me to go with you?" he asked. "You may need help when you get there."

"Thank you, but you've done enough already," Gail Saunders said. "Dr. E.C. will give us a hand if necessary."

Morgan nodded. "I hope he's good with gunshot wounds. Shab-on-day-sh-king's leg is torn up pretty badly."

Something, a special kind of warmth, softened Gail Saunders' features. "Dr. E.C. is not only a fine doctor," she replied, "he's a fine man, a friend of mine and of the Chippewas. Someday, I'll tell you about him. Like back in Colorado Territory in 'sixty-four, when a thousand Sioux, Cheyennes and Arapahoes attacked an ordnance train he was with and . . ."

"Ready, Miss Gail," the clerk, Allison, called. He had the delivery wagon drawn up in front of the store with Shab-on-day-sh-king aboard and the driver already on the seat.

"Thank you." She started to turn, hesitated, and then just stood there regarding Morgan with a quiet, grave expression. "Mr. Morgan, I don't know quite how to say this without being misunderstood, but"—color rose from her throat to stain her cheeks—"well, you've been a kind of knight in shining armor to me since I was sixteen years old and I first read about your unrelenting fight for Indians' rights. Now to have you turn up here to help Bog-o-nay-ge-shig and his people is like meeting a living legend. My father was a great admirer of yours. I wish he could have lived long enough to . . ."

"Miss Gail," the driver called patiently.

"All right, Tom." Before Morgan could move to assist her, she climbed quickly to the driver seat. From there, she smiled down at him and she was, he thought, not merely attractive but beautiful.

"Mr. Morgan, I'd like to help you in your investigation. If you'll drop by this evening, say, around seven-thirty, perhaps I can clarify the situation here for you. Meanwhile, I want to thank you for defending Shab-on-day-sh-king. That was a brave thing you did. You could have been killed, you know." Then, in a low voice, "You will come?"

"Yes." Morgan nodded, and stepped back as the wagon got under way. Not until it was far down the street did he realize that he had not asked where she lived. He wondered ruefully if she affected every man she met the same way.

By now, Lake Street had returned to normal with people once more going about their business. Only the fast drying prints of Shab-on-day-sh-king's bloody moccasin on the boardwalk in front of Saunders' Mercantile and the man in a shapeless suit and a black Homburg slouched against Quam's Photography remained as witnesses to the violence of a quarter of an hour ago.

Casually, Jason Bradshaw pushed away from the photography shop and sauntered toward Morgan. He stood silently observing the Oregonian with those shrewd, miss-nothing eyes; then tipping the Homburg back, he smiled amiably.

"Want to tell me about it?"

Always the story first, Morgan thought. Not that Jason Bradshaw didn't like people; it was just that his perspective was different. To him, it was the event, not the people who made it that deserved top priority.

"Where in hell were you?" Morgan demanded. "You seem to have a talent for turning up *after* trouble has passed."

Unperturbed, Bradshaw shrugged. "I was there, but you didn't seem to need any help."

"That damn fool, O'Connor, came close to shooting me."

"But he didn't," Bradshaw pointed out. "So why are you so upset?"

It was impossible to ruffle the reporter, Morgan decided. Or to stay angry with him for very long. Still, a trace of irritation lingered in his voice when he replied.

"If you were there, then you saw what happened," he said. "O'Connor definitely meant to kill that Chippewa. At least we now have some proof that Bog-o-nay-ge-shig's charges against the Marshal have a basis in fact." He began walking toward the Pameda Hotel with Bradshaw keeping pace beside him.

"What about your visit to the Agency?" A note of irritation sharpened Bradshaw's words. "What did Meir say when you told him who you were, and why you were there?"

Pausing in front of the Pameda, Morgan turned to the *Globe* reporter, his manner serious. "He warned me that if I started poking around in his and Hugh Stark's business, I could end up dead. He suggested that I go back to Oregon and let Minnesota handle its own Indian troubles."

"Well," Bradshaw remarked dryly, "that's laying it on the line. How did you handle it?"

"I told him to have the Agency's books ready for an audit when I came back. He called me an Indian-loving bastard and told me to get out."

Unbuttoning his coat, Bradshaw thrust his hands into his pockets, rocked back on his heels and pursed his lips. "Are you going through with the audit?"

"I doubt it would do any good," Morgan replied. "He's too smart to get caught with doctored books. If he is embezzling Chippewa funds he'll have receipts for nonexistent supplies, materials, and never-performed administrative services. And if you question those people they'll back him up. It's the old kickback game." His smile was grim. "For the moment, I want Meir to sweat. He's not the kind to panic. But he has no idea of how much I know nor how far I'll go to get at the truth. He'll waste no time working out strategy with Stark on how to deal with me. Threats, violence, bribery . . ."

"Murder." Succinctly.

"Perhaps," Morgan agreed. "Only he'd not call it murder; he'd call it killing. He still thinks 'Dodge City, Abilene, Tucson, Leadville, Hornitos, Fort Laramie,' trail drive towns, tough mining camps and Army outposts where men settled their differences with the gun. He packs a forty-five slung from a full ammunition belt, and you can be sure he knows how to use it."

For once, Jason Bradshaw lost his cynicism. "You make him sound dangerous."

"He *is* dangerous," Morgan warned. "Remember that if you ever clash with him."

"And O'Connor?"

Unconsciously, Morgan's lip curled. "He's a bully hiding behind a badge. However, for that very reason, he also has to be considered dangerous." Troubled, he turned and stared out across the waters of Leech Lake. "The more I think about it, the more I'm inclined to agree with you that someone's using O'Connor to keep the Pillagers stirred up. It *has* to be Stark. But why? He's not only giving Leland political ammunition to shoot him down with; he's risking criminal exposure as well. He stands to lose everything."

"Or," Jason Bradshaw said calmly, "to gain everything."

Morgan's eyebrows shot up in startled reflex. He had been thinking of Stark as simply another get-a-big-piece-of-the-pie grafter with perhaps, as Leland claimed, ambitions of controlling the timber industry. But what Bradshaw was suggesting carried much darker implications.

"Everything?" He stared inquiringly at the reporter. "What, exactly?"

For a moment, Bradshaw concentrated on the toes of his dusty shoes; then he shrugged and glanced up at Morgan with a frustrated expression.

"I don't know," he said frankly. "I've just got a feeling that whatever's brewing out there on that lake—on Sugar Point, Bear Island, Ottertail Point, even here in town—is only the tip of the iceberg. And that if you try to reach the base, Hugh Stark will bring all his wealth, power and political influence to bear against you. If that fails, I'm convinced he'll have you killed."

They stood there in the bright autumn morning staring soberly at one another. Then Jason Bradshaw reverted to his usual tough, objective self. "What's your next move?"

"I'm calling on Gail Saunders tonight," Morgan replied. "She's promised to brief me on the overall situation here. Tomorrow, I'm going over to Sugar Point to talk to Bog-o-nay-ge-shig. If I come up with anything, I'll contact you. Meanwhile, what about you?"

The familiar cynicism, the crooked smile returned to Jason Bradshaw's hollow-cheeked face. "While you're stalking the tiger, I'll circle the jackals—disgruntled employees, men with secret grudges, and those who hate Stark because they're afraid of him. Maybe one of them will dig up some bones for us."

"Us?" About to turn into the hotel, Morgan paused. "Or you?"

Slowly, Bradshaw removed his hands from his hip pockets, buttoned his coat, and when he smiled it was with stiff lips and unfriendly eyes.

"You still don't trust me, do you?"

A faint breeze, autumn-chilled, ruffled Morgan's hair, blowing a few dark strands across his face. He brushed them back and stood there, thinking, feeling Bradshaw's resentment coming at him, not wanting to antagonize the *Globe* reporter, yet not wanting to lie either. Finally, he said what he had to say, quietly, calmly.

"I'll trust you, Bradshaw, when you give me your word that,

no matter what we turn up, you'll hold your story until I okay its release."

"Hell," Bradshaw exploded angrily, "I can't promise anything like that! I'm sitting on what may prove to be the story of the year. If I get scooped on it, I'd lose my job."

The story first, last and always, with the human factor ignored or secondhand.

"And if you wreck my investigation for the sake of a one-day newspaper headline," Morgan said harshly, "you'll leave Hugh Stark, Meir and O'Connor free to continue cheating and harassing peaceful Indians. You do that, by God, and you are no better than they are! In fact, worse, because you're the one who told me that if I was here to help the Pillagers, you'd back me all the way. What kind of man are you, anyhow?"

In that instant, he thought that Bradshaw was going to strike him. Blood ebbed from the reporter's spare-fleshed face; the shoulders inside the ill-fitting suit lifted, squared and, somehow, created an illusion of greater width and depth.

Yet beneath Bradshaw's anger, Morgan sensed the inner conflict within the man. The desire for a sensational news scoop versus a deeply ingrained sense of social justice; the thought flicked through his mind that wasn't this, after all, what life was about? The constant struggle between good and evil within every man?

Slowly, the color returned to Jason Bradshaw's face; the truculent set of his shoulders disappeared. He stared at Morgan with a frustrated what-the-hell's-happening-to-me expression.

"Damn you," he said bitterly. "Why did I have to get mixed up with you anyway?"

"It was your choice," Morgan reminded him. "Not mine."

"And one I regret." Sourly, but without any real sting. "All right. I'll go along with you so long as no other paper scents the story. But with this understanding. We share whatever evidence of criminal conspiracy either of us turns up. And the *Globe* has the exclusive right to run the story twenty-four hours in advance of your report of your findings to the Commissioner of Indian Affairs."

Studying the reporter's uncompromising features, Morgan knew that Bradshaw had gone as far as he was going to go.

Even the temporary suppression of a possible nationwide news scoop was, to Bradshaw, the ultimate compromise.

Yet remembering his own refusal to meet a similar demand by Senator Leland, Morgan hesitated. But then, he reasoned, the Senator's motive had been political assassination, whereas Bradshaw, as a reporter, firmly believed that the public had "the right to know."

"All right." He thrust out his hand. "Exclusive rights to the story before I notify the Commissioner. You understand, though, that Stark and Meir may be innocent of any criminal acts?"

"You don't really believe that, do you?"

"There's always the possibility." Morgan motioned toward the Pameda. "You want to join me for dinner?" Without waiting for an answer, he went inside, with Bradshaw following.

Pollock, the desk clerk, looked up from his mail sorting as they walked into the lobby. "Good morning, gentlemen." His eyes, bright, inquisitive, switched from one to the other. Shoving aside the mail, he rested his arms on the counter top and smiled broadly.

"Well, Mr. Morgan, that was an exciting incident. I mean the way you handled Marshal O'Connor. A brave thing, sir, standing between him and Shab-on-day-sh-king. He'd have killed the Chippewa, for sure. Now you understand why I said he was an Indian hater. And why"—he switched subjects without breaking the flow of words—"when I saw you talking to Miss Gail I knew right away you were planning to . . ."

"Mr. Pollock," Morgan cut in crisply, "I can appreciate your interest; but this is an official investigation concerned with facts, not with idle speculation. I'm sure you understand."

Leaving the embarrassed clerk to his mail sorting, Morgan and Bradshaw went into the dining room. A waitress took their orders and disappeared into the kitchen.

Only then did Morgan become aware that the pleasant buzz of conversation had died away, leaving behind a homogenous silence; a blend of curiosity, unease and—or perhaps he simply imagined it—a trace of fear.

The silence held throughout dinner and followed Morgan and Bradshaw out into the lobby. There they parted, with Bradshaw off on some personal mission of his own, and Morgan electing to relax an hour before any further move.

A still red-faced clerk gave him his key, and he sensed the clerk's mild-mannered resentment directed toward him. By tomorrow he knew that it would be gone. The little man was incapable of any sustained emotion.

At the foot of the stairs, he looked back. Pollock had come from behind the desk and was standing in the doorway peering up and down the street.

Shaking his head, Morgan went upstairs. The Pollocks of the world viewed life vicariously from the safety of countless doorways, experiencing it secondhand from their snug, insulated little "four walls and a roof caves" without ever realizing what they were missing. He didn't know whether he pitied them or despised them, or whether what he felt for them was a combination of both.

In his room he draped his coat over a chair and sat down on the edge of the bed to think. Viewed in retrospect, what was happening to him seemed somehow like a bizarre dream. Only thirty-six hours before, he had been comfortably relaxed in his Pullman compartment while the train rushed through the night bearing him home to Oregon. Then the conductor's knock on the door, a murmured apology, and Senator Leland's telegram thrust into his hand.

Now, eighteen hours after his arrival in Walker, he was deeply involved in an investigation of one of the most powerful timber men in the nation with nothing to gain except the satisfaction of helping a small band of Chippewas.

Whatever Hugh Stark's goal, like Leland he seemed to have drawn others into his net: Meir, the Indian Agent, who was absolutely necessary to his exploitation of the Chippewas; possibly the moonshiner, Mike Davitt; and, finally, U. S. Marshal Richard O'Connor, who used the New Ulm massacre and his lawman's badge as an excuse to harass a conquered people for no other reason than that their skin was red.

If, as Jason Bradshaw suspected, O'Connor's rabid racism was being deliberately fanned by Stark to the point where the Chippewas' tempers were wearing thin, then the Pine Ring leader had to have a deeper, far more reaching objective than simply control of the timber industry.

But what, dammit? What?

Impatiently, Morgan rose and walked over to the window. He stood staring down upon the sunlit street and the people moving leisurely along the boardwalk; and, inexplicably, Senator Leland's warning slipped into his mind.

"I don't believe even the Commissioner realizes the danger inherent in the situation. My God, how could anyone who had ever read about it ever forget what happened at New Ulm!"

At the time, he had rejected it as a melodramatic scare tactic. Now it no longer seemed an absurd improbability. He shivered, not liking to think of what might happen if the heat of Bog-o-nay-ge-shig's anger set off a conflagration among the several thousand Chippewas on the reservation.

As he started to turn away from the window, a candy-striped barber's pole across the way reminded him that he needed a shave and a haircut before calling upon Gail Saunders. Retrieving his coat, he went downstairs. Stepping outside, he crossed the street to the barber shop.

Conscious of the curious stares turned upon him, Morgan took the only empty seat, crossed his legs, and sat back to wait his turn. Silence swallowed all sound for a good ten seconds. Then Joe Pruitt, a small, neat man with a good-natured face and a brown mole on his left cheek, waved a greeting with a loaded lather brush.

"Afternoon." And then added with his usual candor, "We were just talking about you. Half of us were arguing that you were a damn fool for crossing Marshal O'Connor over that Chippewa. And that you were lucky you didn't get your head blown off. The other half, mostly the ladies, claimed you were a hero. And that you were never in any real danger because the Marshal is a bully, a coward and just plain scared of you."

Morgan smiled, an easy smile that relaxed the initial tension created by his entrance. "And which side did you take?"

"Never take sides," the barber said. "I've got my own opinions. You want to know what I think . . ." He paused, the lather brush poised in midair. "For once, I think they're all right. You're a damn fool, a brave man *and* lucky you didn't get your head blown off." He grinned. "I'm Joe Pruitt. I'll get to you as soon as I can."

"Soon as I can" turned out to be an hour and a half.

During that time, Morgan gained a "town's-eye" view of the kettle-on-the-fire situation. Virtually everyone agreed that Bog-o-nay-ge-shig had plenty of room for complaint. That the Indian Agent, Frank Meir, was undoubtedly dipping his fingers into the Chippewas' annuity. That U. S. Marshal Richard O'Connor was a bully whose harassment of the Pillagers was brutal and mostly uncalled for—although some did argue that the Pillagers had brought a good deal of it upon themselves by refusing to testify against the whiskey peddlers. And, finally, that Hugh Stark *might* be guilty of the things of which he was accused.

"Might be," Joe Pruitt clarified, speaking for those present, "means 'probably is'; but you'll not find anyone willing to stand up and swear to it. That doesn't mean people approve of what's going on. It's simply a case of survival. The Pine Ring, which Stark heads, is a big outfit. Its logging crews and sawmill hands spend just about every dollar of their pay right here in Walker. We can't afford to antagonize Stark and risk having him order his crews to take their business to Akeley, Brainerd, or some of the smaller towns. It's, well, it's just not practical."

"Especially," Morgan spaced his words carefully between razor strokes, "over a bunch of Indians with very little money to spend, and no political power with which to fight back. Isn't that what it all adds up to? Greed?"

A steaming hot towel dropped over his face, muffling his words, but not shutting out the smothering silence. Immediately, he regretted his action. It had accomplished nothing except to chill the warmth which these people had offered him.

He blinked his eyes as Joe Pruitt removed the hot towel, dried his face, and raised him to a sitting position. In the suspended silence, the barber splashed on lilac water, used a clean towel to cool the sting, patted on a little talcum powder, and then said evenly:

"Mr. Morgan, most of us are plain, ordinary people who work hard, mind our own business, fight our own battles, and expect others to do the same. No one ever said the world was fair, or that what's going on here is right. But if you've got to blame someone, blame the politicians in Washington." Unpinning the neckcloth, he whisked it away and stepped back. "That will be forty cents." He gave Morgan his change, hesitated, then asked quietly, "You have a family, a wife and children?"

"No."

Pruitt shook his head. "That's your trouble, Mr. Morgan. You've got no responsibilities to keep you busy; so you go around trying to solve other people's problems. And then you get mad because men with families won't jump on your bandwagon like you think they ought to. You can't understand what it's like. I mean worrying about those you love; and how you're going to feed and clothe them, and keep a roof over their heads, and . . . well, you just don't understand."

"Maybe not." Morgan slipped into his coat, opened the door and, pausing, laid a steady glance upon the barber. "But I expect any Chippewa would know far more about it than you do. He lives with it every day of his life. Good day, Mr. Pruitt. Ladies and gentlemen."

Outside, he paused, undecided, in the early afternoon sunshine. One thing was becoming painfully clear. Until he learned to keep his mouth shut, he would do well to keep to himself. By the time news of the incident in the barber shop spread, resentment against him would further mount.

Although he had made many enemies over the years because of his Indians' rights philosophy, never had he made so many, so fast. And all this growing hostility toward an investigation which he had not as yet really begun, he had accomplished in a single day! He had moved too quickly, too soon. It was time to think, to exercise caution and, if possible, to relax.

At Wright Bros. he rented fishing tackle and spent the afternoon working likely spots up and down the forested shoreline, tossing his catch back into the river.

Around five-thirty, he walked back through the gathering dusk, returned the fishing tackle, and then had supper in the Pameda's dining room. Afterward, he changed into a dove gray suit, slipped into a light coat and, after receiving directions to Gail Saunders' home from an almost-friendly-again Pollock, stepped out into the chill night air.

The hands of his gold Hamilton watch showed a quarter past

seven when he left the stable in a rented buggy. Driving west on Lake Street until the last house fell behind and the street merged into a narrow dirt road, he continued under the star sheen for another quarter of a mile. There the road forked, the main branch going straight ahead, the smaller branch swinging right and climbing steeply up a knoll overlooking the lake. Atop the knoll, a light filtered down through the trees.

Taking the hill road, Morgan followed it until it ended in a moonlit clearing at the crest. Here, high above the lake, the wind was stronger and very cold. Morgan wrapped the reins around a small sapling, draped the woolen lap robe over the mare's back, and then walked toward the house.

It was a big house, surrounded on three sides by trees, with a wide, deep porch that offered a sweeping view of the lake, and window shutters that could be closed against the bitter winds. Hung from a raftered beam overhead, a square, glass-sided hurricane lantern swung back and forth in the wind, its warm yellow light fanning out in all directions.

Morgan took a deep breath, and then knocked.

A dog barked somewhere inside, quieting immediately at a soft-spoken word. A moment later, Gail Saunders opened the door and stood silhouetted against the light from within.

"Come in, Mr. Morgan!" Quickly, she drew him into the foyer. "Here, give me your coat." Hanging it on a rack, she turned back to him with a half-amused, half-quizzical expression. "Do you always stare at a woman that way the first time you call on her? Frankly, I don't know whether to feel flattered, insulted, or . . ."

Her voice faded away and she just stood there, the warm glow from the brass-shaded kerosene lamp playing over her hair, the smooth olive skin, and the full, ripe mouth. Suspended from a narrow blue ribbon around her neck, a golden "robin's egg" ball nestled in the hollow of her throat. She wore no other jewelry; she needed none.

Morgan flushed, not knowing quite how to answer. Kneeling in the street beside the wounded Chippewa, she had seemed much slimmer, almost girlish, but now at close range with the fashionable sky-blue dress molding her breasts and hips, she was clearly much a woman—and an attractive, sophisticated one at that.

"I'm sorry," he said awkwardly. "It's just that this afternoon . . . well, frankly, you don't look like the same person."

Her eyes smiled up at him like warm blue crystals. "This afternoon, Mr. Morgan, I was a businesswoman, a plain little wren." The full mouth quirked at the corners. "If the wren's transformation into a bluebird startled you, then I suppose you're entitled to stare. Come."

Slipping her arm through Morgan's, she led him into a comfortably furnished parlor with a tall, slim man standing before an open fireplace staring down into the leaping flames.

"Dr. E.C. . . ."

The physician turned, a smile so transforming his grave features that Morgan experienced the odd feeling that he was seeing the man as he must have looked in his youth, handsome, intense, driven.

Then, suddenly, the illusion was gone. Perhaps because the smile which had created it had withdrawn behind a polite, guarded reserve, a subtle change reflected in the cool, impersonal eyes that observed Morgan from beneath thick, heavy eyebrows.

And in that instant of first confrontation, Craig Morgan understood why Gail Saunders had spoken of Dr. E. C. Lindley with such warmth and admiration. For never had he seen a man's life etched so starkly, so poignantly upon his face, feature by feature, for those with the sensitivity to read it.

The high forehead of the thinker; the deeply lined cheeks; the firm mouth, which could not hide its sensitivity; the fine gray eyes, shadowed by the suffering they had witnessed; the failures that not even the brilliant mind nor the skilled surgeon's hands had been able to avert; the frustration, the sometimes depressing sense of inadequacy, of self-condemnation; the deep-seated resentment against a medical science which did not, could not, provide better diagnostic aids and miracle drugs to save those whom, somehow, he felt should have been saved; the reverence for life, the never-ending, uncompromising battle with death; and the "little death" within him every time he lost.

A shy, lonely man who, out of a sense of self-preservation, threw up a barrier between himself and his patients because there was only so much of their pain, their heartbreak, that he could endure without it shattering him and, along with him, his usefulness as a doctor. A deeply troubled man because he had not found the answer to the unanswerable Question, not realizing that, as a part of the totality of Being, he was the unanswerable Question . . . and its Answer.

It was all there in bone, in muscle, and flesh, and marked by the spirit of the man himself. Morgan read it and understood in that fleeting moment before Gail Saunders repeated, "Dr. E.C., I want you to meet Craig Morgan. Mr. Morgan, my good friend, Dr. E. C. Lindley."

"I've heard a great deal about you, Mr. Morgan," Lindley said, offering his hand. "Much of it from Gail, a great deal more from newspaper articles over the years. Frankly, I like to think of you as a thorn in the side of the national conscience." The cool gray eyes warmed ever so little, and a trace of that warmth crept into his voice as he continued.

"You're a remarkable man, sir, to have risked your life for Shab-on-day-sh-king the way you did. Incidentally, he was very lucky. Another inch and the femoral artery would have been severed. He asked me to thank you for him."

"It was nothing," Morgan replied. "However, I will want a sworn statement from him regarding the incident as soon as possible. Also"—he turned to Gail Saunders—"since you were a witness, Miss Saunders, to what actually took place in the store . . ."

"Please, not yet!" Smiling, Gail Saunders motioned Morgan to a sofa before the fireplace. "Sit down, the two of you. Dr. E.C., your favorite chair. Mr. Morgan, you can sit with me. Now, coffee, wine, a liqueur?"

"Coffee, please," Morgan said, seating himself before the fire.

Lindley nodded. "Coffee will be fine, Gail." Then when she had disappeared into the kitchen, he leaned back, his face serious.

"Gail has told me you're here to investigate Bog-o-nay-ge-shig's charges against Hugh Stark and the others."

"It's a temporary assignment," Morgan explained. "As soon as my investigation is completed I'll be returning to my own logging interests in Oregon."

"I see." The physician measured him with a thoughtful look. "I wonder if you fully understand the true nature of the issues involved here, as well as the very real danger in which you have placed yourself by coming to Walker."

"It would seem that the issues have been clearly defined by the people involved," Morgan replied. "Chief Bog-o-nay-ge-shig, survival; Leland, politics; Stark, ambition; Meir, profit; Marshal O'Connor, racism; Mike Davitt, whiskey peddling; and the town, at least a part of it, a self-serving greed and indifference."

"Bravo, Mr. Morgan!" Gail Saunders said softly from the doorway, where she had stood listening. "And the danger? What about the danger to your life, as well as to your own financial interests?" She set the silver coffee service on a low table beside the sofa, filled china cups and served Morgan and Lindley in turn.

"Now." Seating herself beside Morgan, she searched his face intently, as though seeking answers there rather than in words. "Aren't you concerned about your own personal welfare?"

Cautiously, Morgan tested the coffee, then shrugged. "This is not the first time my life has been threatened, Miss Saunders; nor, I'm sure, will it be the last. However, at thirty-five, I'm still very much alive, and I fully intend to stay that way. As for my business . . ."

Damned pretty hair for a squaw, ain't it?

"When I was seventeen years old, I was bucking timber in Oregon for twelve, fourteen hours a day, six days a week for fifty dollars a month and found. All I owned were the clothes on my back, and a dream. If I should lose everything I own because of this trouble, I would still have the dream, and peace of mind."

He hesitated, not wanting her to think him dramatic, yet, at the same time, compelled to speak frankly. "However, I am not sure that it would be for the reasons you think, justice and human dignity, although I would like to think so."

Gail Saunders leaned toward him, her eyes darkening to a near violet. "You know, Mr. Morgan, you really *are* a knight in shining armor. Don't be embarrassed. I'm a very impulsive, uninhibited creature. You'll simply have to get used to me."

Without taking his eyes off the fire, Dr. E.C. remarked dryly, "I've known her since she was fifteen years old, Mr. Morgan, and I still haven't gotten used to her. She has a child's wisdom, a tomboy's brashness, a woman's cunning, her mother's idealism, her father's shrewdness and a fierce independence that drives most men away." That rare, youthful smile showed itself briefly. "Now that he knows all about you, Gail, I suggest that you get down to the business of why you invited him here."

"I'm sorry." Gail Saunders smiled ruefully. "I just didn't want to plunge right into this mess the minute you arrived. But then Dr. E.C. is right." She settled herself comfortably on the sofa.

"To begin with, what's happening here now is nothing new in itself. For the past nine years, ever since they were forced to cede valuable timber and mineral rights to the federal government in 1889, the Chippewas have been preyed upon by the whites. Because of crooked Indian agents, they have been forced to live off the land. Hunting, fishing, picking berries in season and harvesting wild rice from their canoes. In the old days that would have been enough; but, in a white man's world, it's a hard life. They've also had to sell some of their timber for cash, although not enough to satisfy the logging contractors, who want it all." Her voice sharpened, taking on a thin-edged resentment.

"Hugh Stark, with his Pine Ring, and Frank Meir, the Indian Agent, are the latest and most ruthless of the predators. They're both corrupt, but I think Stark is the worst. As an educated, successful businessman, he doesn't need to cheat and rob the Pillagers the way he's doing. He's got his eyes set on the U. S. Senate and, later, on a Cabinet post. To date, he's been building up his organization with money gained by cheating the Chippewas. But that's a slow process, and he's a man in a hurry. Now he's deliberately trying to stir them up, hoping that the Army will be sent in to put down the uprising." Her lovely face darkened with anger, long restrained.

"You know what's happened in the past when Indians who raised the lance were defeated. They were rounded up and sent to unhealthy climates where most of them soon died. Their lands were taken from them and opened up to settlement, with the railroads and unscrupulous speculators acquiring most of it. Working hand in glove with the railroads, the speculators made fortunes overnight by laying out town sites, often in the middle of nowhere, and then selling lots at exorbitant prices to the hordes of people who poured into the area."

Carefully, she placed her cup and saucer on the table. "Now do you understand what's happening here? Hugh Stark is playing with fire and either doesn't realize it or simply does not care. He wants the Chippewa lands, timber, everything; and he'll go to any lengths to get it, even to setting off an Indian uprising."

Morgan frowned. Again that ominous word, *uprising*. Yet seated beside this beautiful, fashionably dressed young woman in the security of her home, the idea seemed somehow ridiculous. Senator Leland, however, had not thought it ridiculous; and Jean Chardin, who did not like Leland, had agreed with the Senator. Now Gail Saunders, who knew Chief Boy-o-nay-ge-shig better than anyone did, was speaking of it as a definite threat.

"An Indian uprising in eighteen ninety-eight!" Morgan made no attempt to mask his skepticism. "Do you really believe it could come to that?"

Gail shrugged. "Ask Dr. E.C. He's been in their wigwams, their cabins and in the woods when they've been hurt. He knows their mood as well as I do."

"Do you agree with her, Doctor?" Morgan turned to the physician. "Is it really that serious?"

The heavy eyebrows pulled down until they almost met in the center. Then Lindley said carefully, "Right now, I'd say they're angry, frustrated, not quite ready to lash out. But the powder keg's there, just waiting for a spark to set it off. Had O'Connor killed Shab-on-day-sh-king today, I think that might have done it." Crossing his arms, he rested his chin on his chest and studied Morgan over the tops of nonexistent glasses.

"What worries me," he added, frowning, "is that an uprising here could spread spontaneously to the Central Plains. A sort of last desperate attempt to revive the Paiute Wovoka's dream of bringing back the buffalo and all the dead warriors and of driving the white man from the land forever. A pathetic gesture, yes; but it could happen and a lot of people could die."

Unconsciously, Morgan stretched his hands out to the fire, seeking somehow to draw the heat into his suddenly chilled mind. This man, E. C. Lindley, was no hack "Ned Buntline" writer, weaving melodramatic tales from a few distorted facts and an overheated imagination, but a doctor with a trained, analytical perspective. His fears could not be ignored or taken lightly.

He swung his attention back to Gail Saunders. "It seems that you both agree that Stark is deliberately trying to incite a riot," he said. "And that there is a very good chance that he may succeed. Has it ever occurred to either of you that all this might be only a means to a greater end? Jason Bradshaw, a reporter for the St. Paul *Globe*, believes that it's simply the tip of the iceberg, and that what lies beneath the surface is so big that Stark will go to any lengths to achieve it."

Observing Gail Saunders closely, he caught a flicker of surprise behind her eyes and sensed that Bradshaw was not the only one to look behind the obvious. He moved carefully now.

"Because of Stark's personal interest in you, you must have grown to know him quite well. Do you have *any* idea of what could be so important to him that he would risk financial ruin, public disgrace and possibly even imprisonment to attain it?"

A hot coal popped loudly in the silence, sending a shower of tiny red and yellow sparks against the brass fire screen; and then as the flames threw flickering patterns of light and shadow across her face, Gail Saunders' mouth shaped itself into a tight little smile.

"Why, the ultimate dream of many men, Mr. Morgan," she said. "The presidency of the United States."

"The presi—" Morgan stared at her, unbelievingly. "You can't be serious!"

"Oh, but I am," she assured him. "What do you think, Dr. E.C.? You've known Hugh Stark as long as I have."

Linking his hands behind his head, Lindley stared thoughtfully at the fire. "You could very well be right," he conceded. "Stark's never concealed his political ambitions, although he's never stated just how high they went. But if a man aspires to the U. S. Senate and to a Cabinet post, well, why *not* the presidency? There's nothing criminal about that."

"No," Morgan agreed, "except that Hugh Stark is not just any man. His political ambitions threaten the lives and prosperity of half a dozen small towns and could, as you've pointed out, result in another Ghost Dance revival throughout the West." He paused to let the full import of his words sink in, then continued.

"If Miss Saunders is correct, then Stark's plan must be a three-stage one, the Senate, the Cabinet, the presidency, with each stage dependent upon its predecessor for its success. If any one stage fails, then the whole thing collapses. With his bid for stage one, the Senate, currently at stake, Stark can't afford an investigation into Bog-o-nay-ge-shig's charges against him. The publicity, even the suspicion of complicity could ruin him."

"Then you admit," Gail Saunders said, "that there is danger here for you?"

This time Morgan made no attempt to laugh it off. "I'd be a fool to deny it," he replied. "A man with a dream that big, especially a man as ruthless as Hugh Stark, is not going to let anyone stand in his way. If he's using O'Connor . . ."

"He's using him all right," Gail interrupted. "Him, and that whiskey peddler, Mike Davitt, and his own daughter, Elaine. She has O'Connor convinced that he's the greatest U.S. marshal in history. And Davitt's whiskey keeps the young Chippewas drunk and troublesome, giving O'Connor the excuse to abuse and arrest them." Impulsively, she laid her hand over Morgan's in a gesture of concern. "Don't underestimate the man you're dealing with, Mr. Morgan. Beneath that cultured, well-bred exterior, Hugh Stark is a very dangerous person, capable of anything, even murder."

"And Meir?" Morgan asked. "Where does he fit in?"

"Meir?" Gail Saunders' face mirrored her disgust. "Meir is not only embezzling part of the Chippewas' annuity; he's also involved in Stark's illegal activities. Since you've read Bog's complaints to the Commissioner, I'll not go into them. Let's just say that they're true."

"It's not enough to say that they're true," Morgan pointed out. "We have to have evidence that will hold up in a court of law."

For the first time, he brought forth the latent fire in Gail Saunders. She stared at him a moment, nonplussed; then the color flooded her face.

"Mr. Morgan, I don't have to have *legal* proof to know that the Pillagers are being cheated. I see it going on every day.

Hugh even admits that he's not paying them the same wages nor providing them with the same accommodations as he does his white sawmill hands."

"That may be unfair discrimination," Morgan told her, "but it's not a criminal offense. What about the specific charges—false scaling, cutting of young timber, arson, conspiracy, embezzlement—those things?"

"Dammit, Mr. Morgan," Gail Saunders flared, "I thought you came here to help Bog and his people! Instead, all you do is sit there and talk about the law, and legal proof, and—" Her voice broke and she brushed angrily at the quick tears. "Perhaps you'd better leave before I say something I'll regret later."

Realizing that it would be futile to try and reason with her at this time, Morgan rose.

"Perhaps I should," he agreed. "If you want to get in touch with me, I'm staying at the Pameda Hotel. Good night."

She did not answer, but sat curled up on the sofa, her face to the fire and he knew that she was crying. He nodded to Lindley, who had risen and now stood with his back to the fire. "Good night, Doctor."

Following him into the foyer, Dr. E.C. waited until Morgan had slipped into his coat. Then he said quietly, "She's an idealist, Mr. Morgan. Unfortunately, she's cast you in the St. George and the Dragon role; and, at the moment, she can't understand why you don't simply don your shining armor and ride out on your white charger and kill the dragon, Stark, forthwith. Be patient. Try and understand how she feels about you, both as a symbol and as a man, and make allowances for what's happened tonight. Then give her a few days and her common sense will take over." He opened the door and held out his hand.

"Go see Bog-o-nay-ge-shig tomorrow. There's not much he can tell you that Gail and Senator Leland haven't already told you. But it's important that you understand his viewpoint. If I can help, my house is a quarter of a mile farther down the main road. Good night, sir."

"Good night, Doctor."

Outside, the wind blew in strongly from the lake, but the sky was clear with bright stars scattered overhead. Retrieving the lap robe from the mare's back, Morgan climbed into the buggy and drove back to town.

It was nine o'clock when he entered the lobby of the Pameda Hotel. Pollock sat dozing behind the desk. Without waking him, Morgan took his key off the board and went upstairs.

He was tired, angry with himself, and frustrated. Nothing was going right. Not only had he antagonized those whom he had expected to antagonize, but he had also hurt and alienated Gail Saunders. He hoped that Dr. E.C. was right and that her hostility would soon pass. Meanwhile, he could not let thoughts of her interfere with his investigation.

In the morning, he would cross the lake to Bear Island to see Bog-o-nay-ge-shig. He considered taking Jason Bradshaw with him, but decided against it. He could not risk Bradshaw, in his eagerness for a story, angering the chief.

Undressing, he slid between the sheets, blew out the lamp and lay there, inexplicably troubled by the silence that filled the room, spread throughout the hotel, and covered the whole town. And then it came to him with sudden nostalgia what was missing.

The swift rush of the Rogue River sweeping around the bend and past his big, comfortable house back home.

Smiling, he closed his eyes and let memory bring the sound of it into his room and fell asleep.

Awakening at five o'clock in the morning, Morgan dressed, had a hasty breakfast in the deserted dining room, and then headed for the dock.

A sullen Chardin was already there, waiting for him. Obviously, the half-breed had somehow learned of his rift with Gail Saunders the night before and was reacting to it.

Settling himself in the bow, Morgan relaxed as Chardin, with a stiff wind at their backs, sent the boat out through the Narrows at a brisk twelve knots. He had no intention of arguing with the fisherman. Let Chardin think what he wanted.

He concentrated on the lake and on Pelican Island as it came up on their starboard bow and then fell rapidly astern. Gradually, the wind, the creak of the rigging and the rush of water muted in his ears. For what seemed only a moment, he closed his eyes. When he opened them again, Bear Island was three-quarters of a mile astern and Sugar Point lay dead ahead.

Carved out of the timber crowding almost to the water's edge, a twenty-acre clearing fronted the lake with a comfortable log cabin, fish racks, drying sheds and a dock forming a compact whole. A canoe was drawn up on the shore and a man, almost as slim as Morgan, lounged beside it, a rifle in one hand.

Shading his eyes against the sun, Chardin studied the man on the shore with a thoughtful frown. "That's 'Colonel' Sheehan," he said. "Wonder what he's doing here?"

"Sheehan?" Morgan stood up in the bow for a better look. "Who is he?"

Chardin lowered the sail and headed for the landing. "He's O'Connor's chief deputy. No one knows much about him except that he's a loner with a taste for good whiskey and beautiful women. He's polite to the ladies and civil enough to men; but he never shows any other signs of being human. I think even O'Connor's a little afraid of him."

Still watching the man on the shore, Morgan said, "Is he mixed up in all this?"

The fisherman shook his head. "No, but he knows what's going on. He has to."

Suddenly, Sheehan spotted the boat and made for the cabin with long, rapid strides. By the time Chardin brought the craft alongside the dock, the deputy had disappeared inside.

"If O'Connor's with him we may be in for trouble," Chardin said, checking the knife at his hip. "You got a gun?"

"In my suitcase at the hotel." Morgan stepped ashore and waited for the fisherman to join him.

"You better start carrying it," Chardin advised. "This may be Minnesota, eighteen ninety-eight, not the wild West; but to Sheehan and O'Connor that don't mean a damn thing."

It was no idle warning and Morgan knew it. He wished that he had brought the pistol, but it was too late to worry about it now. With Chardin keeping pace beside him, he walked toward the house.

Suddenly, a squaw broke from the cabin and ran toward them, screaming in Ojibway. A moment later, Marshal O'Connor and Sheehan emerged and hustled a stocky, middle-aged Indian toward the dock.

For the first time, Morgan got a look at Chief Bog-o-nay-ge-shig, Hole in the Day, who had, indirectly, involved him in all this trouble. By any standards, the Chippewa chief had to be considered "colorful." Lumberjack waist trousers; wide red suspenders worn over a red, white and black checkered shirt; his head, with his hair braided in a single loose coil worn down his back, adorned with feathers; a necklace of bear and panther claws encircling his muscular neck and a tortoiseshell rattle fastened to a French *voyageur* sash around his waist.

Mission educated, Bog-o-nay-ge-shig had reached a compromise, in dress at least, with the white man. But there was no compromise in the black, defiant eyes that flicked to Morgan, then to Chardin, and back to O'Connor.

Here was a fighting chief, Morgan realized. A man who would take only so much, and no more. Right now, O'Connor, the fool, had him pushed to the ragged edge.

At sight of Morgan, the Marshal pulled up short, his face darkening with anger. "What the hell are you doing here?"

"None of your business," Morgan said curtly. Then speaking directly to Bog-o-nay-ge-shig. "I'm Craig Morgan, an inspector for the Bureau of Indian Affairs. I'd like to talk to you."

"You want to talk to Bog, you'll have to do it in Duluth." O'Connor flashed him a silver-eyed challenge. "He's a material witness in a whiskey peddler's trial. Come on, Sheehan"—he jerked his head toward his chief deputy—"let's get the bastard into the canoe."

"No." Morgan held his ground. "I'd like to talk to him now."

"You go to hell," O'Connor said, and drew his gun. "Sheehan—"

Drifting to the left, Sheehan put himself on Morgan's and Chardin's flank. A handsome man, bearing a faint likeness to the Civil War guerrilla Quantrill, he stood easily, making no move to line up his rifle.

Unarmed and outflanked, Morgan's position was untenable. Yet he masked his chagrin behind an unruffled calm.

"Interfering with an official investigation, Marshal, is not going to put you in a favorable light," he said. "And especially since you're one of the suspect individuals."

The blood rushed, cherry red, to O'Connor's face. "Get out of my way, Morgan. You give this red bastard any ideas of starting trouble and I'll kill him." He nodded to Sheehan. "Let's go."

"*No!*" With an angry cry, Bog-o-nay-ge-shig broke free and backed away. "First, I will talk to this man, Morgan. Then maybe I will—"

O'Connor's left caught him on the jaw, dropping him. "By God, I warned you!" The Marshal whipped up his pistol and fired.

"You fool!" Morgan knocked aside his hand, deflecting the shot. "You crazy damn—"

Without warning, the forest erupted Indians, a hundred and fifty of them, armed with war clubs and repeating rifles.

Sheehan tried unsuccessfully to bring his rifle into play before he was overpowered. O'Connor, wrestling with Morgan, never had a chance. As half a dozen others grabbed Morgan, Chardin cried out sharply, "*No!* He is a friend of the Chippewas!"

In the tense silence, Bog-o-nay-ge-shig got slowly to his feet. He looked at Morgan, then at Chardin. "This is the man who saved Shab-on-day-sh-king's life?"

Chardin nodded. "He is a friend of Indians everywhere. That is why men like O'Connor and Meir hate him. Miss Gail believes in him. Dr. Lindley trusts him."

"And you?" Bog-o-nay-ge-shig asked. "Do you trust him?"

The fisherman gave him an intense look. "He saved Shab-on-day-sh-king's life. He has just saved yours. And you ask me if I trust him. Are those the words of a chief?"

To know that Jean Chardin trusted him came as a relief to Morgan. For beneath Chardin's pleasant exterior lay something wild and dark and chilling, something that was constantly warring against the man's normally peaceful nature. He, Morgan, had no desire to clash with that mysterious alter ego.

"All right." Bog-o-nay-ge-shig swung back to Morgan. "We will talk. But, first, you will see how a 'savage' treats white men who try to kill him. Pugonny-koshig . . ." A brave handed him a tomahawk. For a moment, he stood swinging it back and forth, his black eyes riveted upon the Marshal's face.

O'Connor licked his lips, watching the pendulumlike swing of the tomahawk with a hypnotized-bird fascination. Tiny beads of perspiration glistened on his forehead.

"*Haaaaa!*" Suddenly, Bog-o-nay-ge-shig brought the tomahawk above his head in a threatening gesture.

"*No!*" With a hoarse cry, O'Connor dropped to his knees, covering his head with his hands. "No!"

"*Waugh!*" Handing the tomahawk back to Pugonny-koshig, the chief spat on the ground in front of O'Connor. "An Indian would have laughed in my face and died like a warrior. But you! Get in your canoe and go. Don't come back. The next time my people might kill you."

Slowly, O'Connor pushed to his feet. His pale eyes were rolled back in rage. He had been humiliated before two white men, a half-breed, and a hundred and fifty Indians, all of whom he hated. He swung on Morgan.

"You meddling bastard!" he cried. "If you hadn't interfered, I'd have killed this red nigger and saved the state of Minnesota a lot of trouble." He started toward the canoe landing, stopped, and turned around. "Goddammit, Sheehan, don't just stand there! Let's get going."

Pushing back his hat until the sun laid full across his face, Sheehan fished a cigar from his pocket, carefully bit off the end and, striking a match, touched the flame to the tip. He waited, letting the seconds drag out, looking at O'Connor until the fire touched his fingers. Then flicking the match away, he walked toward the landing, deliberately taking his time. It was a challenge, a gesture of contempt and the ultimate insult before Indians.

O'Connor's color changed from cherry red to putty white; and, watching, Morgan knew that Sheehan would be wise to watch his back in the future. On the other hand, the Marshal's position was now precarious. For if Sheehan decided that he would make a better U.S. marshal, he might well use his gun to make that job immediately available.

Not until the canoe, with O'Connor and Sheehan at the paddles, was well out and headed for Walker did Morgan turn back to the clearing, empty now save for Jean Chardin and Bog-o-nay-ge-shig. The Pillagers had faded into the forest as silently as they had come; but he knew that they were still there.

He walked over to Bog-o-nay-ge-shig, looked him straight in the eyes and said, "I came here in peace. If you don't want my help just say so, and I'll leave. I've got a business in Oregon to run."

It was, in a sense, an ultimatum.

Bog-o-nay-ge-shig took his time answering. Finally, apparently satisfied, he offered his hand, white-man fashion, and said in simple English, "I am glad you come, Mr. Morgan. We do need help. I am glad my friends, Miss Gail, Dr. E.C. and Jean Chardin trust you. That is good. Now, we talk."

Leading the way to the cabin, he sat down cross-legged on the ground in front of it and motioned Morgan to follow suit. Seated thus, the three of them formed a small, rough circle. Subtly, the circle changed the entire atmosphere. Although there was no peace pipe, it was no longer a meeting but a powwow, a council.

Across from Morgan, Bog-o-nay-ge-shig's broad, high-cheekboned face assumed an alien dignity. The white man's checkered shirt and waist overalls and bright red suspenders seemed to fall away, leaving a Chippewa war chief sitting there, naked save for breech clout and moccasins, with the feathers in his braided hair, the bear claw and panther necklace and the tortoiseshell rattle adding a wild, barbaric touch of color.

The sun crept across the clearing but brought no warmth to it. Chardin sat quietly, his face impassive. Morgan waited, knowing that when the Chippewa was ready to talk, he would talk. A jaybird squawked raucously from somewhere among the trees.

Abruptly, Bog-o-nay-ge-shig leaned forward; and when he spoke, his voice betrayed the long festering resentments which he had carried bottled up within him for years.

"I have written many letters to the Commissioner, Mr. Morgan. My chiefs and I have even gone to Washington to ask for justice. We have been treated like children, sent home with a pat on the back by men with big smiles and lies in their hearts. Of our million-dollar annuity more than seven hundred and fifty thousand dollars had been spent to 'look after our interests.' We have been cheated by the Indian agents of most of the rest of our money."

He looked around the clearing, at the cabin, the fish racks, the drying sheds, the maple trees, each with its little birchbark container to catch the sap for the sugar and the maple syrup he loved so well, at the potato patch with its rail fence to keep out the wild pigs. He looked at all these things, and the lines of bitterness around his mouth deepened.

"We are poor, Mr. Morgan; we live hard. We sell some timber for a little money. But this man, Stark, and his people want it all. He hires bad Chippewas to set fires in our timber to scorch it a little; then the Agent, Meir, sells it to him as 'dead and down' timber. He sends his crew in to scale our timber where it lies. He ought to wait until it is out where it can be scaled right. Most of the time, the scales never leave his company offices. He pays my people fifty cents a day in his sawmills and the white workers two dollars. For those who work in the deep woods, the food is not fit for a dog." The wide mouth thinned into an ugly slit and, for the first time, his manner became belligerent.

"My people are angry, fed up with the white man's lies and broken promises. They grumble and make threats. The whiskey peddler, Mike Davitt, keeps the young men stirred up. Then Marshal O'Connor and his deputies threaten and arrest us. We go to Meir and we tell him all this and he does nothing because he is a part of it. Is there *any* white man, Mr. Morgan, including you, who is not a part of it? When will it stop? When the last Indian is dead?"

He lapsed into silence, his mood dark, brooding, and Morgan could feel the hate building up inside him. Even to speak in this moment could be dangerous. Morgan glanced at Jean Chardin. The half-breed frowned and shook his head.

Again, the waiting, with the chill from the ground reaching through to stiffen his muscles; and the sun wheeling slowly across the sky. It must have been this way in the old days, Morgan thought, with long, tense silences and sudden impassioned outbursts.

Fifteen minutes. Half an hour.

With a quick impatience, Bog-o-nay-ge-shig brushed aside his dark mood. The glance he now threw Morgan was challenging, rather than hostile, and his voice was calmer.

"We have complained to the Commissioner before; and he has sent in other inspectors to look into this matter. But nothing ever comes of it. They look, but they do not see. They see, but they do not understand. They are fools. They go back and they say to the Commissioner, 'That Bog is a liar and a troublemaker. Pay no attention to him.' But the smart ones, they know better. Stark pays them money and they cover their eyes and see nothing. Then the Commissioner says, 'They are right. That Bog *is* a liar and a troublemaker.' "

Resting his hands on his crossed knees, he rocked back and forth, his eyes half closed, thinking. When he opened them, he laid it squarely on Morgan.

"Now, *you* come here. It is said you know timber. Gail Saunders, Dr. E.C., even Chardin here tells me that you are a friend of the Indian, of the Pillagers. But I, Bog-o-nay-ge-shig, do not know this to be so. Maybe you are only another fool. Or another crooked white man. Maybe you are both. I will find out sooner or later." A thin-edged warning aimed at Morgan like an arrow.

"Me—I have not lied to you, Mr. Morgan. Where is the proof, you ask? The proof is out there in the deep woods. If you know timber you can find it. But *will* you? Or will you, like the others, sell out to Stark and his Pine Ring? Don't answer, Mr. Morgan; lies come easy to the white man's lips. I warn you; the Pillagers will stand for no more of the white man's greed and cruelty. Unless something is done to stop it . . ." His face ridged, squared into a merciless war mask that carried the message better than words.

"An uprising is not the answer," Morgan said quietly. "It would only give Meir an excuse to call in the Army, which is exactly what Stark wants. In the end, you would lose everything, your homes, your lands, perhaps even your lives."

Bog-o-nay-ge-shig crossed his arms over his chest and viewed Morgan with open scorn. "Does a Chippewa fear the Shadow Land? To die in battle . . . is that not better than to live no life?" He came to his feet in a single motion. His eyes burned with that same wild, fierce fire as when he had swung the tomahawk over his head and brought Marshal O'Connor to his knees in panic.

"The white man calls me 'Bog' or 'Bug' in the same way he calls a black man 'boy'! But I am Bog-o-nay-ge-shig, Hole in the Day, a Chippewa war chief. And I say to you again: if you are a friend of the Pillagers, you will send Stark and Meir to prison before it is too late.

"If the tomahawk *is* raised, I will remember that you saved Shab-on-day-sh-king's life—and mine. More than that, I cannot promise. Now I have said enough, too much." He made a peremptory gesture toward Jean Chardin. "You will tell Miss Gail and Dr. E.C. what I have said. And you will tell them that I am their friend. You will tell them that."

"I will tell them that the storm clouds gather," Chardin said, "and that soon the lightning will strike the Pillagers' enemies and destroy them."

Bog-o-nay-ge-shig frowned, a trace of irritation sharpening his voice. "Is it the Indian in you, Jean, who hates Stark? Or is it the white man? I have warned you before; I warn you now. If blood must flow, let it be because of the wrongs done my people and not for your personal revenge."

The fisherman flushed but kept his temper. "I am an Indian," he said, "and your friend. You ought not to talk to me that way."

"You are a half-breed," Bog-o-nay-ge-shig said, "and the white in you hates the Indian because you are not all white, and the Indian in you hates the white because you are not all Indian. You do not know who you are or what you are, Jean Chardin. Sometimes your hate for Hugh Stark is greater than your friendship for me, and then, like a mad wolf, you become dangerous even to your friends. Your heart is good; your tongue is straight; no man questions your bravery. But there is a sickness in you that gnaws at your belly like a weasel. Kill it, Chardin, before it kills you. Now go, both of you. We will talk again when the time is right."

Putting his back to Morgan and Chardin, he went into the cabin. The powwow was over.

Thoughtfully, Morgan returned to the boat landing. He had come here hoping to win Bog-o-nay-ge-shig's trust. But despite the fact that Gail Saunders, Dr. Lindley and Jean Chardin had all vouched for his integrity, he had the feeling that the Chippewa was still skeptical and not overly impressed. To further heighten tensions, Bog-o-nay-ge-shig had reiterated his charges against Hugh Stark, Meir and O'Connor, and had then followed through with a blunt ultimatum.

Stop what's going on here or blood will flow.

He took his place in the bow as Jean Chardin worked the boat away from the shore and picked up the wind. Still smarting from the sting of Bog-o-nay-ge-shig's harsh words, the fisherman withdrew into himself, discouraging further talk.

Observing him, Morgan wondered what dark secret lay behind Chardin's hatred for Hugh Stark. Whatever had happened between them, Stark was still alive only because Chardin had not yet found a way to kill him. But if Stark knew that, and he undoubtedly did, why hadn't he gotten rid of Chardin? To a man with money murder was no problem.

Why did Chardin hate enough to kill? And why didn't Chardin protect himself from that hate?

Morgan studied the fisherman with a troubled frown. Chardin's eyes were fixed on the sail; his mouth was set. Clearly, he was in no mood to talk. Following the half-breed's example, Morgan withdrew into a shell of silence that lasted the remainder of the voyage.

At dockside, Chardin tied up the boat and then stood staring moodily out across the bay. "You'll have to find yourself another boatman," he said. "I'll not be carrying you anymore."

"Why?" Morgan asked, surprised. "You're not quitting because of that little run-in with Bog-o-nay-ge-shig? I thought you more of a man than that."

"By God, he had no right to talk to me that way!"

"He was thinking of what was best for his people."

"And *I*"—Chardin jabbed a blunt forefinger against his chest —"am thinking of what is best for me."

Morgan shrugged. "Then perhaps it's best this way. I'm sorry. I needed your help."

The mildness of his reply took some of the fire out of Chardin. "It's nothing personal, Mr. Morgan," he said. "It's just that, well, a man cannot walk two trails at the same time."

Complex, Morgan thought, *and torn. What are you, Jean Chardin, white or Indian? Or are you, as Bog-o-nay-ge-shig said, nothing?*

"Why didn't you let me know about this from the beginning?" he asked. "I thought you wanted to help send Stark and Meir to prison. Wouldn't that satisfy you?"

For a moment, Chardin remained silent, his thoughts turning inward in self-search. Then he said quietly, "When I first offered to help you, I thought that it would be enough. But I was wrong. I am a simple man, Mr. Morgan, not smart like you. I think with the heart, not with the mind. This hate inside me—I have to deal with it the only way I know how. Whether it is the best way, I do not know. But it is my way, and, for me, it is good." His dark eyes rested on Morgan, somber, challenging.

"Now everyone will think I have betrayed the Pillagers because I cannot put them above this other thing, and that may be so. But I tell you, I can have no peace so long as Hugh Stark is alive. I am going to kill him, Mr. Morgan, and neither you, nor Bog nor anyone else can stop me."

"Why?" Morgan fired the question at him like a bullet. "What is this thing between you and Stark anyway?"

Chardin stiffened and, for a fraction of a second, that same wild look Morgan had glimpsed on Bog-o-nay-ge-shig's face blazed back at him from the half-breed's eyes. Then, as suddenly as it had come, it was gone.

"That, Mr. Morgan," Chardin said evenly, "is none of your business," and walked away, leaving Morgan standing there.

Staring after the fisherman's retreating figure, Morgan shook his head. The list of "spark strikers" who could, at any moment, set off the dynamite-laden situation was growing steadily. Meir, O'Connor, who was not going to let his humiliation at Sugar Point go unchallenged, Bog-o-nay-ge-shig, and now Jean Chardin. Of them all, Chardin offered the most immediate threat. For if the half-breed made an attempt upon Stark's life, it would bring about the very crisis Stark sought.

Morgan's shoulders slumped. Of those whom he had counted upon to help him only Jason Bradshaw, Dr. E. C. Lindley and Gail Saunders remained. And with both Gail and Lindley lacking the needed experience, that left only Bradshaw. If anything happened to the *Globe* reporter, he might as well pack his bags and go home.

Buttoning his coat, Morgan walked back to town. By the time he reached the Pameda his dark mood had lifted and his natural optimism had taken over. He had built up his own logging company from nothing, without help. If he had to, he would take on Stark, Meir, O'Connor and Davitt alone.

At the desk, a once again affable Pollock gave him his key, a faintly scented letter, and a conspiratorial smile. Addressed simply to "Mr. Craig Morgan," the letter bore no postmark, which meant that it had been hand delivered.

"Well," Pollock asked eagerly, "aren't you going to open it?"

Damn the little man, Morgan thought. *He should have been a cheap tabloid reporter.*

"Mr. Pollock," he said evenly, "don't let me keep you from your work. I'm sure you have plenty to do."

Leaving the clerk open-mouthed and red-faced, he sat down in a chair overlooking the street and opened the letter. The single page was filled with flowing script. He read it quickly.

Dear Mr. Morgan,

Apologies are such futile things since they never say what we really mean. And "Sorry" can't make up for my conduct last night. I think you understand why I acted as I did. But that's no excuse. It's not your fault that I built you into an invincible hero, and then expected the real-life man to live up to the impossible image. It's just that with this trouble going on so long and nobody doing anything about it that, well, I foolishly expected you to rush in and resolve the matter overnight.

Won't you please have dinner with me tomorrow—will seven o'clock be all right?—and give me a chance to make up for my bad manners and ill temper?

Gail Saunders.

Slipping the letter into his coat pocket, Morgan sat staring out the window, feeling a warmth such as he had not experienced since the death of his wife, Anna, six years before. It was a good feeling, and it reminded him of just how lonely the years had been, and but for those Nez Percé on the reservation, and the squaw whom he had never known, how meaningless his life would have been.

The barber, Joe Pruitt, had been partially right. With no family to worry about, he *had* become involved in other people's lives. But Pruitt had not known about the squaw's scalp, or about the deeper sense of moral responsibility that weighed so heavily upon his conscience. Not even Gail Saunders knew that.

Quietly, he rose and went upstairs. He knocked on Jason Bradshaw's door, but there was no answer. The reporter evidently had not returned. However, it was still a couple of hours until dark. He would see Bradshaw later at supper.

Jason Bradshaw was not in the dining room when he went down at six o'clock, nor could any of the waitresses recall having seen the *Globe* reporter.

Morgan dined alone, surrounded by a spreading circle of silence. Word of the incident in Joe Pruitt's barber shop had obviously spread. Before it stopped, half the town would be lined up solidly against him. It was too late to do anything about it. All he could do was to make certain he didn't blunder again.

At seven o'clock, after his third cup of coffee, he paid his bill and left with little tendrils of animosity following him even into the lobby where Pollock sat sulking behind the desk.

"Mr. Pollock—"

The clerk kept his head buried in his newspaper, pretending not to hear.

"Mr. Pollock," Morgan said calmly, "I'd hate to see you lose your job, but then you don't seem to care whether you keep it or not."

The newspaper dropped with a dry, crackling sound; the balding head popped up, and Pollock regarded him with "I've been stabbed" eyes.

"I'm doing just what you told me to do." Pollock's tone was aggrieved. "Minding my own business."

Morgan found it impossible to stay angry with the clerk. Pollock was a paradox: a good-natured, mild-mannered little man who would not deliberately hurt anyone, yet who could, with his tongue, stir up all kinds of trouble without realizing it. Like an alcoholic to liquor, he was addicted to gossip and almost certain to die that way.

"Good." A faint smile crinkled the corners of Morgan's eyes. "Then you should be able to tell me if you've seen Mr. Bradshaw today."

"Not since this morning," Pollock answered reluctantly. "He left about half an hour after you did."

"Did he say where he was going? Or when he would be back?"

"No, sir; and I didn't ask him."

"Well, when he comes in tell him I want to see him immediately. I'll be in my room."

"*If* he comes in," the clerk replied darkly. "The way you two are poking around, you'll both likely end up dead. But then that's your business, not mine."

"You're learning, Mr. Pollock," Morgan said pleasantly. "Keep it up and we'll get along fine. Good night."

Pollock did not answer. His head was back behind the newspaper, only the top of his balding head showing above the edge.

Smiling, Morgan left him to nurse his resentment, but the smile did not reach the top of the stairs. The sense of nagging unease which had been with Morgan since Bradshaw's failure to turn up at supper continued to plague him. Had the *Globe* reporter come up with evidence so incriminating that he had been murdered to silence him? Or was he simply hot on the trail of a new lead?

At the head of the landing, Morgan checked Bradshaw's room, hoping to see a sliver of light from beneath the door. But the room was dark, and there was no sound of movement inside.

He hauled out the gold Hamilton watch, checked the time. *Nine-thirty*. The premonition that something was wrong persisted. He slipped the watch back into his pocket and, in that moment, made up his mind.

If the proof of a Stark-Meir conspiracy was out there in the deep woods, as Bog-o-nay-ge-shig claimed, he would go looking for it—and Jason Bradshaw—tomorrow morning.

Emerging from Saunders' Mercantile, Morgan stood, khaki clad, on the boardwalk, flexing his feet to break in the new logger's boots. A rolled-up ground sheet and blanket were slung over one shoulder, and he carried a Mackinaw on one arm.

In the early morning silence, with the sun just now beginning to splash across the shadowed store fronts, the gun at his hip seemed somehow out of place, almost obscene, until the pungent smell of sawdust and the high pitched rasp of saws down at the sawmill reminded him of why he was here. Then the weight of the holstered .45 was suddenly comforting, reassuring.

Shifting the Mackinaw under his arm, he walked down the boardwalk, conscious of the stares of the merchants standing in their shop doorways. He suspected that they knew Jason Bradshaw was missing. That would be Pollock's work. He was not surprised, recalling the excited gleam in the clerk's eyes when he had come down at five o'clock and inquired if Bradshaw had returned.

"No, sir," Pollock had said, "and it's my opinion—mind you, I do have a right to my opinion—that he won't be back. You're a brave man, Mr. Morgan, and I like you even if you do give me a bad time. But you're up against some dangerous, powerful people. A lot more powerful than you realize. Why don't you pack up and go home before it's too late?"

It was good advice, Morgan thought. And with the hostile stares of Walker's merchants reminding him that he was not wanted here, he wondered why he didn't take it. Senator Leland had woven his little net and then left him, Morgan, behind to do the job, or get killed. *The unscrupulous bastard!*

Ahead of him, he saw Joe Pruitt standing beside his candy-striped barber's pole. He slowed his steps, knowing that if anyone knew where Bradshaw might have gone, it would be the little barber.

As he came abreast of the shop, he stopped and smiled pleasantly. "Good morning, Mr. Pruitt. I'm looking for Jason Bradshaw. Have you seen him this morning?"

Normally, Joe Pruitt was a good-natured, easygoing man, but Morgan's parting remark the day before had upset him. He did not like being forced into the position of having to examine his own conscience.

"I haven't seen Mr. Bradshaw since day before yesterday," he replied with cool civility. "But if I do see him, I'll tell him you're looking for him."

"Do you have any idea where he may have gone?" Morgan asked. "Or to whom he may have talked? It's important, Mr. Pruitt. Jason Bradshaw may be in grave danger. He may even be dead."

The barber's face settled into an inscrutable mask. But beneath the mask, Morgan sensed the fear of Hugh Stark's retaliation which Pruitt had voiced the day before. Whatever Pruitt might know, he would tell nothing.

"Mr. Morgan," Pruitt said in a flat tone, "Jason Bradshaw's business is no concern of mine. I don't know who he's talked to, nor where he's gone. What's more, I don't want to know. Like I told you yesterday, folks here mind their own business. You'd be wise to do the same thing. Good day, sir." He went back into his shop.

Picking up his bedroll, Morgan headed for the livery stable. It would be a waste of time to question anyone else. The town would do nothing to hurt him; it would simply refuse to help him.

At the livery stable, Len Archer, the owner, turned out to be the exception.

"Sure, I remember Bradshaw," Archer, a rawboned, gray-haired man with an easy smile, said in answer to Morgan's query. "He came in here around six-thirty yesterday morning. Had a blanket roll and a change, like you. Rented a horse for three days, saddled up, and rode out."

"Did he say where he was going?" Morgan asked. "Or when he would be back?"

"Nope." The livery stable owner ran a hand through his hair with a wry smile. "Come to think of it, for a man who asked so many questions, he didn't answer a single damned one. He is smart, that reporter. If—" Archer snapped his fingers in sudden remembrance. "Almost forgot. He said tell you not to worry. He'd get in touch with you when he had something."

Bending, Archer picked up a straw and stood chewing thoughtfully on it, not saying anything, just studying Morgan with shrewd eyes. Then tossing the straw away, he said, "Mr. Morgan, not all of us see things the way Joe Pruitt and some of the others do. Course you can't blame them too much. Joe's a good, kind man. It's just that he's got a big family to worry about. And the rest are pretty much in the same boat. Ah, hell, that's no excuse! Any way I can help, I will." An underlying concern shadowed his rawboned face.

"You're taking on some dangerous men, Mr. Morgan," he said.

"Men who don't live by civilized rules. You can die out there in those woods. Remember that. Now, come on." He led the way into the livery stable. "You look like a man who knows how to ride. I've got just the horse for you."

Fifteen minutes later, Morgan rode out of town astride a steel gray stallion, bedroll and Mackinaw strapped behind the cantle, his change in the saddle bags, and the weight of the gun at his hip both a defense and an offense.

It was cool and quiet and dusky in the timber with the tall pines so closely spaced that they did not branch until near their tops, making them grow very straight and free of boles. A logging contractor from British Columbia had once told Morgan that the white pines in Minnesota were the finest in the world; and, observing them now, he had to agree.

Riding easily in the saddle, he relaxed, feeling at home for the first time since his arrival. From the age of fifteen, when his mother, giving up hope that his Army father would ever return, had disappeared with another man, his life had been a succession of logging camps, with the ring of double-bitted axes, the rasp of crosscut saws and the cry of "Timber!" as the big trees came crashing down with a mighty *whooshing* sound filling his days.

Nights had been spent around a red hot, pot-bellied stove in the rough planked bunkhouse with the winter wind, pouring in through hand-thick cracks in the walls, freezing his backside, and the sour smell of damp socks and long johns strung on overhead clothes lines sharp in his nostrils, and the steam dimming the printed words until he had to lay the book aside and lie quietly listening to the tall tales of the older men until someone drew out a harmonica and livened things up with a bit of music. Then it was lights out, a hard bunk, the sound of exhausted men's breathing, and, finally, sleep.

Morgan breathed deeply now of the clean, crisp air, pungent with the smell of the pines, and smiled, remembering those years. Whistle punk at fifteen, grease boy at sixteen, a chopper at eighteen, bucking at nineteen. Twelve hours a day, six days a week, with nothing to break the monotony of the long months except a once-a-year spree in Portland that lasted just long enough for the whores, the gamblers and the saloonkeepers to empty the crew's pockets and to drop a few bodies into the dark, swirling waters beneath the riverfront dives.

Hard, dangerous work; rough, tough men; low wages and no future, unless, like Craig Morgan, a man dreamed of something better. He had saved his money and, at twenty-one, had bought a small one-man sawmill for five hundred dollars from a disgruntled operator. He had then promptly hired the ex-owner to teach him the business end of logging.

That had been the beginning of the realization of the dream. After that, more hard work and a lot of self-sacrifice with the dream never fading.

His marriage in 1889 to Anna West, daughter of a Salem banker, had marked the second important milestone in his life. For although she had been unable to give him a child, she had furthered his education, to this point largely self-acquired. A well-bred, well-educated girl, she had taught him the social graces, polished his grammar, opened his mind to the greater world of knowledge, and saw to it that her father, Martin West, instructed him in the precise, logical world of bookkeeping, accounting, loans, mortgages, profit and loss. Then, having done all this, Anna Morgan had developed pneumonia in December of 1892, and had died a week later.

For Morgan, her death had very nearly ended the dream. Only the memory of her unswerving faith in him during the three short years of their marriage had kept it alive. Had it not been for that, he might have turned his head on the dream and lost himself among the nameless, faceless men who moved aimlessly through the big woods without goal or expectation beyond the next big spree in town.

However, even the memory might not have been enough had not his long suppressed sense of guilt for his father's murder of the young Cheyenne squaw chosen this time to surface. Perhaps it had needed this moment of weakness, this distraction from the dream to break through the barrier which his mind had set up to keep it hidden.

When it did break through, it became a Greater Dream, adding to, rather than diminishing, his world. Resolutely, he had put the past behind him. Anna was dead; nothing he could do would bring her back. But he could use the background, the education she had given him as a living memorial to her.

And so he had become a fighter for lost causes, a Don Quixote who, more often than not, shattered his lance against the windmills of hate, bigotry, and racism. But not always. Occasionally, he won. And that had made it all worthwhile.

How quickly those years had passed, with the small, one-man sawmill growing into a prosperous business of logging camps, mills and wholesale-retail lumberyards throughout Oregon. The dream had become a reality, and the Greater Dream an act of contrition and a justification of his, Craig Morgan's, own existence. There had, of course, been . . .

The stallion stumbled, throwing Morgan forward against the saddle horn and back into the present, reminding him of where he was, and why he was here. Involuntarily, he shivered. Because of the Greater Dream, and the hooped scalp of a long-dead Cheyenne squaw whom he had never known, the small empire he had spent his life building was threatened with destruction, and him along with it.

Remembering Len Archer's warning, he rode carefully now, his free hand close to the gun at his hip, his eyes searching the shadows for some sign of movement. Once, he spotted a bear on the shore of a small lake, flicking a fish out of the water with its paw, and, a hundred yards away, a deer drinking. A mile farther on, the sharp slap of a beaver's tail betrayed the presence of a dam nearby. Intuitively, he sensed that, for the moment, there was no danger for him here.

Near dusk, he made camp on the shore of a small lake about three miles north of Steamboat Bay. In half an hour, he'd caught a pike and picked enough berries to make a meal. He broiled the fish over a bed of hot coals and had the berries for dessert. Then with the light already fading, he picketed the gray, carefully banked the fire, and, with his saddle for a pillow, lay watching the first stars appear in the sky.

He wondered if Jason Bradshaw was also camped out somewhere. And, if so, whether the *Globe* reporter was on the trail of something. Or was Bradshaw already dead, his body buried far back in the timber? Senseless speculation that could accomplish nothing.

So far, he had avoided the logging camps, although there

were plenty of signs of logging operations going on around the area. With October almost here, the crews had already swamped out and brushed roads through the woods. Now the choppers with their double-bitted axes and springboards had moved in and started felling the big trees. Several times, Morgan had heard the warning cry, "Timber!" in the distance, and the rasp of the crosscuts as the two-man bucker crews sawed the trees into the proper lengths.

With the coming of snow, the logs would be skidded to the nearest water or railroad spur. Logging would go on until the January thaw. Then the butt logs, those with the most board feet of lumber in them, would be taken out. If a sudden thaw set in, thousands of logs would be left to rot.

It was this senseless waste, this felling of trees so far from any water or railroad spur that it did not pay to get them out, that angered Morgan. Bad enough in itself, when linked to Bog-o-nay-ge-shig's other charges it threatened not only the Chippewas, but the legitimate timber industry as well.

Everyone knew what was going on; nobody did anything about it. The ones who could have stopped much of it, the Bureau of Indian Affairs inspectors, were either too inexperienced or had been bought off. Yet, as Bog-o-nay-ge-shig insisted, the proof was out there. The problem was to find it.

With the .45 within easy reach, he pulled the blanket up around his shoulders and lay listening to the splash of fish upon the lake. Just before he fell asleep, he remembered Gail Saunders' dinner invitation and that he had forgotten to leave word with Mr. Allison, the mercantile clerk, that he would not be able to come. He seemed to have developed a real talent for antagonizing or hurting others. But why Gail Saunders, of all people?

Damn!

Smoke, stinging his nostrils and sucked deep into his lungs, awakened him. He sat up, coughing, his mind not yet fully alert. On the opposite side of the lake, the tall pines stood silhouetted against the lightening sky. Across the now-dead camp fire, the stallion moved nervously back and forth on its picket line, ears perked, nostrils flaring.

Morgan threw aside the blanket, grabbed the .45 and pushed to his feet. The cold bit at him, setting his teeth to chattering. He saddled the skittish gray, tied the bedroll behind the cantle and swung up. Despite the chill, he was perspiring beneath the khaki shirt. He understood the stallion's fear. He felt it, too.

Forest fire! The nightmare of loggers everywhere.

By now, the smoke had begun to drift out of the timber to the northeast. Not bad yet, but already thickening, spreading. He put the gray to a trot and headed back for Walker, hoping to skirt the fringes of the fire before it cut him off. A half mile farther and the smoke began to diminish, thinning to trailing wisps that hung motionless in the still air.

He rode more slowly now, the gray's hoofs clip-clopping a monotonous cadence in the silence. Heat wrapped around horse and rider, and, once again, smoke stung Morgan's nostrils and set his eyes to watering. The gray began to dance around nervously, tossing its head and fighting the rein.

Pulling up, Morgan fished a pair of binoculars from the saddle bags and swept the area to the east with a growing unease. A score of small fires were still burning in a five-hundred-acre tract of white pine, with trees everywhere scorched and blackened by the heat. Fortunately, with no wind to fan them, they seemed to be dying out.

Morgan stuffed the binoculars back into the saddle bags. He didn't like it; he didn't know why, but he didn't like it. Lightning from thunderstorms often set off forest fires during dry, hot summers. But *twenty* small fires, intended to scorch, not to destroy, scattered over five hundred acres of valuable timber land in early fall . . .

It had to be arson. Predawn, no witnesses, limited acreage, no wind to spread the fires nor to cause them to "crown."

Carefully, he shifted in his saddle, his right hand resting on the cantle, close to the gun at his hip. In the dim light, the trees on either side of the road looked dark and menacing, potential shelter for . . .

A hundred feet ahead, a tree trunk bulged, shoulder high, started to separate.

Morgan brought the stallion up, rearing, its hoofs beating the air, and felt the great body shudder as the bullet slammed into its heart. As it toppled backward, he kicked free of the stirrups and hurled himself clear. A second shot struck a tree, spearing him with a shower of pine splinters. Then he was flat on his belly in the shadows, the .45 in his hand.

From there, he commanded a clear view of the skid road and of the timber on the other side. He lay motionless, listening for some whisper of sound. The minutes crawled past with the sun dappling the ground beneath the trees. The heat and smoke began to diminish as the fires burned themselves out.

Was this, he thought, what had happened to Jason Bradshaw? Had the *Globe* reporter also stumbled onto the arsonist and been killed to silence him?

Gradually, the patterns of dappled light began to play tricks upon him, sculpting pieces of shadow into imaginary heads, arms, even moving figures. He forced himself to concentrate on the tree from behind which the first shot had come. *Or had it been the one next to it? Or perhaps the one behind it?*

He closed his eyes for an instant. When he opened them he thought he saw a swift-moving shadow cross the road and disappear among the trees ten yards to his left. He thumbed back the hammer of the .45.

Just when he thought he had been mistaken, the Chippewa came at him, bent low and running on silent moccasins. At ten feet, Morgan caught a glimpse of the raised rifle. Rolling on his side, he fired across his chest. The bullet struck the Chippewa beneath the chin and drilled out through the top of his head. He fell backward, the rifle flying from his hands.

For ten minutes, Morgan stayed where he was. Then satisfied that the arsonist had been alone, he got up and walked over to the dead man. The Chippewa wore fringed buckskins and a fur-banded necklace. An ugly V-shaped scar marred his right cheek.

Morgan stood there, conscious of the silence, of the sun filtering down through the trees, of the stallion lying on its side in the middle of the road, of the dead Chippewa at his feet; and, suddenly, all the tensions and frustrations of the past two days caught up with him.

Goddammit, he'd killed the one man who could have put Hugh Stark and Meir behind bars!

He kicked savagely at a broken tree branch. Maybe he just

wasn't right for the job. Or maybe, as the desk clerk, Pollock, and Len Archer had warned, he was up against people and forces too powerful for him or any other man to handle. It was a humiliating thought and he quickly rejected it.

Returning to the dead stallion, he salvaged his gear. Then with the Mackinaw draped over one shoulder and the binoculars strap-hung over the other, he moved out. Chardin had said that there were more than a hundred lakes within a dozen miles of Walker. According to the map Len Archer had given him, he had ridden between Swamp Lake and Steamboat Bay and then, swinging north by east, had passed Crooked Lake, Welsh Lake and the tiny unnamed lake where he had seen the bear scooping a fish out of the water, and had spent the night on the shore of Little Moss Lake.

Now, he reasoned, if he retraced his route, bearing almost due south, he would skirt the southwest tip of Crooked Lake, and there in Crooked Creek, connecting the lake and Steamboat Bay, he would probably find the dead Chippewa's canoe.

Around mid-morning, he reached Crooked Lake and, within an hour, had located the canoe drawn up on the bank of Crooked Creek. He had hoped it might contain some bit of incriminating evidence, but he found nothing.

Stowing the Mackinaw, he clambered aboard, and promptly ended up in the water. The birchbark, he discovered, was like a spirited horse. Unless you understood its delicate balance, staying aboard was all but impossible. But once understood, it became a part of you, and you of it, and man and canoe flowed effortlessly together.

Captured by the magic of the moment, Morgan thrust aside for the time being his repeated failures, increasing danger and growing concern for Jason Bradshaw's safety. The problem was not going away. It would be waiting for him when he reached Walker.

It was late afternoon when he beached the canoe near the dock at the end of Lake Street. Several fishing boats were already in, but he saw no sign of Chardin's boat. The half-breed was evidently somewhere on Bear Island, nursing his grudge against Bog-o-nay-ge-shig and his hatred for Hugh Stark.

Chardin's unstable nature troubled him. Trying to anticipate the fisherman was useless; worrying about the matter was a waste of time. Let Chardin do what he would. He, Morgan, had his own job cut out for him.

The desk was deserted when Morgan entered the Pameda Hotel. A sign on the counter informed the public to "Ring Bell For Service." Morgan took his key off the rack, walked over and looked into the dining room. Pollock was sitting in a corner, talking to one of the waitresses. There was no sign of Jason Bradshaw.

Upstairs, he knocked on Bradshaw's door, but received no answer. Something had gone wrong. Bradshaw was either dead or in real trouble. Yet Morgan could do nothing but wait and hope.

In his own room, he undressed, tossed the grimy, smoke-permeated khakis on a chair, and stretched his long frame out on the bed. His hands were blistered; his arms and shoulders ached from the unaccustomed paddling; and the feeling of angry frustration had begun to build up again.

He sat up on the edge of the bed, remembering that there were things he had to do. Tell Archer about the loss of the stallion and his saddle, and reimburse him. Request the local constable to send out a party to recover the Chippewa's body. Also ask that Marshal O'Connor be notified since the entire matter fell under federal jurisdiction. He doubted that O'Connor would take any action, but he wanted to be on record as having reported both incidents.

Bog-o-nay-ge-shig should also be told. If Jean Chardin turned up, perhaps he could be persuaded to carry the news to the chief. Or if not Chardin, then Dr. E.C. or Gail Saunders.

Slipping on the sweaty khakis, he went out into the hall, found a maid, and ordered water for a bath. An hour later, shaved and wearing the Western-style whipcord suit, he left the hotel.

At the livery stable, he settled with Len Archer for the dead stallion. Archer refused payment for the saddle, saying that he would have one of the hostlers ride out and recover it.

"Important thing," he said, "is that, for the first time, someone has struck back at Stark. He has to know now that you mean business. Course, that's going to make him all the more dangerous."

"You're probably right," Morgan agreed. Then, "Any word on Bradshaw?"

"No." Archer shook his head. "But if I hear anything, I'll get in touch."

"I'd appreciate that."

Archer gave him a slow, easy smile. "Like I told you, not all of us feel the same way Joe Pruitt does."

From the livery stable, Morgan went to the constable's office where he reported the arson incident and the death of the Chippewa. The constable promised to pass on the information to O'Connor when he saw him.

"He hasn't been around since the Shab-on-day-sh-king shooting. He don't have much use for small town constables nor Chippewas. One of these days though, he's going to pick on the wrong Indian and end up dead."

"You think he's mixed up in this trouble?"

"Maybe he is; maybe he isn't. But he's sure not helping matters by stirring up Bog's people."

"What about Hugh Stark?"

"Now, look, Mr. Morgan"—the constable shifted uneasily in his chair—"I don't intend to get involved. It's a federal matter, and you and the Marshal are federal people. You two handle it."

Morgan left without mentioning Jason Bradshaw's disappearance. It would have done no good. For that, too, would have been a "federal" matter for the U. S. Marshal to investigate. An investigation O'Connor would almost certainly ignore. O'Connor would like to see both him *and* Bradshaw dead.

Outside, Morgan paused a moment in the bright autumn sunshine, looking up and down the street. At the stores with their neat white fronts, well-kept boardwalks and merchandise-filled windows, and the people going in and out of the awninged doorways; at Joe Pruitt's red-and-white-striped barber's pole and the old man lounging in front of Joe Frost's saloon; and, suddenly, the sense of unreality which he had experienced in Gail Saunders' living room returned.

He found it difficult to believe that greed, hate, fear and death, like a silent wind, swirled and eddied in emotional currents throughout the town, swept across Leech Lake to invade the wigwams and log houses of the Chippewas and, not stopping there, whipped around the Indian Agent's house at Onigum.

Yet it was there, threatening to develop into a tornado that would touch down and destroy everything in its path. In passing, it would lift the Chippewas off their lands and set them down in a hostile environment where they would die; and, behind them, their lands, stripped of timber and unsuitable for farming, would also die; and there would be nothing left but Hugh Stark and his Pine Ring; and then they, too, would move on to destroy other regions, other Indians—other human beings—until the last warrior of the last tribe was gone, and white men read about him and his culture in history books, and said, "My God, what savages, what animals they were!"

It was inevitable, Morgan realized. He knew it; he just couldn't accept it.

"Love ye one another" . . . "Star-Spangled Banner" . . . "Battle Hymn of the Republic" . . . "dedicated to the proposition that all men are created equal" . . . "with liberty and justice for all" . . . *so long, by God, as your skin is white!*

Crap!

He wished he could feel like Gail Saunders' knight; but he couldn't. He wasn't a hero. He was nothing but a damned fool bent on self-destruction because of a Cheyenne squaw's shining black hair woven into his conscience.

Down the street, the sign swinging over Saunders' Mercantile shone whitely in the sunlight.

Morgan walked toward it.

A bell tinkled over the door as he entered.

Near the rear of the store, Gail Saunders stood with her back to him, returning a bolt of dress goods to the shelf. At the sound of the bell, she turned and said pleasantly, "Good afternoon. May I . . ." She stiffened, and Morgan saw the color rise to her face and the full lips thin ever so slightly.

"Oh." She drew a deep breath. "You know I should be very angry with you, Mr. Morgan. Do you realize I left the store early and spent two hours preparing a special treat for you, and another hour turning myself into a bluebird; and then you . . ."

She broke off, regarding him with feminine outrage. Then,

suddenly, her eyes filled with laughter, her mouth curved in a rueful smile, and she said softly, "Did you simply forget?" She came from behind the counter and extended her hand. "Or did you have a reason?"

Although she did not have the animal sensuality of many women, she possessed that distracting feminity of the total woman. She was, he realized, quite capable of arousing men without being aware of it.

"I had a reason," he said, still holding her hand. "But that's no excuse. I'm sorry."

Gail Saunders' eyes held steady with his. "Did Mr. Pollock give you my letter? I asked him to."

"Yes, and thank you."

"I'm so ashamed of the way I behaved," she said. "You must know how much I admire and respect you for what you're trying to do here. It's just that I get so frustrated. So . . . forgive me, please."

A faint smile crinkled the corners of Morgan's eyes, animating his normally still features. "Would you believe that I almost broke my foot this morning kicking a tree branch for the same reason? If the tree had been a man, I'd probably have taken it out on him."

Gail Saunders colored. "You're being kind," she murmured. "I can't imagine you doing anything like that. Unless, of course, something really went wrong."

"It did."

Briefly, Morgan told her of Jason Bradshaw's disappearance, and of the incident near Little Moss Lake. When he mentioned the V-shaped scar on the dead Chippewa's cheek, she caught her breath.

"Why, that's Whiskey Joe!" she exclaimed. "He's a—was—a drunken troublemaker who encouraged the young men to drink, and who wouldn't leave other men's wives alone. The Pillagers have ostracized him for the past two years. He's worked for Hugh Stark ever since." Her eyes widened. "Mr. Morgan, Stark had to have been paying him to set those fires. There's your proof!"

"My proof is dead," Morgan reminded her. "Damn!"

Gail Saunders' hand tightened on Morgan's arm. "Even if you

had taken him alive, he wouldn't have talked. Or if he had, Stark would have had him killed before he could testify."

"If that's true," Morgan replied, "then no one is going to talk, this whole investigation is a farce and I'm risking my life for nothing."

"No!" she protested. "What I'm saying is that I doubt we can ever convict men like Hugh Stark in the courts. Their power will have to be curbed by congressional legislation with the help of men like you and Jason Bradshaw.

"Craig"—it was the first time she had ever used his given name—"Senator Leland doesn't care whether Stark is convicted, or even indicted, just so long as you publicly link him to a rumored conspiracy to defraud the Chippewas. Leland knows that the newspaper coverage alone would destroy Stark as a viable candidate at the polls. Perhaps"—her glance was shrewd, direct—"we should learn something from the Senator."

There was no mistaking her meaning, nor did Morgan pretend to do so. "If you're suggesting that we join forces with Leland, forget it," he retorted. "I've no use for the man."

"I'm not suggesting that we join him," Gail Saunders assured him. "What I *am* suggesting is that you turn over whatever evidence you now have against Hugh Stark to Jason Bradshaw and let him run a feature article on it in the St. Paul *Globe*."

"That would guarantee Leland's return to the Senate," Morgan reminded her. "I'll be no party to that."

"Would you rather have Hugh Stark there?"

Tall as she was, she had barely to look up at Morgan, and the impact of her eyes at such close range disturbed him. He wished he were back in the secure, well-ordered routine of his bachelor's existence in Oregon.

"No"—he shook off the thought—"but I'm not sure that destroying Stark politically would put out the fire here. It may already be too late for that. Also, you're forgetting that Bradshaw may be dead. If he is, I'll be next on Stark's list."

"Not yet."

"What do you mean?"

"He'll try and bribe you first."

Morgan pondered the idea; it made sense. "Perhaps I should call on Stark," he said. "Since Whiskey Joe worked for him, that ought to be excuse enough."

"Perhaps you should," Gail agreed. "I've a feeling that he's expecting you. But be careful, Craig. And don't underestimate him."

"I never underestimate anybody," Morgan assured her. "Now where can I find Stark?"

"At this time of day, he should be in his office at the Red River Logging Company," Gail replied. "Do you want me to go with you?"

"No, I'd rather handle this alone." Morgan smiled, tentatively testing her mood. "But, first, can we bury the hatchet and start over again?"

Mock fire burned behind the quickly lowered lashes, but behind the fire lurked a secret laughter. "I'm willing," she agreed, "provided you drop by tonight and help me eat all that food I spent hours preparing for you yesterday."

Quicksand, Morgan thought. *Stay away from her, you fool;* but found himself answering warmly, "Seven o'clock. And I promise I won't forget this time."

He was halfway to the Red River Logging Company before he realized that he had not mentioned the trouble at Sugar Point. Nor his nonproductive council with Bog-o-nay-ge-shig. *Dammit, he couldn't even think around her!*

She was still on his mind when he entered the office of the Red River Logging Company.

A pale-faced young man, wearing a pinstriped suit and gold-rimmed glasses, rose from his desk and came forward to meet him. "Yes, sir? May I help you?"

"Craig Morgan, Bureau of Indian Affairs. I'm here to see Mr. Stark on official business."

The eyes behind the gold-rimmed glasses chilled. "I'm Robert Gillispie, Mr. Stark's secretary. Perhaps I can help you."

"You can," Morgan replied pleasantly. "You can tell him I'm here."

The secretary's thin lips flattened until they lost all color, then he turned and disappeared behind a door marked: Hugh Stark, President.

Curiously, Morgan looked about him. Half a dozen clerks

wearing green eye shades and black sleeve guards sat on high stools at a work desk running the length of the room. From their furtive glances, he knew that they had overheard the conversation between him and Gillispie.

Walking to the window overlooking the mill works, he saw that saws, planers and steam boilers were mostly shut down. But with the January thaw, all this would change. Butt logs would be skidded to the narrow-gauge spur tracks, winched aboard waiting flatcars and hauled to the nearest lake. From there, they would be floated down to Walker Bay. Then mills all over the area would go into full operation with the high, rasping whine of the big saws tearing at the eardrums and the smoke from the kilns rising above the town to be whipped away by the wind.

Gail Saunders had told him that the mills in Walker and Akeley turned out pattern timber, thirty-six to forty inches wide, that could be squared off, and eight to sixteen feet long. Straight-grained, beautiful wood, free of boles, it was shipped by rail to Minneapolis, floated down the Mississippi, and then by ship across to London where, sliced paper thin, it was used for patterns in the garment factories. No wonder Stark and his Pine Ring found it profitable to . . .

"Mr. Morgan." He swung around. "Mr. Stark will see you now." Gillispie's voice was as frozen as his eyes.

On the threshold of Hugh Stark's private office, Morgan paused. His eyes swept the big room with its walnut-paneled walls, oil paintings, luxurious carpet, rich draperies, half drawn against the late afternoon sun—and finally came to rest upon the man seated behind the massive desk.

Hugh Stark was not as tall as he had appeared outside the Agency headquarters building; nor as young, although his full, firm-jawed face showed no signs of wrinkles. Fifty-five, probably; not more than five feet ten, but with a muscular body that suggested tremendous strength. It was the dynamic flow of power from behind the pleasant features, however, that gave one the impression that he was standing even while he remained seated behind that carefully selected massive desk.

The whole setting, the luxurious furnishings, the half shadowed atmosphere, the impeccable suit, complete with guardsman's tie and diamond stick pin, was deliberately created to impress and to intimidate.

Meeting Stark's eyes, dark brown like his thick, as yet unstreaked hair, Morgan smiled faintly, and Stark, reading his mind, smiled in appreciative understanding.

"Come in, Mr. Morgan." Rising, the Pine Ring leader shook hands, then motioned Morgan to a seat. "I've been wondering when you would get around to calling on me." He sank back and regarded Morgan with open interest. "You're not the first Indian Affairs inspector to come up here, but you are the first timberman to get involved. Quite frankly, sir, I think you are a well-meaning fool who's not only creating problems for the timber industry, but for the entire nation."

His voice was cultured, his accent a marked contrast to that of the Oregon country.

"This entire situation is a farce. Instead of sending you up here to further complicate matters, the Bureau of Indian Affairs or the Department of the Interior should request that troops be moved in to take disciplinary action before things get out of hand. The whole country would benefit if you were to recommend such a course of action to the Commissioner."

Listening, Morgan realized that nothing he could do or say would touch this man, for Hugh Stark was amoral, beyond good or evil. He did not hate Indians as O'Connor did; he merely viewed them as obstacles in his path to be removed. If he could create a situation whereby the Army would come in and annihilate them, he would do so. He was not only dangerous to Indians; he was dangerous to society.

"The situation here is a tragedy, not a farce," Morgan said. "I think you know that, but just don't care. How much more you know is a matter of question."

Selecting a fine meerschaum pipe from a half dozen in a rack on the desk, Stark filled it from a cedar humidor and lit up. Then he rested his elbows on the desk top and let the smoke curl up between them. His eyes were cool, guarded.

"Let's get to the point, Mr. Morgan," he said. "Why are you here?"

Morgan settled himself comfortably in the big leather chair

and asked, "Do you have a Chippewa working for you named Whiskey Joe."

"Why, yes," Stark told him. "He's worked for me off and on for the past year or so." His glance was inquiring. "Why do you ask?"

"He tried to murder me this morning when I caught him firing timber near Little Moss Lake. I had to kill him."

"I'm not surprised." Stark's handsome features remained inscrutable. "He's been nursing a grievance against the Pillagers ever since they kicked him out several years ago. However, he never gave me any trouble other than to go on a drinking spree now and then."

"What kind of work did he do for you?" Morgan asked.

Stark shrugged. "Odd jobs mostly. Cleaning up around the mills. Hauling supplies to the camps when logging operations are underway. Chopping wood for the camp cooks' stoves and for the bunkhouses. That sort of thing."

"Why would he fire the Pillagers' timber?"

"As I said, for revenge."

"How about for profit?" Morgan said. "The day I visited the Agency, Whiskey Joe and another Indian were arguing with Meir. Money was scattered over the floor. Whiskey Joe kept yelling, 'No more, Meir! No more!' The argument could have been over what he was being paid to fire the Chippewa timber."

Stark sat rubbing the meerschaum's bowl with the palm of his hand for a moment. Then, for the first time, his manner took on a challenging quality. "Are you suggesting, Mr. Morgan, that Meir is hiring renegade Chippewas to commit arson?"

"It's a distinct possibility," Morgan replied. "Five hundred acres of prime timber were scorched by those small fires Whiskey Joe set. Under the dead and down timber law, the Indian agent is empowered to sell that timber as though it were fallen. If a logging contractor makes it worth his while, he can sell it without a bid. That's one of Bog-o-nay-ge-shig's complaints."

The meerschaum became a smoke screen from behind which Stark spoke with an imperturbable calm. "What you're suggesting, Mr. Morgan, is criminal conspiracy on two counts. Arson, and fraud against wards of the federal government. You have also implied that a member of the Pine Ring, of which I am president, is bribing Meir in order to gain those dead and down contracts. Are you prepared to name that contractor, Mr. Morgan? And to prove your charges in a court of law?"

"Not yet." Morgan rose and stood staring down at Stark. "But I will before I leave Walker. Good day, sir."

"Wait." Stark pushed back his chair and stood up. Entrenched behind the massive desk, he radiated power; yet, for the moment, he chose diplomacy.

"You're trying to move too fast, Mr. Morgan. The situation here is more complex than perhaps you realize. So far, you have heard only the Chippewas' side. I'd like for you to hear mine; not here, but in a more relaxed atmosphere." A brief pause, then he continued in the same smooth, urbane manner.

"My daughter, Elaine, and I are staying at my summer home on Front Point. We would be pleased to have you spend the weekend with us. Frankly, I think it would serve a constructive purpose. Besides"—this time, Stark's smile was genuine—"Elaine is eager to meet you. She's convinced that you're motivated by some dark tragedy in your past, and she's determined to discover what it is. Will you come?"

Morgan's mind worked quickly. If he accepted, what would he gain? How much of his hand would Stark show? It was worth finding out.

"If you're willing to talk seriously, yes."

"Good." Stark appeared relieved. "I'll have a carriage pick you up at the Pameda at four o'clock Friday afternoon."

"That will be fine." About to leave, Morgan remembered Jason Bradshaw. "By the way, have you seen Bradshaw recently?"

"Bradshaw?" Stark pursed his lips, concentrating. "Oh, you mean that reporter from the St. Paul *Globe*? No. I've never even met the man. Why do you ask?"

"He's missing."

"I wouldn't worry about it. He's probably on Bear Island or Sugar Point digging up a story."

"You're no doubt right."

With a brief nod, Morgan went out, closing the door behind him. The secretary, Gillispie, gave him a cold glance from behind the gold-rimmed glasses, then returned to his work. Morgan smiled. Gillispie hated everything and everybody, and probably didn't even know why.

The smile broadened, not because of Gillispie nor anything in particular. He just felt good. For the first time, he had the feeling that things were beginning to break for him. If Hugh Stark tried to bribe him during the weekend, he would know that the Pine Ring leader was worried. And when a man started to worry, he became careless. Eventually, he made a mistake. Hugh Stark was no exception.

Shadows had begun to lengthen across the boardwalk when Morgan stepped outside. The gold Hamilton watch read six o'clock. He walked briskly back to the hotel.

Thirty minutes later, wearing the Western-style suit, he left the Pameda and hurried toward Len Archer's livery stable. While Archer backed the same gentle mare between the buggy's shafts, Morgan informed him of the latest development.

"He's worried, all right," Archer agreed. "But don't forget that you're dealing with a very dangerous man. If he does offer you a bribe and you turn him down, he'll order you killed. That may have already happened to Jason Bradshaw."

"I asked him if he'd seen Bradshaw," Morgan said. "He claimed he'd never even met him. I believe him."

Archer stared at Morgan with a baffled expression. "Then where the hell *is* Bradshaw? Nobody's seen him, or has any idea where he might have gone. I don't like it." He handed Morgan the reins. "You'd better get moving. Gail Saunders is a damned good-looking woman. You turn up late tonight and you won't get another chance."

Climbing into the buggy, Morgan flicked the mare with the buggy whip. Dust rolled off the wheels in a yellow cascade. Here and there, a merchant, closing up shop, watched the buggy pass with inscrutable eyes.

To Morgan, the half-mile ride to the big house on top of the hill was the longest he had ever traveled. The three hours he then spent with Gail Saunders seemed the shortest of his life. Not since Anna's death had he felt so relaxed, so comfortable in the company of a woman. Although what he felt for her was not yet love, he was beginning to appreciate her more and more for the warm, genuine person she was.

Len Archer had gone home when he returned the buggy to

the livery stable. He handed the reins over to the sleepy-eyed hostler and walked slowly back to the hotel. He had not realized how tired he was, nor how much had happened in the past twelve hours.

He had killed a renegade Chippewa arsonist, and had almost gotten killed himself. He had found a friend in Len Archer, met Hugh Stark, been invited to the Pine Ring leader's home for the weekend, and, despite his determination not to get involved with Gail Saunders, was much closer to her than he cared to admit.

Things were beginning to happen.

The big clock on the wall read ten-thirty when Morgan returned to the hotel. Pollock had already retired. A sign on the desk informed guests to "Ring Bell For Service." Morgan took his key off the rack and climbed the stairs.

A light showed from beneath the door of Jason Bradshaw's room.

He knocked on the door. "Bradshaw!" He kept his voice low. "It's Morgan. I need to talk to you."

A man groaned and mumbled something in a garbled voice.

"Bradshaw, are you all right?" Morgan opened the door, stepped inside—and stopped.

Jason Bradshaw lay sprawled face down on the bed, one arm tucked under him, holding his stomach. A blood-stained towel in his free hand still dripped on the carpet, and the water in the wash basin beside the bed was a bright red.

"My God!" Morgan bent over the reporter. "What happened to you, man?"

The one visible eye opened, blinked, and, with an effort, focused upon Morgan. Bradshaw ran his tongue across his puffed lips. "Where the hell have you been? I think I'm busted up inside."

"Let's have a look at you." Carefully, Morgan rolled the reporter on his back. "Maybe . . ." His voice faded in shock.

Only the torn, bloody, off-the-rack suit and the single swollen gray eye staring up at him from the Halloween mask was familiar. From forehead to chin, bloody furrows crisscrossed Bradshaw's hollow-cheeked face. His left eye was completely closed; a hen's egg-size lump on the cheekbone gave his whole head a grotesque appearance; his nose had been broken; air whistled between his puffed lips through a tooth-missing gap. He kept coughing and hacking as bloody mucus clogged the half-blocked nasal passages.

"Sometimes"—he looked at Morgan and tried to grin—"I wonder if it's worth it."

"Who did this to you?" Morgan asked in a tight voice.

"Drew Larkin, Stark's general superintendent."

"Why?"

"He caught me snooping around near Lake May and ordered me to leave. We had some words, and—"

"Was Stark there?"

"No."

"You think Larkin was acting on orders from Stark?"

Bradshaw hacked and blew a gob of bloody mucus from his flattened nose. "Maybe. I don't know."

Had Stark lied about not seeing the reporter? Morgan wondered. *Or had Larkin acted on his own?* He was inclined to believe the latter.

"Did you find out anything?"

"The usual gripes, long hours, poor pay, lousy food, bunkhouses not fit to live in." Bradshaw breathed cautiously, slow, shallow gasps. "A few have real grudges. Men crippled by falling timber who were fired, with nothing to tide them over until they recover—*if* they recover. The woods boss lets them sleep in the bunkhouse, and the cook sneaks them food from the kitchen. I talked to half a dozen of them. They swear that false scaling of Chippewa timber is a common, widespread practice, and that both Stark and Meir know about it.

"I also ran into a couple of renegade Pillagers. We had a few drinks"—somehow Bradshaw managed the old crooked smile—"and they boasted that Meir paid them 'plenty money' for setting 'little fires that scorch.'"

It was difficult for Morgan, watching the reporter's battered features contort with pain, but he did not try to spare him. He couldn't afford to.

"Will they testify to that in court?"

"No." Bradshaw tried to shake his head. "Anyway, who the

hell would believe a few disgruntled loggers and a couple of drunken, no good Indians?"

"Then we're just wasting our time," Morgan retorted. "Without witnesses, we can't prove anything in court. Gail Saunders pointed that out to me a few hours ago. She thinks our only chance is to expose Stark in the newspapers."

Bradshaw's one good eye gleamed with appreciation. "That woman's smart. Print what we've found out, but can't prove in court, and the publicity will destroy him."

"What about a libel suit?"

"That wouldn't help him."

"Would all this prevent an insurrection?"

"I doubt it." The reporter's breath whistled through the tooth-missing gap. "The Chippewas are not going to be satisfied with anything short of some sort of correction of their grievances." Then, "What have you come up with?"

"That can wait," Morgan said. "I'm going after Dr. E.C."

"Now." Stubbornly. "Ten more minutes won't kill me."

Always the story first, even if he was dying. To argue with him would take more time than to tell him.

"All right." Briefly, Morgan summarized the incident at Little Moss Lake, his meeting with Hugh Stark, and his acceptance of Stark's weekend invitation at Front Point.

"Be careful," Bradshaw warned. "You could be walking into a trap."

"Perhaps," Morgan conceded. "Then, again, I may just turn up something."

He rose, flexed his cramped legs, and moved toward the door. There he paused, grave faced. "You're a tough, hard-boiled reporter, Bradshaw; and, sometimes, you grate on my nerves. But I'm glad you're still alive."

Bradshaw smiled with his one good eye and his puffed lips. "Thanks."

Downstairs, Morgan routed a disheveled, sleepy-eyed Pollock out of his quarters just off the lobby.

"Jason Bradshaw's been badly hurt," he told the clerk. "You'd better send someone for Dr. Lindley."

"I knew it!" Pollock slapped his hand down on the desk with a kind of grim triumph. "I tried to warn you both; but you wouldn't listen. The next time, it'll be you, and maybe dead."

"The doctor, Mr. Pollock."

"There's no one here but me," the clerk protested. "And I can't leave my desk until I'm relieved."

"Mr. Pollock," Morgan said gently, "you're not going to have a desk unless you get moving."

"But—!"

"Now, Mr. Pollock!"

He waited until the clerk slipped into a coat and hurried out into the night. Then he went back upstairs.

Jason Bradshaw had not moved. His breathing was stertorous, and he did not answer when Morgan spoke to him. He was either sleeping or unconscious.

Drawing up a chair, Morgan sat down and waited. He looked at the *Globe* reporter's battered face, at the hundred and forty-five pound body, at the torn, bloody suit. He looked a long time, remembering the way Bradshaw had tried to shape the puffy lips into a cocky smile. Then the anger came. It took him a long time to bring it under control.

He was still sitting there when Pollock returned with Dr. Lindley.

Bradshaw aroused long enough to answer questions, grunt, goan and swear as Lindley palpated, probed, checked his pupils, and listened to his chest with the stethoscope. Then he rolled over on his back and went to sleep.

For a moment, Dr. E.C. observed him with a faint frown, then rose and nodded to Morgan.

"He's taken a savage beating," Lindley said. "Luckily, his vital organs seem to be all right. However, he has a couple of fractured ribs that could give him trouble. There's always the danger of pneumonia." Closing his black leather bag, he slipped into his coat and stepped out into the hall. Morgan followed.

"How long will he be out of action?"

"Barring complications," Lindley said, "at least ten days' bed rest. After that, he'll need to take it easy for a month. I'll drop by in the morning and check on him. Meanwhile, I've given him some laudanum for pain and to make him sleep." The cool eyes rested on Morgan. "If you've needed proof of the danger you're in, sir, you have it now."

"I know," Morgan replied. "And thank you, Doctor, for coming out in the middle of the night."

The physician shrugged. "That's my job, Mr. Morgan."

Watching him descend the stairs, Morgan wondered how long it had been since E. C. Lindley had had a decent night's sleep, and what inner strength kept the man going.

With a final look-in on Bradshaw, he returned to his own room, leaving both doors ajar should the reporter need him.

For a long time, he stood at the window, staring out across the darkened town, thinking. The brutal beating of Jason Bradshaw had upset him. He had not realized how much he respected the reporter, nor how indispensable Bradshaw was to his investigation. Now with Bradshaw out of action, his own position was definitely threatened. For that reason, his visit to Front Point now took on greater importance.

Hugh Stark, his daughter, Elaine, and he, Morgan. A peace conference, an attempted bribe, or a trap?

Tomorrow, he would find out.

Promptly at four o'clock the following afternoon, a shiny surrey drawn by a spirited black thoroughbred pulled up before the Pameda Hotel. The driver, a carbon copy of Gillispie, minus the frigid manner, carried Morgan's valise to the surrey and then waited while he spoke to Gail Saunders and Dr. Lindley.

"I wish you'd let me come with you, Craig." Concern shadowed Gail's voice. "I don't like you going out there alone."

"Don't worry," Morgan assured her. "I have a feeling that this will be a battle of wits, not of violence."

"But can you be sure of that?" Dr. E.C., his suit rumpled and with dark circles under his eyes, voiced his skepticism. "Don't forget Jason Bradshaw."

"No," Morgan admitted. "However, it's worth the gamble. Either we come up with some solid evidence that the Commissioner of Indian Affairs can submit to a federal grand jury, or we'll be forced to give the public such evidence as we have through the *Globe* and let them return their own verdict. I'd prefer the legal route if possible. Now I'd better go before the man in the pinstripes drives off and leaves me."

As he started to walk away, Gail Saunders laid her hand on his arm. "Remember what I told you, Craig. Elaine Stark is brilliant and ruthless. She's also a beautiful hussy. Watch out she doesn't turn your head."

Her candidness shattered Morgan's sober mood. "Please, give me credit for not being a total fool. You keep an eye on Jason Bradshaw for me; and I'll promise not to be snared by Elaine Stark."

The intense blue eyes rested on Morgan, unconvinced. "I wish I was as confident of that as you are," she said. "Come back to us, Craig."

With a brief nod, he walked over to the surrey. "Sorry to have kept you waiting," he told the driver.

Sun bounced off the gold-rimmed glasses, and in the eyes behind them lurked some secret amusement.

"Waiting, Mr. Morgan, although I don't know exactly what for, seems to be the story of my life."

As they drove down Lake Street, Morgan was conscious of the flat stares of merchants standing in their shop doorways, and of people on the boardwalks turning their heads and whispering to one another. Aware of what had happened to Jason Bradshaw, they were now wondering what his next move would be. With odds, no doubt, being offered that he would not come back from Front Point alive.

He doubted whether, if he were a gambler, he would cover those bets.

Set back from the shore of Leech Lake, Hugh Stark's summer home, a two-storied white mansion with French doors, a flagstone terrace, and a smooth carpeted lawn, reflected the same calculated design to intimidate as his Walker office.

As the surrey swept up the graveled drive, Morgan glimpsed a score of people seated on the terrace with white-jacketed waiters, moving among the ornate wrought iron tables, serving refreshments, and a dozen buggies and surreys clustered around the carriage house beyond.

Separating himself from the group, Hugh Stark hurried forward to meet his guest.

"Welcome to White Pines, Mr. Morgan," he said, shaking hands. "Bruce"—to the pinstripe-suited young man—"have one of the staff take Mr. Morgan's luggage to his room. Come." He grasped Morgan's arm. "I want you to meet some of my associates."

"I wasn't expecting other guests." Morgan nodded to the group on the terrace. "It's hardly the atmosphere for serious discussions."

"They own summer homes around the lake," Stark reassured him. "They'll all be leaving soon."

As they approached the terrace, Morgan felt cool eyes appraising him from beneath the gayly colored lawn umbrellas. They all knew who he was and why he was here. With Stark guiding him, he moved from table to table, politely acknowledging the Pine Ring leader's introductions.

"Mr. and Mrs. James van Buskirk. Jim is vice-president of Red River Logging Company . . . Mr. and Mrs. William Garner. Bill is secretary-treasurer of the company . . . Mr. and Mrs. Thomas Randall . . . Senator and Mrs. Dean Aldrege of Wisconsin . . . General and Mrs. Jack McCall . . ."

"How do you do? Nice to meet you, Mr. Morgan." "Charmed, sir." "I've heard so much about you, Mr. Morgan! You must come to see us while you're here." "Tell me, sir, is it true . . ." Banal inanities masking the fear, resentment and contempt which they harbored for one of their own kind who would destroy their snug little world to help a bunch of ignorant savages.

As their peer, Morgan returned their contempt and hating, white-toothed smiles and derived a certain satisfaction from their discomfort.

"And now"—Stark paused before an umbrella-shaded table facing the east—"I want you to meet my daughter, Elaine. Elaine, this is Mr. Craig Morgan."

Whatever Morgan had expected, it was not this. Slim, elegant, with touch-the-shoulders blond hair and jade-green eyes that seemed to have no depth, Elaine Stark, even seated, displayed the poised sophistication of the born-to-wealth woman. Five feet three, small-boned, fair-skinned and with almost classical features, she reminded Morgan of an exquisite Dresden figurine.

"Ah, the champion of Indians' rights!" She extended a slim hand, her mouth curving into a half mocking smile. The jade-green eyes slanted up at him, cool, challenging. "You're going into battle against my father, aren't you?"

"Your father and I have different philosophies and different goals," Morgan countered. "Hopefully, we may be able to reach an equitable agreement."

"You can talk business tomorrow," Elaine Stark said. "Today, you can talk to me." She glanced toward Stark. "May I borrow him until dinner, Father?"

"Why not wait until all these people leave," Stark suggested. "Then, if you wish–" He broke off, staring past Morgan with a worried frown. "I'm sorry, Mr. Morgan. I should have warned you that Marshal O'Connor is here, as Elaine's guest. I couldn't very well ask him to leave. Now, I'm afraid he's going to create a scene. Please let me handle him."

Casually, Morgan turned. O'Connor was crossing the terrace toward them with purposeful strides. The Marshal was clearly in a belligerent mood. Morgan turned to Elaine Stark.

"Perhaps you'd better leave."

"No."

By then, it was too late.

O'Connor halted a yard away. His quicksilver eyes flicked from Morgan to Elaine Stark. A dull flush rose to his cheeks. He swung angrily on Stark.

"What the hell is *he* doing here?"

Stark stiffened. "Mr. Morgan is my guest." His voice was brittle. "Now I think you'd better leave. I'll not tolerate your belligerence at White Pines."

O'Connor's mouth set in a stubborn line. "Not until I've had my say." He looked to Elaine Stark for support, received none. "Elaine, do you know who this man, Morgan, is? He's a Bureau of Indian Affairs inspector, working hand in glove with Senator Leland to ruin your father. A damned fool who wants to turn the country back to a bunch of savages! I don't want you having anything to do with him!"

Elaine Stark tilted her blond head and ego-shriveled him with those jade eyes. "Marshal, you'd better leave–*now*."

"By God, don't treat me like dirt, Elaine!" O'Connor cried in a strangled voice. "You know you're not the only woman in Minnesota!"

She stared straight through him.

"You green-eyed bitch!" He pivoted on Morgan. "You stay away from here or, by God, I'll make you wish you had!"

He strode away, brushing guests roughly aside, and disappeared behind the carriage house. A minute later, he raced down the drive, roweling his horse cruelly into the timber.

Stark watched him go in silence. Although he remained calm, the incident had clearly disturbed him. "I'm sorry, Mr. Morgan. It should never have happened." He glanced at his daughter. "It was foolish to invite him here, Elaine. The man can be dangerous when he loses his temper. Do you realize that a tragedy at White Pines could have ruined me politically?"

"You're forgetting *why* I invited him, Father," Elaine retorted. "Why I've tolerated him for the past year. Certainly it has not been of my choosing."

The open defiance in her voice and in the proud set of her head took Morgan by surprise. For an instant, the mask had dropped, revealing the real woman beneath. Intelligent, calculating and driven by an ambition that would let nothing, not even her father, stand in her way. It showed in her face—the fire, the ice and the steel.

She must have sensed his thoughts for the mask slipped smoothly back into place and, once again, she was the poised, sophisticated hostess.

"Forgive me, Mr. Morgan," she murmured, "for my bad manners and lack of foresight. I had no idea that this would happen."

"You're not to blame," Morgan told her. "Nothing could have kept O'Connor away once he knew I was here."

"Thank you for understanding." Elaine slipped her arm through his. "Now why don't you unpack and relax awhile before dinner?"

The three of them crossed the deserted terrace. By the time they reached the house, the last of the guests had gone.

In the spacious foyer, a maid waited to show Morgan to his room. Stark excused himself and went to his study. Elaine accompanied Morgan to the foot of the stairs.

"I'm looking forward to an exciting weekend," she said, smiling up at him. "I must warn you, however, that my father's interests are also mine. Whatever threatens him, threatens me. I hope that it won't come to that. But if it should . . ."

"If it should?" Morgan prompted.

"Then you will have to fight me, too." The pink-lipped smile remained in place. "And I must warn you, Mr. Morgan, that I can be as dangerous as my father."

"I'll remember that," he said, and followed the maid up the stairs. On the landing, he turned. Elaine Stark had not moved. The smile was still in place.

"Dinner is at seven, Mr. Morgan."

"Thank you."

He followed the maid down the hall.

Dinner was an informal affair with only Morgan, Stark and Stark's daughter present. Yet despite Stark's easy manner and Elaine's sometimes brilliant conversation, memory of the clash with O'Connor still lingered, creating new tensions.

Throughout the meal, Morgan was conscious of the silent battle of wills between Stark and his daughter, a subterranean overflow of anger from the sharp exchange on the terrace. He wondered why no one had mentioned the deep-seated hostility between them, for it was there, just below the surface, and it intrigued him.

Two people bound together by blood, expediency, and a common goal whose too-much-alike natures kept them engaged in a constant state of attack and defense.

Could he, somehow, turn that distrust and animosity to his advantage?

The thought stayed with him throughout the evening.

It was eight o'clock when they returned to the drawing room with its Persian carpet, crystal chandeliers, period furniture and magnificent rosewood grand piano. This was no ordinary summer home, Morgan realized, but actually a townhouse made all the more impressive by its rustic setting. Here—not in St. Paul, Duluth, or in Washington—Hugh Stark worked out the strategy for his Great Dream, and issued the orders to cheat, defraud, harass, commit arson, and, if necessary, to kill.

"You have a beautiful place here," he said. "Few men could afford it."

Stark shrugged. "It serves its purpose."

"Like your office?" Morgan challenged. "To intimidate people, and to perhaps soften resistance?"

A touch of admiration flickered in Stark's eyes. "If you want to put it that way, yes. You would be surprised just how effective it is." He turned to his daughter. "Elaine, my dear, will you excuse us? I'd like to take a walk with Mr. Morgan."

Elaine Stark's Dresden features sharpened. "Can't your business wait until tomorrow? It's already past eight."

"There's a full moon," Stark replied. "You can take Mr. Morgan for a stroll when we return. I'm sure he wouldn't mind."

The pink lips shaped themselves into a porcelain smile. "You always win, don't you, Father? Mr. Morgan, I'll wait up for you."

Nodding, Morgan followed Stark through the French doors and onto the deserted terrace. Moonlight lay white across the wrought iron furniture and spread outward over the lawn. Already a crisp tang in the air foretold the changing of the seasons.

For a moment, the two men remained silent, letting the night come to them. Then Stark led the way across the terrace and down the graveled drive. A hundred feet from the house, he paused beside a three-tiered fountain dropping rivulets of water from basin to basin into the pool surrounding it.

"I invited you to White Pines, Mr. Morgan," he said, "to acquaint you with the other side of this Indian problem. As you know, logging in Minnesota is big business, and is expanding rapidly. In communities such as Walker, the economy is dependent upon it. Naturally, people resent any outside interference which threatens their prosperity. Your investigation here *is* a threat to that prosperity."

"To their prosperity, sir," Morgan challenged, "or to your political ambitions?"

Stark smiled faintly. "The two are inseparable, Mr. Morgan. As I go, so goes north central Minnesota." A faint breeze blew fine spray from the fountain against his face. He wiped it away with the palm of his hand.

"For that very reason, Mr. Morgan, I am concerned about this investigation. An unfavorable report from you to the Commissioner of Indian Affairs could conceivably lead to a congressional probe damaging to me and my associates. And with elections coming up, bad publicity is the one thing I cannot afford."

"Then why did you have your general superintendent, Drew Larkin, beat Jason Bradshaw half to death?" Morgan asked. "You seem to have little respect for the power of the press."

Stark stared at him with a genuinely shocked expression. "I can't believe that," he said. "Larkin has been with me for years. He would do nothing to jeopardize my interests."

"Perhaps he thought he was protecting your interests," Morgan suggested. "I understand he's an aggressive man."

"Only when he's provoked," Stark replied. "Bradshaw must have said or done something to set him off. Exactly what did happen?"

In a few terse sentences, Morgan gave him the details.

By now, Stark had regained his composure. "Frankly, Mr. Morgan, I can't see where Larkin was at fault. Although I disapprove of the way he handled the matter, he *was* acting in my interests, and Bradshaw *was* trespassing. However, since I need the *Globe*'s support, not its animosity, I'm willing to offer Bradshaw an apology and a reasonable financial settlement provided he stops prying into my affairs. But that's as far as I'll go." He buttoned his coat and walked back toward the house, with Morgan following.

"What's happening here is progress, Mr. Morgan; and neither you nor anyone else can stop it. I regret that you can't accept that because, despite our differences, we have a lot in common." A pause, with the splash of the fountain lost now in the night sounds. "A man with your ability could go a long way in my organization, Mr. Morgan. It's no secret that I want nationwide control of the timber industry through high political office. Once I achieve that—and I will—you could virtually name your own position."

"And the price?" Morgan prompted.

At the edge of the lawn, Stark stopped and faced him in the moonlight. "Only that you place the Pine Ring's activities here in the proper perspective."

It had been a long time coming; but now it was out.

"In other words"—Morgan kept his voice level—"close my eyes to what's going on here and go back to Oregon."

"I didn't say that, Mr. Morgan," Stark replied. "I merely suggested that you face up to what Polk, half a century ago, referred to as this nation's 'manifest destiny.' Unfortunately, I can't seem to communicate that fact to you. I can only hope that you change your mind before the weekend is over."

"You would be better served if you changed yours," Morgan said. "You're not only risking criminal indictment; you're playing with fire as well. In the event of an uprising, you would be Bog-o-nay-ge-shig's first target. Also"—he spaced his words carefully —"there is Jean Chardin to worry about. He has threatened to kill you."

"Mr. Morgan"—Stark shifted position so that his face was in shadow—"many men have threatened to kill me. Most of them are dead. Jean Chardin does not concern me. As for the other risks you mention, what is at stake makes them seem very insignificant. Now"—he started back across the terrace—"I think we'd better go inside. Elaine will be waiting for you. She won't be happy until she's figured you out."

They did not speak again until they entered the great entrance hall. There Morgan paused, listening to the faint sound of music from the drawing room.

Stark smiled. "I told you she's persistent. Now if you will excuse me, I have some paper work to go over in my study. I'll see you at breakfast. Good night."

When he had gone, Morgan followed the sound of the music across the foyer. Outside the drawing room, he paused, took a deep breath, and entered.

"'Come into my parlor, said the spider to the fly.'" Seated at the piano, Elaine Stark smiled as Morgan crossed the room. "Did you enjoy your walk?"

Standing beside her, Morgan watched her slim hands play lightly over the keys and wondered how such a woman could evoke so much beauty from felt-padded hammers and tightly strung steel wires. Cold, she might be; talented, she certainly was.

"Your father and I did not reach an agreement," he replied, "if that's what you mean. But then that wasn't why I was invited here. Nor why"—his eyes ranged cooly over her small, exquisite figure, sheathed in an ice-blue satin dress with a daringly low-cut bodice—"why the spider has invited me into her parlor."

Elaine Stark laughed, soft, amused laughter that curved her small pink mouth into a provocative *O*. "And just why *have* I invited you into my parlor?"

"Why, to spin a web of glittering promises around me," Morgan said calmly, "to try and persuade me not to drop my investigation of your father."

It was Debussy now, gentle, poignant, intended to cover her surprise. "Why on earth would I do that, Mr. Morgan?"

Morgan leaned his tall, spare frame on the piano and looked straight into her eyes. "Because you're a brilliant, ambitious woman trapped in a man's world with no hope of ever fulfilling your dreams. And so you spin webs to try and trap a man who will help to destroy your father, so that you can take over his empire."

Smoothly, the porcelain mask slipped back into place. "You are a very perceptive man, Mr. Morgan. I suspected as much during dinner. Tell me. Are you going to sell out to my father? Or are you going to continue to play Don Quixote?"

"I'm going to continue my investigation."

She rose and crossed to the great fireplace where she stood, slim and lovely, with the flames playing like sun and shadow across her face.

"Suppose, Mr. Morgan, I were to link my father to a conspiracy to gain control of Chippewa lands by inciting them to insurrection?"

It was a dramatic break, and, for that reason, Morgan questioned it. Was it a trap within a trap, designed to somehow snare him? Carefully, he cast his own net.

"We'd need solid evidence," he replied. "Records, correspondence and reliable witnesses."

"I understand. However"—an expressive lift of the rounded shoulders—"I can't guarantee all that overnight. My father is a brilliant man. He's not likely to have put anything incriminating into writing. But given a little time . . ."

"Time is the one thing we don't have," Morgan informed her. "We're sitting on top of a powder keg that could blow up any day."

Elaine Stark bit her lip. She slanted Morgan a speculative glance, her eyes smoking up to hide the struggle going on behind them.

He waited, saying nothing to upset the delicate balance of her mind, leaving it up to her to make her own decision. Suddenly, with a little shrug, she broke the silence.

"You leave me no choice, do you?" she said. "Well, this much I can tell you. For the past year, my father has been using me as a lure to blind Marshal O'Connor to what's really going on here, and to encourage his harassment of the Chippewas in the hope of stirring them up. During that time, I've sat in on meetings between my father and the Indian Agent, Frank Meir, at which arson, false scaling and the purchase of dead and down timber without competitive bidding was discussed. I've no proof of this; but it's the truth."

"So," Morgan said, not really surprised, "you *are* a part of the conspiracy."

"A pawn, Mr. Morgan." Bitter, self-mocking. "Nothing more."

"Why are you telling me this?" Morgan asked. "Don't you realize that it could send you to prison, along with your father? Do you hate him that much?"

A lovely Dresden figurine framed in light and shadow, yet now subtly different. Steel, not clay, beneath the rich, delicate colors and matchless glaze.

Slowly, Elaine Stark turned her head and in a voice devoid of emotion said, "Hate? Mr. Morgan, I hate my father as I've never hated any man in my life. He's used me, as he used my mother before me, to decorate his home, inflate his ego and, when he's stood to profit from it, to arouse other men's desires. In one way or the other, I've been a pawn all my life." She fell silent a moment, then continued in that same frozen voice.

"I want him dead, Mr. Morgan. Alive, he would always be a threat to me. But, first, I want him broken, his Great Dream destroyed—did you know he wants to be President of the United States?—and I want him to know that it was I who brought him down. Do I frighten you, Mr. Morgan?"

"No," he said. "You intrigue me. Just how do you expect to accomplish all this?"

He was never quite sure how it happened. One moment, she

was standing in three-quarter profile against the backdrop of the firelight, her jade eyes glowing with frozen flames; the next, her slim body was pressed against him, her arms around his neck and her lips reaching up to him in open invitation.

"Why, through you and the press, Mr. Morgan," she said cooly. "When you leave here Sunday evening it will be with my full written confession. You are to turn it over to that *Globe* reporter, Jason Bradshaw, and let him run a front-page exposé of the conspiracy against the Chippewas." She smiled, her arms tightening around his neck. "Within three days after the story hits the street, my father will be dead."

"Suicide?" Morgan rejected the idea. "He's too much of a man for that."

"*Not* suicide, Mr. Morgan; although the press will draw that conclusion."

Staring down into the jade eyes, dispassionately passionate, Morgan realized that, as her father had used her, she would attempt to use him, Craig Morgan, to achieve her goal.

Dangerous. More dangerous, in her way, than Hugh Stark. Yet she was Stark's Achilles' heel, the only apparent means of breaking the Pine Ring leader's power and of stopping the rape of the Pillagers. He *had* to have her confession.

"Are you suggesting that I murder your father?"

"Murder is an ugly word," she countered. "People die up here all the time from accidents in the deep woods, in the mills, or even while hunting. I'm only suggesting that if something *should* happen to him . . ."

"You would inherit everything."

"Your Indian friends would also profit." She slicked a small pink tongue across her lips. "And if you and Jason Bradshaw expose a conspiracy to incite a Chippewa uprising, the press will make you a national hero overnight. As a champion of the underdog, you will be a natural candidate for the U. S. Senate from Oregon. Later, if you're interested, perhaps . . ."

"What about you?" Morgan asked. "You still may well be indicted for conspiracy."

Imperceptibly, a sweet, naïve expression dissolved the porcelain mask. "With my father's death and the conspiracy broken up, interest in the affair will die. No grand jury would think of indicting Hugh Stark's daughter, the frightened pawn of a ruthless father."

The blond head tilted up to him, her eyes seawater green. "Think about it, Craig."

She was, indeed, a deadly spider, Morgan thought, *spinning a web to trap him. Let her spin until he got her confession. Then let her try and escape the web she'd spun around herself.*

"I'll think about it," he agreed. "And I'll give you my answer in the morning."

"By morning, Mr. Morgan"—he spun around as Hugh Stark spoke coldly from the parlor doorway—"if you're wise, you'll be on your way back to Oregon." He stood there in his smoking jacket, caressing his favorite meerschaum.

"You disappoint me, Mr. Morgan," he said. "I thought you too intelligent to be drawn into my daughter's murderous intrigues. I've known of them for years. Don't delude yourself; you're no match for my daughter. You'd be wise to remember that." He stepped aside and motioned with his hand. "A carriage will be waiting outside in ten minutes."

In the foyer, Morgan swung around. "I came here to try and reach some sort of compromise that would prevent an Indian uprising and, at the same time, keep you out of prison. Obviously, it was a waste of time. Good night."

Upstairs, he closed his still unpacked valise, and returned to the foyer.

Elaine Stark was nowhere in sight. Any hope of a confession from her was gone. Stark would keep her a virtual prisoner until he could send her out of the country.

Crossing the foyer, he went outside.

"Gillispie II" was waiting beside the surrey. The gold frames of his glasses glinted in the moonlight; the amused, secretive smile was gone. He stood silent while Morgan climbed aboard; then he swung up and drove down the graveled drive.

Arriving in Walker, he reined up before the Pameda Hotel, and said cooly, "I was in Oregon once, Mr. Morgan. It's beautiful country. If I had what you have, I'd go back and enjoy it. But then I'm just a man who spends his life waiting for other people, opportunity, something. Still, think about it, Mr. Morgan."

With a flick of the buggy whip, he was gone.

Down the street, a man came out of Joe Frost's saloon and stood smoking a cigarette under the dim glow of the electric street lights, installed the previous April. As the surrey drew up in front of the Pameda, he ground out the cigarette and walked toward Morgan with a lazy arrogance.

"I'm Mike Davitt." Tipping back his hat, he motioned toward Morgan's valise. "You and Stark come to an agreement that quick? Or did that jealous fool, O'Connor, run you off? Hell, don't look so surprised. I know everything that goes on here."

Morgan had expected him to be a lanky, lantern-jawed hillbilly. He wasn't. Thirty, handsome, with a to-hell-with-you arrogance that made one smile; and then, without knowing exactly why, stop smiling. Perhaps it was his eyes. They were like a lynx's, alert, watchful, devoid of emotion. Like Sheehan's, only somehow different.

"I've heard about you," Morgan told him. "None of it good. Is Stark paying you to keep the young Chippewas drunk so that Marshal O'Connor can harass them? Or are you on your own?"

The lynx's eyes grew very still. "I don't trust Stark. I don't have any use for Meir. And I hate O'Connor's guts. But whatever they do is their business. I want no part of it; it's bad for my trade."

"Maybe."

The to-hell-with-you smile was back again. "You're a fool, Morgan. You saw what happened to Bradshaw. The same thing could happen to you. If you meddle in *my* business, I'll kill you."

As silently as though he were on moccasins, he disappeared into the night.

Now he'd met them all, Morgan thought. *Each motivated by his or her own special goal. U. S. Senator, timber baron, Indian Agent, newspaper reporter, Chippewa chief, U. S. Marshal, whiskey peddler, gunman, beautiful storekeeper, doctor, fisherman, socialite, barber, livery stable owner.*

The list sounded like characters in a traveling actors' troupe; only this was no cheap music hall melodrama, but a rapidly developing real-life tragedy involving real people.

Picking up his valise, he went inside. Ignoring Pollock's open-mouthed surprise, he motioned for his key. Then, without explanation, he mounted the stairs.

Light splashed from beneath the door of Jason Bradshaw's room. He knocked lightly.

A pleasant, middle-aged woman opened the door and informed him that Mr. Bradshaw was asleep. Dr. Lindley and Miss Saunders had dropped in to see the patient around nine o'clock. Yes, Mr. Bradshaw had inquired about him.

"How is he?"

The smile faded. "Dr. E.C.'s worried. He's running a fever."

It was not what Morgan had hoped for. "If he grows worse during the night, let me know. Meanwhile, when he wakes up tell him Morgan is back. Good night."

He waited until she closed the door; then he crossed the hall to his own room.

Star sheen outlined the window overlooking the lake, filling the room with dark shadows. He put the suitcase in the closet, removed his coat, and stretched to ease the tension in his neck and shoulders. Then he settled himself in a chair, lit a cigarette, and stared thoughtfully at the glowing tip.

Jason Bradshaw's condition worried him. It was becoming increasingly obvious that the power of the press might be the only way to destroy Stark.

His visit to White Pines had reinforced that belief. He had brought Stark into the open, which had been his purpose in going there. And Elaine Stark's "confession" had implicated Stark, Meir and herself. Unfortunately, Stark's discovery of his daughter's treachery now ruled out any possibility of obtaining a written confession. Or of a peaceful solution to the problem. With the situation dangerously volatile, positive action had to be taken, and quickly.

He ground out the cigarette on the heel of his boot and dropped it into the brass cuspidor. In the morning, he would unleash the battered Bradshaw to scoop every other newspaper in the nation. Then he would turn his findings over to the Commissioner of Indian Affairs and go back to Oregon, while Minnesotans destroyed Hugh Stark's Great Dream at the polls.

But that would not be the end of it. Stark's vengeance would reach out for him, as it had for others in the past. He must spend the rest of his life constantly on guard, not knowing when or from where the attack would come.

A dark tunnel with no light at the end.

Restlessly, he rose and walked over to the window. At the end of the block, the street light went out, leaving the town in darkness. He stood thinking, piecing together the events in his life which had led him into the morass which could eventually destroy him.

Events? People, really. The Nez Percé warriors with their slumped shoulders and apathetic eyes, waiting for their monthly handout . . . his father, Sergeant Jim Morgan, U. S. Cavalry . . . his mother, a blurred, shadowy figure in his memory, perhaps because he wished it that way . . . the long-dead Cheyenne squaw whom he had never known, but whose dark, shining hair on the cabin wall had haunted him all these years . . . his wife, Anna, whose love had opened the doors of knowledge and success, and whose remembered faith in him had given him the incentive to fight for the Greater Dream . . . and, finally, his compassion for the underdog.

All those things had led him here to this moment in time and space. But what was it that made him stay? What forces combined to cast him into a different mold than other men?

Certainly not his father; although, by Western standards, Sergeant Jim Morgan had been neither better nor worse than the average soldier on the frontier. Nor his mother, neglected and virtually deserted, who had run off with another man, leaving a fifteen-year-old boy to cut his stick alone, without brothers, sisters or friends.

Friends had come later; yet even these had been guarded relationships. He had not wished it that way; nor could he have explained why it was so. Sometimes, he experienced the feeling that he was separated from the rest of the world by an unbreakable, one-way glass wall. He could see and hear people on the other side, but no matter how hard he pounded on the glass, or shouted in desperation, no one ever seemed to be aware of him.

Save for his acceptance over the years by people such as Gail Saunders, Dr. E. C. Lindley and a growing number of legislators in Washington, he might have questioned his competence to relate to society. Gradually, as his controversial activities began to gain support, he had come to recognize the glass wall as one of the spirit, rather than of the mind . . . and the reason behind it.

He was a humanist, an idealist in a pragmatic, dog-eat-dog world. It was that simple. What had made him that way, he did not know. It didn't matter. If he had any sense, he would get the hell out of this mess before it was too late.

Suddenly, he thought of Jason Bradshaw sprawled on the bed, bloody, savagely beaten, staring up at him with that one good eye and mumbling through puffed lips, "Sometimes, I wonder if it's worth it!"

He laughed, soft, easy laughter. Bradshaw had been talking through his hat and had known it. They both knew it.

Of course, it was worth it. Every damned bit of it!

It was Marshal O'Connor who struck the match.

He did it so quietly that not even Morgan knew when he and "Colonel" Sheehan took the train for Duluth the following morning. Nor was Morgan aware of the fact that Chief Bog-o-nay-ge-shig, brought in from Sugar Point during the night and hidden in the conductor's cubicle, was already aboard.

Only one man, a spy of Mike Davitt's, saw the chief smuggled aboard. Not waiting for daylight, he stole a canoe drawn up on the shore and paddled toward Ottertail Point. It was daybreak when he beached the canoe there, and full dawn by the time he reached Mike Davitt's temporary camp near a small, isolated Pillager village.

Davitt listened to the spy's report in tight-lipped calm. Then with a brief nod, he said, "Stay here. Don't sell any more whiskey. I'll be back tomorrow."

"Where are you going?"

Davitt gave him a cold-eyed stare. "Into Walker to see a man named Craig Morgan. I may have to kill him."

It was seven o'clock when Morgan stepped out of the hotel and walked west through the gathering dusk. As he came abreast of the Walker Saloon, the street lights went on, pale yellow eyes of progress, accentuating the dark shadows where they could not probe and, somehow, making his fears seem a ridiculous fantasy.

An Indian uprising here in the civilized northeast! Electric lights, running water, beer ordered by telegraph from Minneapolis one evening, arriving on the M & I the next day; and in Chicago, New York and in the nation's capital even a few of the exciting horseless carriages!

The idea was ridiculous!

Joe Frost, owner of the Walker Saloon, gave him a cool nod as he entered. He ordered bourbon. Frost served him in silence, rang up his money, and moved to the far end of the bar.

"Morgan!"

Seated at a table against the wall, Len Archer motioned him over. Morgan dropped into a chair. "Hello, Archer."

Archer shoved aside his beer. "I heard about Bradshaw," he said. "I can't say I'm surprised. How is he?"

"Dr. E.C. is afraid he's developing pneumonia."

"That's bad." The stable owner frowned. "What's this going to do to your investigation?"

"I'd planned to let Bradshaw break the story in tomorrow's edition of the *Globe* of what's actually happening here," Morgan answered. "Unfortunately, that's out for the moment."

Archer sipped his beer, wiped the foam from his mouth with the back of his hand and said, "Why don't you wire the *Globe* to send up another reporter to write the story?"

"He'd need specific details of what Bradshaw uncovered," Morgan pointed out. "If Bradshaw could dictate to another reporter, he could write the story himself."

"What about your own testimony?"

"Not enough, alone," Morgan told him. "But that's not the problem. We've got enough evidence for an indictment if our witnesses would testify. They won't. They're scared of Stark. Without witnesses, we have no case. That's why Bradshaw is so important. He's a top reporter with the guts to go after Stark. And in the *Globe,* he has a paper and an editor who will back him up. This couldn't have happened at a worse time."

Abruptly, Archer sat back in his chair. His expression was strained. He looked like a man who would have preferred to have been elsewhere, but couldn't leave.

"I don't quite know how to put this." He cleared his throat. "Until Bradshaw was taken out of action, I thought you might prevent an uprising here. I was wrong. No one can stop it. It's like a boil that's come to a head; it has to be lanced to get rid of the corruption before it can heal. It's not your fault. It's . . . well, that's just the way it is."

"I never thought I'd hear you talk like that," Morgan said quietly.

"Hell, man, face up to facts," Archer protested. "So far, you've antagonized a lot of people who don't like Stark, but now like you even less. You've gotten nowhere with Meir, except to call his bluff. You've backed Marshal O'Connor down in public, but you haven't stopped him from harassing the Pillagers. Mike Davitt's still peddling his rotgut whiskey to the young Chippewas. Bog-o-nay-ge-shig's more belligerent than ever. Jean Chardin is somewhere out there in the woods trying to figure out a way to kill Stark. Your witnesses won't testify. And Bradshaw is too sick to wipe Stark out in the *Globe*. Dammit"—he ran a hand through his hair in a harried gesture—"what did you expect me to say? Tell you you've got Stark on the run? Keep egging you on until you get yourself killed? I'll not do that. You've fought tough battles before. Why don't you admit this is one you just can't win?"

Carefully, Morgan put down his whiskey glass. He sensed Archer's distress. Had he been in the livery owner's place, he might well have felt the same way. At least, Archer wasn't motivated by fear or self-serving interests.

"You're forgetting, Len," he pointed out. "I wasn't sent here to prevent an armed uprising, but to conduct an investigation of charges brought by Bog-o-nay-ge-shig against certain individuals. I'll not quit until I've finished it."

A rueful smile cleared Archer's long face. "Sometimes," he said, shaking his head, "it's hard to believe that you're real. You're a lot like Bradshaw. Get your teeth set in a man's butt and you won't—" The smile went sour. "Mike Davitt just came in. He's headed this way."

Without turning, Morgan said, "Let me handle him, Len."

The whiskey peddler hooked out a chair and sat down. The to-hell-with-you smile was missing. A tiny tic tugged at the corner of his mouth.

"I warned you to keep out of my business, Morgan," he said. "You didn't do it. You talked Bog into going to Duluth to testify against one of my men. Why?"

"What are you talking about?" Morgan retorted. "I haven't seen Bog-o-nay-ge-shig since he ran O'Connor off Sugar Point."

The devil-fire flickered in Davitt's eyes. "You're a liar or a damned fool. O'Connor and Sheehan sneaked Bog out of town this morning on the M & I. By now, they've got him jailed in Duluth as a material witness."

"I don't believe it," Morgan said flatly. "Bog-o-nay-ge-shig hates the Marshal's guts. He wouldn't go anywhere with him. Or do anything to help him."

"Unless O'Connor sold him a pack of lies," Archer suggested. "Such as, for instance, promising to tear up the warrants for Pugonny-koshig and Shab-on-day-sh-king. That would outlaw Meir's ultimatum."

"Bog's no fool," Morgan told him. "He'd never buy a story like that."

"When a man is thinking of his people's survival," Archer pointed out, "he sometimes closes his eyes to the truth."

A man who wanted only peace and justice might do just that.

Thoughtfully, Morgan eased back in his chair.

"Did it ever occur to you, Davitt, that O'Connor might just have put one over on both of us?"

"Shut up." Soft, deadly, but thinking hard just the same, the lynx's eyes never leaving Morgan's face. Abruptly, he shoved back his chair and stood up.

"If you've lied"—his voice was deceptively soft—"you'd better start carrying a gun. You'll need it."

He was gone, quiet as an Indian—almost as quiet as an animal.

"Well." Len Archer reached for his beer with a hand that was not quite steady. "What do you think?"

"I think I almost got killed."

"No," Archer remarked dryly. "I mean what's O'Connor up to? Something smells."

Morgan pondered the question, not liking the answer that came to his mind. O'Connor wasn't the kind to forget his humiliation at Sugar Point. Was this a carefully planned scheme to murder Bog-o-nay-ge-shig during an "attempted escape" en route to Duluth? The Marshal was capable of it.

He finished his drink, then met Archer's inquiring glance across the table.

"I've got a gut feeling that O'Connor's about to blow the lid off things. And that there's not a damned thing we can do about it."

"But you won't leave Walker?"

"No."

Archer shook his head. "I wish to hell I could figure you out."

"It's simple," Morgan explained. "I don't like to see a dog kicked, a deer gut shot, a fox run down and torn to pieces by dogs, a coon caught in a trap, chewing its leg off . . . or human beings treated worse than animals because of the color of their skins."

"Well, now I know." Archer rose, wincing as the arthritis in his knees reminded him of the coming winter. "You know where to find me."

"Thanks."

He was still sitting there when Joe Frost closed up.

It was nine o'clock when Morgan returned to the hotel. Pollock, who had not yet retired, greeted him with an "I've-got-a-secret" smile and nodded across the lobby.

"You've got a visitor," he said. "She's been waiting for half an hour."

"Good evening, Mr. Morgan." Gail Saunders rose from a sofa near the stove. Her voice was strained and he read the concern in her face. "I know it's late, but I had to see you." She glanced toward Pollock. "Can we talk in private?"

"Of course." Morgan led her to a sofa across the lobby and sat down beside her. She was clearly under stress.

"What's happened?"

She breathed deeply. "It's started."

"Tell me about it."

"It began yesterday when Marshal O'Connor ordered the arrests of Pugonny-koshig and Shab-on-day-sh-king on bench warrants. Deputy Marshal Morrison picked them up this morning. The Pillagers forcibly freed them before he could get them off Bear Island. O'Connor went into a rage when he heard about it. He sent Morrison to Onigum to demand the return of the fugitives. His timing was bad." Her hands spread in a mute storytelling gesture.

"With the Chippewas gathered at the Agency for their annual payment, and in no mood to be bullied, Morrison got a flat 'No,' from the chiefs. He appealed to Meir for help. Meir laid down an ultimatum. The Pillagers have one week to surrender Pugonny-koshig and Shab-on-day-sh-king. If they don't, Meir will ask for troops to restore order." Frustration sharpened her voice. "Things are working out just the way Stark planned them—what with Elaine maneuvering O'Connor into laying the trap, and now Meir about to spring it. What are we going to do, Craig?"

Morgan stared at her, his mind seeking some way out of this morass into which so many people, white and Indian, had been drawn.

"I don't know," he replied honestly. "If Bradshaw was well, we'd incinerate Stark in the *Globe*. Perhaps we can still do it. We have a week, maybe a little more, left."

"And if you can't?"

"Then there's no question but that the Army will move in and that fighting will occur," Morgan said. "Have you talked to Bog-o-nay-ge-shig recently?"

Gail Saunders concentrated on her slim, brown hands. "Bog has disappeared. Shab-on-day-sh-king sent a runner to me with the news. No one knows what's happened to him. There's talk of foul play. The chiefs are in an ugly mood."

Obviously, she knew nothing about O'Connor's latest move. Morgan decided not to tell her. It would only upset her more. He switched the subject.

"How is Bradshaw?"

"Dr. E.C. is worried about him. He's still running a high fever." She refused to be diverted. "Craig, would the Commissioner of Indian Affairs listen to you?"

"What could I tell him?" Morgan asked. "That the arrests of Pugonny-koshig and Shab-on-day-sh-king were illegal? That their forcible release was justified? That Meir, as Indian Agent, has no authority to demand their surrender? I was sent here to investigate, not to interfere with legitimate law enforcement."

"Then what are you going to do?" Gail Saunders tossed her

head with a show of anger, her long black hair swirling around her shoulders. "Sit here and twiddle your fingers? What's happened to the great Indians' rights fighter! You're . . ." Her voice faltered; she buried her face in her hands.

"Now I've really given Mr. Pollock something to gossip about!" she cried in a muffled voice. "Why do I have to be so hot-headed? It's just that everything seems to be falling apart and we can't stop it!"

Sensing her anguish, Morgan found it impossible to be angry with her. "I think it was too late from the beginning," he said, deciding that the truth would make things easier for her later. "Senator Leland knew that. I think everyone knew it but me."

The life went out of Gail Saunders' face. Her shoulders drooped. "Are you saying it's all over?"

She looked so crushed, Morgan had to fight down the impulse to take her in his arms. "No!" He was surprised at the intensity of his reply. "Even a battle lost would focus national attention upon the situation here. And that's how legislation gets passed."

"Please! Don't talk to me about . . ."

"We have to talk," Morgan told her firmly. "Gail, I'm no head-in-the-clouds idealist. I deal with the realities of dreams. I realize that sending a few people to prison, getting a few more fired, and using public outrage to curb the power of ruthless logging contractors isn't going to solve the Chippewas' problems. There will always be Starks, Meirs, O'Connors and Mike Davitts. But the constant heat of publicity will make it more difficult and less profitable for them to operate." He rose abruptly. "It's late. I'd better take you home."

For a moment, she searched his face intently. Then with an indrawn breath, she said, "Dr. E.C. is waiting for me outside."

Lake Street was deserted when they stepped into the night. A light rig was drawn up in front of Quam's. Slipping her arm through Morgan's, Gail matched her stride to his, long, free and easy.

Beside the buggy, she stopped and, rising on tip toes, kissed him on the mouth. "Thank you for being so understanding," she whispered. "Now will you please help me up?"

"I warned you she was unpredictable, Mr. Morgan," Dr. E.C. remarked dryly. "Let's go, Gail."

Lifting her into the buggy, Morgan stepped back as Lindley flicked the mare lightly with the reins. He waited until the buggy disappeared into the darkness, then returned to the hotel. Pollock, who had been peering out the door, could not make it back to his desk in time. He stopped, red-faced, staring at Morgan like a trapped fox.

"I . . . I was just . . ."

"I know what you were doing, Mr. Pollock." Morgan followed the clerk to the desk, waited until Pollock handed him his key, and then said coldly, "For the last time, Mr. Pollock, keep your nose out of my business, and out of my private life." At the foot of the stairs, he paused, one hand on the newel-post. "You're not a bad man, Mr. Pollock. You just need something to keep you occupied. Why don't you get married?"

"*Why don't you?*" The words were out before Pollock could shut them off. "Maybe then you'd go back to Oregon and mind *your* own business!"

Silence, with Pollock, tongue-tied with fright, looking as though he might faint. Morgan, frozen-faced, one foot on the bottom step. The pendulum clock on the wall behind the desk ticking off the seconds.

Morgan, remembering that moment with Gail Saunders, thinking, *Pollock, you're not the only one running away from reality.*

"Mr. Pollock," he said quietly, "I've never run away from a battle in my life. I don't intend to begin now. But when I've finished my investigation, I'll consider what you've said. I may even take your advice."

Upstairs, he spoke briefly with Jason Bradshaw's nurse. She had just given the reporter a sleeping draft. His condition was unchanged. Yes, she would tell him that Mr. Morgan had inquired about him.

"Thank you," Morgan said. "Good night."

In his room, he lit the lamp, turned up the wick, and looked about the comfortably furnished surroundings. Until now, it had been a place to rest, to think, to relax. Suddenly, it had become a tiny fortress with him, the sole defender, besieged and virtually out of ammunition.

To hell with it! To hell with the whole damned mess!

He dropped into the big chair, slipped off his boots, and let his head fall back against the cushioned rest. He was tired. God, he was tired!

He fell asleep.

On September 15, 1898, Marshal O'Connor avenged his humiliation at Sugar Point by betraying Bog-o-nay-ge-shig. He did it with a calculated cruelty, hiding behind a long time precedent established by U.S. marshals in the past.

Craig Morgan, dropping into Cole's General Store around ten o'clock, just as J. W. Bailey, the manager, and his half-breed clerk, Henry, were closing up, was the first to learn what had happened.

"Evening, Mr. Morgan," Bailey said, turning out the front lights. "You're out late. What can I do for you?"

"A half-dozen apples." Morgan smiled. "I get hungry at night."

The merchant flashed him an unexpected grin. "You've got lots of company. Half the men in town drop in to stock up on cheese, sardines, crackers, dill pickles—you name it."

It was the first show of friendliness from a Lake Street merchant that Morgan had encountered. It lifted his spirits.

Sacking his merchandise, Bailey handed it to him. "That will be fifteen cents."

"Thanks." Morgan handed him the exact change. "Have a good night."

As he turned to leave, an Indian in a red, black and white flannel shirt and red suspenders staggered inside, bringing with him a rush of cold air. For a moment, the Chippewa stood blinking his eyes against the light; then, with an effort, he walked toward Bailey, his worn-out moccasins leaving bloody footprints upon the floor. At the counter, he laid his hands upon the top, and said simply:

"Mr. Bailey, I have walked all the way from Duluth. I am cold, I am sick, I am hungry. Will you help me to get home?"

"My God!" Bailey stared at him, unbelievingly. "What happened to you, Bog? Henry, go upstairs and tell Mrs. Bailey to heat up some food and brew a pot of fresh coffee! Tell her Bog's here, sick and hungry. I'll be up and explain later. Then I want you to harness the team, pile some blankets in a wagon, and take Bog home." He turned to Morgan. "Will you help me get him over to the stove?"

Between them, they half carried the Chippewa to a chair close to the fire. Had it not been for the red, black and white shirt and red suspenders, Morgan would never have recognized him. He had lost twelve or fifteen pounds; his face was dirty, haggard, his eyes red-rimmed from lack of sleep. His whole body sagged from exhaustion. His hands, when he held them out to the stove, were trembling.

Drawing up a chair, Bailey sat down. "What happened, Bog? What were you doing in Duluth anyway? I didn't even know you'd left Sugar Point."

Bog-o-nay-ge-shig stared at him with fever-bright eyes, not yet able to frame his thoughts into words. Morgan answered Bailey's question for him.

"Last week, Marshal O'Connor talked him into going to Duluth to testify against a whiskey peddler. When I heard about it from Mike Davitt, I suspected O'Connor was up to something, but there was nothing I could do about it at the time." He addressed himself to the chief. "Why did you go to Duluth with O'Connor, a man whom you hated?"

With his hands still reaching for warmth, the Chippewa said harshly, "The Marshal promised that if I spoke against the whiskey peddler, he would tear up the warrants for Pugonny-koshig and Shab-on-day-sh-king and tell the Agent, Meir, not to call in the soldiers. But when I sat in the white man's court, I read the lie in his face; so I did not tell what I knew." He was racked by a spasm of violent coughing. When it passed, he continued.

"I was turned loose on the streets without money for food, lodging or train fare home. I hung around Duluth for a couple of days trying to get someone to help me. Then I headed back for Walker, living on whatever roots I could dig up, and sleeping out in the open at night."

Bog-o-nay-ge-shig's head snapped up, his eyes flaming with that same fierce fire as when he had swung the tomahawk above his head and brought Marshal O'Connor to his knees in terror.

"I, Bog-o-nay-ge-shig, Hole in the Day, am a fool! Any Indian is a fool to believe the white man. You, Mr. Morgan . . . you knew the Marshal's heart was bad. Why did you not come to Duluth and help me? I tell you why. Because you are like the politicians in Washington, with their big, bear-toothed smiles and their lying hearts. Only you are worse. You use the Indian to make a name for yourself. You are like a summer storm, much wind, much thunder and lightning, but no rain to give life to the land and its people. Go back to Oregon, Mr. Morgan. The whites do not want you here! The Chippewas do not want you here."

Bailey frowned and shook his head. "Maybe you ought to leave, Mr. Morgan. You can see he's sick and upset. He needs some hot food in him. Then I'll have Henry take him home. Tomorrow, maybe he'll feel differently."

"All right," Morgan agreed. "But is there anything I can do before I leave?"

"You can help me load some groceries in the wagon for Bog's family."

Bog-o-nay-ge-shig broke his silence. "How is my family, Mr. Bailey? I have worried about them."

"They're fine," Bailey assured him. "We'll have you home by daybreak."

The harsh planes of the Chippewa's face softened a little. "You are a kind man, Mr. Bailey. You ought to have been a Chippewa."

"All white men are not bad, Bog," Bailey said evenly. "And all Indians are not good. Mr. Morgan, are you ready?"

Following the merchant to the rear, Morgan helped carry a week's supply of groceries to the loading dock. By the time they finished, the smell of food and coffee drifted down from the upstairs living quarters, and the clerk, Henry, had a team and wagon drawn up outside.

"Henry, you can load those supplies now," Bailey ordered. "Then you can close up while I see that Bog's fed. Don't forget to bank the fire. Nights are getting cold."

He followed Morgan to the door, his face shadowed. "That fool, O'Connor, may have stirred up a hornet's nest. Bog's well liked and respected in all the small towns in this area. I don't know how people are going to react to all this. Especially the Pillagers." He nodded toward Bog-o-nay-ge-shig, sitting before the stove, dark-faced, brooding.

"If I told folks what I think, they'd call me crazy and laugh me out of town. But I think there's going to be an Indian uprising."

"I agree with you," Morgan replied. "If the government moves in troops, the Pillagers will fight. And he"—nodding toward Bog-o-nay-ge-shig—"is not helping by turning his back on me. Perhaps you can reason with him; I can't."

"Don't expect miracles," Bailey advised him. "What happened in Duluth may have been the straw that broke the camel's back." Unexpectedly, he thrust out his hand. "If it's any help, Mr. Morgan, you do have friends."

"Thank you." Morgan made one final gesture of conciliation to the silent figure before the stove. "You're right, Bog-o-nay-ge-shig. I should have gone to Duluth to check on you. But I, too, am a fool. I couldn't see the forest for the trees. I'm sorry."

The Chippewa did not move or speak.

With a resigned shrug, Morgan closed the door behind him. The town slept quietly under a three-quarter moon as he walked along the deserted boardwalk. But for how long, he wondered. How much longer before the throb of the big war drums carried across the lake; and people stopped laughing at the idea of a little band of Chippewa warriors starting an uprising in this era of incandescent lights, fast passenger trains and Henry Ford's marvelous two-cylinder horseless carriage, capable of traveling twenty miles an hour.

Not long, he thought. *Not long at all.*

On the reservation, the fuse lit by O'Connor raced toward the powder keg. Within hours after Bog-o-nay-ge-shig's return to Sugar Point, word of his mistreatment in Duluth had spread throughout the reservation. Angry chiefs met in council with their sick leader. Then, singly and in small groups, the Pillagers slipped into Walker, Akeley, even Brainerd and began quietly buying new repeating rifles and ammunition. Some even sold personal property to raise the necessary cash. Others, sensing that war was inevitable, had prepared for it weeks before. By sundown, most of the Pillagers were armed and ammunitioned. The rest would be combat-ready within a few days.

With warrants for a score of Chippewas, Marshal O'Connor stepped up his harassment, sending deputy marshals to distant parts of the reservation and, by boat, to the lake islands.

The Chippewas simply disappeared.

Angry deputies threatened entire families living near the

Agency with arrest for "obstructing justice." Two, who pushed their way into the deep woods north of Ottertail Point, finally found some Indians—and wished they hadn't.

"Some day," they were warned, "you come in here, and you no go back."

The badge bearers beat a hasty retreat.

Otherwise, the Chippewas made no hostile move, contenting themselves by refusing to be served subpoenas or warrants or to have anything to do with the Agency.

Inevitably, however, the deep resentments harbored by those who worked for Stark and other Pine Ring contractors surfaced. Angered because the money from the very logs they were handling in the sawmills had not come down to the tribe, they now openly demonstrated their frustration. Contractors' crews were hampered, roads were blocked, and, finally, outright threats were made to drive the Pine Ring off the reservation.

O'Connor, more belligerent than ever, declared the Indians were in a state of insurrection and blamed Bog-o-nay-ge-shig for their increasing hostility.

Reinforced by Meir's ultimatum, Stark brought heavy political pressure to bear upon the Commissioner of Indian Affairs, the Secretary of the Interior, and the Secretary of War.

The Pillagers, Meir wired the Secretary of the Interior, had refused to surrender the fugitives, Pugonny-koshig and Shab-on-day-sh-king, and had declared that they would ignore his ultimatum to abide by the law.

"They have boasted to reservation missionaries, Mr. Secretary, that they will fight if Army troops are sent in to enforce the law. I believe they mean business. The danger to white communities in the area cannot be ignored. Therefore, Mr. Secretary, I urgently request that sufficient troops be dispatched to the reservation to put down this uprising."

Convinced that the threat was both real and imminent, the Secretary of War made his decision. A handful of troops, preferably cavalry, dispatched to the reservation, should be sufficient to cool the Pillagers' tempers and bring them to their senses.

He was wrong.

Forty-eight hours to showdown.

In his office at the Agency headquarters, Meir sat with his boots propped on the scarred desk, waiting patiently for his ultimatum to run out and for the Army to move in.

At White Pines, Hugh Stark, hoping to prevent the Bog-o-nay-ge-shig scandal and the brutal beating of Jason Bradshaw breaking in the newspapers, tried unsuccessfully to contact the *Globe* reporter.

On the terrace, Elaine Stark slanted a cold, hating glance at her pinstripe-suited guard, considered one final attempt to bribe him into carrying a written confession to Craig Morgan, then shrugged off the thought. Her father owned Gillispie, just as he owned everyone who worked for him. And simple escape would be pointless. Without money, she could go nowhere, do nothing. She could even lose her chance to be comfortably exiled abroad.

Damn you, Morgan, why don't you kill him!

Walking along the shore of a tiny lake near Walker with Gail Saunders, Craig Morgan, too, waited and thought, *Bradshaw, you cocky little bastard, get well fast!*

Bringing his boat into Walker Bay at dusk, Jean Chardin, who had made his peace with Bog-o-nay-ge-shig, headed straight for Saunders' Mercantile. There Mr. Allison, the clerk, informed him that Gail Saunders had left early.

"She's having company tonight," Allison explained. "I believe Dr. E.C. and Mr. Morgan."

Chardin nodded his thanks and left.

It was seven-thirty when he reached the top of the hill. Two rigs were drawn up before the house. One he recognized as belonging to Dr. Lindley; the other was a rented buggy from the local livery stable.

Padding silently across the porch, he knocked on the door.

Relaxed in his favorite chair before the fireplace, Dr. Lindley regarded Morgan with frank skepticism. Their after-dinner conversation had inevitably focused upon the crisis created by the Bog-o-nay-ge-shig incident.

"Are you suggesting, Mr. Morgan, that Jason Bradshaw is the only newsman qualified to break the story?"

"Under the circumstances, yes," Morgan replied. "Bradshaw is the only reporter in the state who even suspects what is happening here. He is aware of the situation, recognizes the danger, and has gathered strong circumstantial evidence against Stark and Meir. Moreover, he has the intuitive genius for putting the bits and pieces together to make a convincing story."

Lindley shook his head dubiously. "I think you should turn whatever evidence you have over to the Commissioner of Indian Affairs and let him act upon it as he sees fit."

Seated beside Morgan, Gail Saunders voiced a quiet dissent. "I have to agree with Craig, Dr. E.C. What we're talking about now is immediate, independent action. I think that Jason Bradshaw is the key to . . ."

The Irish setter, dozing before the fire, jumped up and began barking furiously.

"Excuse me." Gail rose. "Someone's at the door."

The two men sat silent, listening to the low murmur of voices in the foyer. When Gail returned, Jean Chardin was with her; and, from her expression, Morgan knew that the fisherman had brought bad news.

"Sit down, Jean." Gail motioned Chardin to a chair, then resumed her place on the sofa. Despite her efforts to remain calm, she was clearly disturbed. She looked at Morgan.

"The Pillagers have been buying guns and ammunition," she said simply. "Feeling is running high, especially against O'Connor. Some of the young men have vowed to kill him." Drawing her legs under her, she turned a troubled face to Morgan.

"Bog-o-nay-ge-shig sent me this message. 'Tell my good friends, Miss Gail and Dr. E.C., that if the soldiers come and try to take Pugonny-koshig and Shab-on-day-sh-king, Chippewa guns will speak and men will die. Tell them that I will not talk to them about this. It has already been decided in council. I, Bog-o-nay-ge-shig, have spoken.'" She caught her breath, then continued.

"He also sent a message for you. 'Tell the man, Morgan, to stay away. I am thinking. I do not yet know. Maybe we can be friends. Maybe. But the time is not now.'"

It was disturbing news, and it destroyed any lingering hopes Morgan had harbored for a peaceful solution. Obviously, the Pillagers were in no mood to heed ultimatums, nor to parley with the Army. The chiefs had drawn a line from which they would not retreat.

"Jean," he asked, "how many people know of this?"

The fisherman shrugged. "No one, I'm certain. Except a Jesuit priest at the Earthome Mission; he just laughed when he heard about it."

Lindley, who had listened without comment, turned his face away from the fire and weighed Morgan with grave eyes. "You believe that conflict is unavoidable?"

"Short of a miracle, yes."

Lindley sighed, the lines of his face deepening. "Jason Bradshaw's fever broke last night. He can do your story for you."

"Thank God!" Morgan was on his feet and moving toward the door even as he spoke. "That's the best news ever."

"Wait!" Gail Saunders rose and hurried after him. "Where are you going?"

"Back to the hotel," Morgan said, not liking what he had to do. "Bradshaw will have to wire that story to the *Globe* tonight. If there *is* bloodshed, I want the whole country to know who was responsible." He opened the door, admitting a rush of cold air. "I'll keep in touch."

"Craig!"

Gail laid her hand on his arm, lifting her face to him, her eyes a more intense blue than he could ever recall. He stopped, thinking how beautiful she really was.

"Yes?"

"Nothing, really." She flushed, covering up her confusion with a little laugh. "It was just that, for a moment, I had the strangest . . ." She gave him a gentle push. "Good night."

The door clicked shut.

Morgan stood there, feeling like a small boy. Dr. E.C. was right. She was the most intriguing, unpredictable woman he'd ever met. Sometimes, he wondered if maybe he wasn't in love with her.

Thoughtfully, he crossed the yard, climbed into the buggy, and drove back to town.

Pollock, reading a newspaper behind the desk, started to get up, but Morgan motioned him to stay put. "I have my key."

Upstairs, he knocked on Jason Bradshaw's door, then entered without waiting for an answer.

Bradshaw, pale and bonier than ever, lay stretched out on the bed, dozing. He looked terrible. The swelling in his jaw had subsided; but his blackened eye had changed color to an even uglier yellow-green-purple. He was clearly not well.

"Bradshaw."

The reporter opened his eyes, turned his head, and said, "Go away. I feel like hell."

"Come on." Morgan swung his legs over the side of the bed. "We've got work to do. The Pillagers have been buying up arms and ammunition. The chiefs have voted to fight if Meir calls for troops. Bog-o-nay-ge-shig won't talk to anyone. I want a *Globe* exposé of what's going on here on the streets of St. Paul tomorrow." He walked over to the dresser, returned with notebook and pencil, and handed them to Bradshaw.

"*Write.*"

Jason Bradshaw's scoop, under his own by-line, hit the streets of St. Paul in a *Globe* "extra" on October 2. Drawing front-page headline rating, the story covered the sweeping Morgan-Bradshaw investigation of an "apparent" conspiracy, involving Hugh Stark, the Pine Ring and the Indian Agent, Frank Meir, to cheat and defraud the Chippewas.

Devoted almost exclusively to the Leech Lake trouble, the "extra" carried two other by-line articles by the ailing Bradshaw. Written with a hard-hitting simplicity, the story on the Bog-o-nay-ge-shig outrage ended with a brief summary of the incident.

> Bog-o-nay-ge-shig was taken to Duluth as a witness to give testimony against a white man. He had been assured that his mileage and expenses would be paid.
>
> When the trial ended he was refused fees and transportation home. Adrift in Duluth penniless, he wandered the streets for a day or two, being unable to secure money, and was forced to walk all the way from Duluth to Walker.
>
> He arrived in Walker in a starving condition and was rescued and carried through the illness that followed by sympathizing whites.

That story is vouched for by the people in Walker. The officials there claim there is nothing in it.

And we might add in support of this that the Commissioner of Indian Affairs states, "The whole matter of arrests by marshals and deputy marshals has come to be a farce, and a handicap to the Chippewas and a disgrace to the community."*

In his other story, Bradshaw highlighted additional incidents which had led to the present crisis . . . the shooting of Shab-on-day-sh-king, his subsequent arrest, along with Pugonny-koshig, their forcible release by Pillagers, the chiefs' refusal to surrender the fugitives to Marshal O'Connor, the Indian Agent, Meir's, ultimatum, the Pillagers' purchase of firearms "to defend their rights and their lands in case the soldiers come." And it called upon residents of Walker and the surrounding towns to remain calm.

> This trouble was not started by Indians, but by unscrupulous whites, with powerful political connections, who want the Chippewas' rich timber lands. If violence breaks out and blood is shed, it will be because of the greed and ruthless ambition of Hugh Stark, his Pine Ring associates, and the current Indian agent, Frank Meir, with the flames fanned by the cruelty of Marshal Richard O'Connor.

It was a bold, explosive indictment, specific charges, supported by strong circumstantial evidence, placing the blame where it properly belonged, and then carefully leaving it up to the public to return its own indictment.

An enterprising news butch aboard the M & I, who had bought up two hundred copies of the *Globe* "extra" in Duluth, sold out his entire stock within twenty minutes after arriving in Walker.

Within an hour, everyone in town knew that the Pillagers were armed and had defied an ultimatum to surrender the fugitives, Pugonny-koshig and Shab-on-day-sh-king. That troops might be moved into the area stirred up a flurry of excitement, but no one really thought there would be a shooting war.

* *St. Paul* Globe, *Oct. 2, 1898.*

Reaction to the entire exposé was much as Morgan had anticipated. Sympathy for Bog-o-nay-ge-shig, anger toward O'Connor, and mixed feelings toward Hugh Stark. On Morgan's role in the matter, Walker remained sharply divided, with people now openly siding for or against him in heated exchanges.

Ironically, Bradshaw, who had actually written the articles, escaped much of the controversy. For one thing, he was a "native," not an outsider. For another, as a newsman, it was his business to report what was going on. The town didn't like it, but they accepted it.

Everyone but Frank Meir.

Crossing over from the Agency at noon the next day, Meir headed straight for the Pameda Hotel. By the time he reached the lower end of Lake Street, the boardwalks were deserted. Merchants stood in their doorways, watching, while customers and clerks peered from the safety of the dim interiors.

If he noticed, Meir gave no sign. The bulldog pipe was missing from his mouth, giving his face a peculiarly naked appearance. He wore the .45 in its plain cutaway holster.

From the hotel's shaded veranda, Morgan spotted him when he reached the Nash Hotel at the far end of the block. A pistol butt showed beneath Morgan's open coat. The pocket of Bradshaw's rumpled suit sagged from the weight of a double-barreled .44 derringer.

Lowering the copy of the *Globe* "extra" he had been reading, Bradshaw watched the Agent's approach with a faint frown.

"I thought it would be O'Connor," he commented dryly. "He's the hot-headed one."

"I wish it had been him," Morgan said. "He's a lot less dangerous than Meir."

Bradshaw drew the derringer from his coat pocket and draped the newspaper over it. Something in his manner, perhaps the look in his eyes, made Morgan think of "Colonel" Sheehan.

"If he wants trouble," Bradshaw said cooly, "why, then, we'll give it to him."

Morgan sat silent.

Down the street, Meir passed Quam's, the click of his bootheels loud in the noonday quiet.

Morgan shifted the pistol until the butt pressed firm against his belly. Beside him, he could hear the faint whistle of air through Bradshaw's tooth-missing gap.

The front legs of his chair touched the floor as Meir stepped onto the veranda and stopped in front of Bradshaw.

"You little son of a bitch!" Meir said tonelessly. "You've got five minutes to get yourself a gun." His eyes switched to Morgan, noting the pistol beneath Morgan's open coat. Abruptly, his held-in anger broke the surface.

"I warned you, Morgan; but you wouldn't listen. You had to stir up a hornet's nest. I don't know what all this is going to do to Stark. It will probably cost me my job and everything that went with it. It's going to cost you a lot more." He stepped back a couple of feet. "Get up!"

With a honey-slow hand, Morgan fished a cigarette from his shirt; just as carefully he lit it, studying the Agent over the flame. He had no intent of getting himself killed in a shoot-out. Tossing the match away, he shook his head.

"This isn't Dodge City, eighteen sixty-six," he said. "And they don't call it killing anymore; they call it murder. If you're smart, you'll clear out of Minnesota while you can. Because this is just the beginning of what you and Stark can expect. I'm not going to quit until I've put you both behind bars."

"*God damn you!*" Meir cried in a choked voice, and reached for his gun.

"Go ahead." The double-barreled derringer poked from beneath the newspaper on Jason Bradshaw's lap. "I'd like to blow your brains out."

Meir hesitated, weighing his chances. By now, he had his temper under control. With a shrug, he let his hand drop to his side.

"Another time," he said, "when the odds are even." His eyes settled on Morgan with a bright hate. "You're not going to send anyone to prison. You still haven't got sense enough to know you can't win." He threw Bradshaw a final hard glance, then stepped off the veranda. Ignoring the people watching from store doorways, he strode rapidly down the boardwalk. When he reached Joe Frost's Walker Saloon, he disappeared inside.

On the hotel veranda, Morgan and Bradshaw sat silent, feeling the warmth of the sun on their faces, and glad that it was so, for they had been very close to death and knew it.

Morgan's breath went out with a little rush. "Thanks," he said quietly.

"Forget it." Bradshaw stuffed the derringer back into his pocket. "I'm sorry I didn't kill him. Do you think Stark sent him?"

"No." Morgan rose, stretched, and stood watching the flow of people resume along the boardwalks. Then with his back still turned, he said, "He'd have no reason to. Meir's ultimatum expires today. The Army will have troops in here by tomorrow evening. If fighting breaks out, the cause of it, and the people who instigated it, could be past history in a couple of weeks. People forget."

"They won't forget," Bradshaw contradicted, pushing slowly to his feet. "The *Globe* will keep hammering away at Stark, Meir and the Pine Ring for having conspired to bring it about."

A smile net-wrinkled the skin around Morgan's eyes. Bradshaw was like a shot of twelve-year Scotch; he gave you a lift when you need it most.

"Would the Commissioner of Indian Affairs intervene?" Bradshaw asked. "His statement to the press was strongly pro-Indian."

It was an idea Morgan had already considered and rejected. "They'll bypass the Commissioner and bring heavy political pressure to bear upon the Secretary of the Interior and the Secretary of War. The Secretary of War will make the decision regarding military action."

"Then why don't you talk to Bog-o-nay-ge-shig?" The bulldog tenacity in Bradshaw's nature persisted. "Try and persuade him to surrender Pugonny-koshig and Shab-on-day-sh-king. Hell, they're not going to be hanged. It doesn't make sense. People losing their lands, their homes, maybe even their lives just to keep two men from going to jail for a few months."

You'll never completely understand, will you, Bradshaw?

"I'd not ask a proud man like Bog-o-nay-ge-shig to betray his people's trust," Morgan replied. "Besides, he wouldn't listen to me. He won't listen to anyone." Buttoning his coat, he stepped off the veranda. "There's going to be fighting, Bradshaw, and we're going to have to report it accurately."

"Where are you going now?" Bradshaw queried.

"To find Jean Chardin. At least Bog-o-nay-ge-shig should know we did what we promised . . . exposed Stark and Meir in the press. What about you?"

The familiar bloodhound-on-the-trail-of-something gleam sparked Bradshaw's discolored eye.

"Have my editor check out what you've said," he declared. "If you're right, reporters will be pouring in, along with the troops, from all over the country. That means this will be the last time I'll have the only wire in town to myself. I'm going to make the most of it."

"Good luck." Morgan shifted the pistol to his hip, and moved down the street.

Lieutenant Chaucer B. Humphrey, 3rd Infantry, U. S. Army, stationed at Fort Snelling, stepped out onto the coach's rear platform as the troop train chuff-chuffed to a halt beside the Walker depot.

For a moment, he stood there, erect and unsmiling, conscious of the startled murmur of the crowd gathered upon the station platform and spilling out onto the open ground separating Lake and Front streets. He had expected a wildly cheering demonstration such as those encountered at all the small towns en route. As though he and his twenty men, all sharpshooters who had performed effectively at Santiago during the recent Cuban War, were some sort of heroes!

Inwardly, he grimaced. There was nothing heroic in being dispatched to subdue a peaceable, middle-aged Indian chief and a small band of Chippewas. He derived a certain satisfaction from the knowledge that his hard-bitten troops shared his feelings. Sergeant Walter Hesbrook had pretty well summed up their attitude when he had heard of their assignment.

"Hell, I can't say I love the buggers, but I've got to admire them for standing up for their rights. *That* makes them men, not animals. You can't blame this Bog, or whatever his name is, for getting his hackles up."

No, Humphrey thought, you couldn't blame him; but, as a

mere lieutenant, you weren't paid to judge. You carried out your orders and tried to make yourself believe that what you did was in the best interests of the nation. You tried, only you didn't always succeed. Your conscience was no fool.

"Lieutenant!" Sergeant Hesbrook stuck his head out the coach door. "You ready?"

"Muster them on the station platform," Humphrey ordered. "And clear those people out of the way."

"Yes, sir."

As the Sergeant ducked back inside, "Colonel" Sheehan emerged and stood beside Humphrey. With Bog-o-nay-ge-shig the principal target, he and two other deputy marshals had been assigned to accompany the troops to Walker.

"Let me handle it, Lieutenant," he said. "I know these people."

"Very well," Humphrey replied curtly. He did not like Sheehan; he tolerated him only so long as he did not interfere. "While you're about it, I'll need shelter for my men."

"Meir, the Indian Agent, has already arranged for them to be quartered in the schoolhouse," Sheehan informed him. "I'll take you there."

Dropping to the ground, he moved among the crowd, snapping, "All right, stand back and give them room! You, Constable"—to the town's law enforcement officer—"see if you can find the Indian Agent. And send someone for Mayor Kinkele. He ought to be here."

"Never mind the Mayor." Humphrey joined Sheehan on the platform. "I'll talk to him later." He walked toward the front of the coach where Sergeant Hesbrook had the detail, carrying full field packs and Krag-Jorgensen rifles, lined up.

"Move them out, Sergeant! We'll quarter them in the schoolhouse for the night." He nodded to the deputy marshal. "Let's go, Mr. Sheehan."

Sheehan frowned, not liking Humphrey's abrupt manner, nor the Lieutenant's deliberate use of "mister," instead of "colonel." With a shrug, he led the way across the open ground toward Lake Street, Humphrey keeping pace, and Sergeant Hesbrook marching his detail smartly behind.

Suddenly, from somewhere back in the crowd, a man shouted in good-natured derision, "Hey, Lieutenant, what you figure to do with them twenty soldiers? You tangle with Bog and he'll make you feel like Custer at the Little Big Horn!"

A roar of laughter burst from the crowd, the sound engulfing the detail like a rolling wave.

Standing in front of the Nash Hotel, Craig Morgan saw Lieutenant Humphrey's shoulders square and knew that the man's professional pride had been wounded. That would only make matters worse.

As Jason Bradshaw joined him on the boardwalk, Morgan said, "I expected a much bigger force, at least a company. Who's in command at Fort Snelling anyway?"

"Brigadier-General John M. Bacon, a brilliant Civil War officer, and now Commander of the Department of Dakota," Bradshaw informed him. "I just got a rundown on him from my managing editor." He dug a crumpled telegram from his coat pocket and handed it to Morgan.

Quickly, Morgan scanned the message.

> Re situation Leech Lake. Secretary War suggested that handful troops, preferably cavalry, sufficient to make Indians back down. No cavalry available. General Bacon dispatching twenty infantrymen under Lt. Chaucer Humphrey. Bacon brilliant Civil War officer, experienced Indian fighter. For reference event actual outbreak fighting refer Bacon biography below.
>
> Bacon, John Mosby, colonel U.S.A.; b. in Kentucky, Apr. 17, 1844. Enlisted 2nd lt., 11th Ky Cav., Sep. 22, 1862. Promoted through grades to col. 8th Cav., June 29, 1897; brig. gen. vols., May 4, 1898. Bvtd. major, Mar. 2, 1867, for siege of Reseca, Ga; lt. col., Feb. 27, 1890, for actions against Indians on the Rio Pecos, Tex., June 7, 1867, and nr. headquarters of Salt Fork of Brazos River, Tex., Oct. 28, 29, 1869. Col. and a-d-c to Gen. Sherman, 1871, 84. Presently Commander, Dept. of Dakota.
>
> Congratulations scoop. Stay on scene. Will keep open line here more stories.

"He's got quite a record." Morgan handed the telegram back to Bradshaw. "Let's hope he understands Indians better than the

Secretary of War." He shook his head dubiously. "Twenty soldiers will only antagonize Bog-o-nay-ge-shig."

"I know." Bradshaw rubbed his sore jaw with tentative fingers. "It's like waving a flag in front of a bull."

Morgan watched Lieutenant Humphrey march his troops across the open ground and turn east on Lake Street. As the detail drew abreast of the Nash Hotel, Morgan called out, "If you take those men over to Bear Island, Lieutenant, some of them are going to get killed."

Humphrey stopped short, wheeled, and came back. He stared coldly at Morgan and Bradshaw. "Who the hell are you?"

"Craig Morgan, Bureau of Indian Affairs." Morgan tapped his chest. "And this is Jason Bradshaw, a reporter for the St. Paul *Globe.*"

The tension eased in Humphrey a bit. "I've heard of you two," he said. "As a matter of fact, you're the reason I'm here. You seem to have stirred up a hornet's nest."

"This time you're about to stir up one," Morgan told him. "If you go to Bear Island and demand the surrender of Pugonnykoshig and Shab-on-day-sh-king, you're asking for real trouble. Bog-o-nay-ge-shig won't talk to you; he won't hand over the fugitives. He has sent word to close friends here that if the soldiers come, he will fight. And with two hundred well-armed men, he's not going to be intimidated by a lieutenant, a sergeant and twenty soldiers."

Humphrey's face clouded. He threw Sheehan a hard look. "Mr. Sheehan says there are only about thirty-five Indians who are actually involved, less than half of them with guns."

"Mr. Sheehan is a liar," Morgan retorted. "He and Marshal O'Connor were almost killed trying to arrest Bog-o-nay-ge-shig several days ago on Sugar Point."

"Why would Mr. Sheehan lie to me?"

In the crackling silence, Morgan met Sheehan's eyes in bold challenge. He half expected the "Colonel" to draw on him, but Sheehan merely killed him with those lynx's eyes.

"For money," he said, "and a promise from Hugh Stark of a better job."

"That's a serious charge, Mr. Morgan." The Lieutenant's eyes switched from one man to the other, seeking the lie hidden in one of their minds. "Can you prove it?"

"I was present when Sheehan and Marshal O'Connor were nearly killed on Sugar Point," Morgan replied. "Dozens of people can vouch for the size of Bog-o-nay-ge-shig's band. And merchants in Walker, Akeley and Brainerd will confirm that the Pillagers have been buying up arms and ammunition for several weeks."

"Mr. Sheehan"—Humphrey's manner was ominously calm—"you have some explaining to do."

"I'm not going to stand here and defend myself against this man's wild charges," Sheehan's voice was cool, unruffled. "And no half-ass Army lieutenant is going to push me around. That also applies to Indian Affairs inspectors and snooping reporters." The lynx-like eyes flicked to Bradshaw. "Don't cross me again."

Brushing past them, he strode down the block and turned into the Walker Saloon.

Humphrey swept the empty boardwalk, his face taking on a hard, tough look. "That son of a bitch," he said, "intended to get me massacred." He was speaking of Sheehan; but Morgan chose to read into the question another meaning, and to use it to express his own growing concern.

"I think you should send for reinforcements, Lieutenant," he advised, "and then wait for their arrival."

Humphrey considered the idea a moment. "You really think Bog-o-nay-ge-shig will fight?"

"He'll fight," Morgan affirmed. "I've talked to him."

"What can he hope to gain?"

"His self-respect, for one thing. And immediate action by the federal government to correct at least some of the Pillagers' grievances."

The Lieutenant's expression soured. "That makes me appear like a bastard, doesn't it? I mean, coming in here with armed soldiers to intimidate already harassed Indians." Some inner resentment, perhaps a subconscious sense of guilt sharpened Humphrey's reply. "I'm career Army, Mr. Morgan. I don't declare wars; I simply fight them." He turned and regarded the detail with an increasing unease.

Twenty men and a sergeant. Tough, seasoned infantrymen, all battle-tested against the Cubans at Santiago. But conventional warfare was one thing; Indian fighting, with the enemy hidden in thick timber, was another. For his tiny force, Bear Island could be a death trap. He pivoted back to Morgan.

"You're a Bureau man," he snapped. "You tell Meir, the Indian Agent, to order the Pillager chiefs in for a council tomorrow morning. They're to be guaranteed safe conduct and freedom from arrest during negotiations."

It was an unwise decision and Morgan told him so. "I'd suggest that you send a runner directly to Bear Island yourself, calling for a parley. They might come. But they'll ignore Meir."

"All right," Humphrey agreed. "Is there an Agency Indian in town I can use?"

"No, but there's a half-breed fisherman, Jean Chardin, a friend of Bog-o-nay-ge-shig's who'll take your message." He spoke to Jason Bradshaw. "Have you seen Chardin?"

"He's at Saunders' Mercantile," Bradshaw replied. "You want me to get him?"

"No, I'll do it," Morgan said. "You take the Lieutenant to the schoolhouse." To Humphrey: "If you go to Onigum keep your detail out of sight. The Chippewa bands there now are in an ugly mood."

Humphrey bristled, his pride already lacerated. "If they start trouble, I will send for reinforcements." He nodded curtly to Bradshaw. "Thanks, but we'll find the schoolhouse ourselves." Stiff-backed, he returned to his troops.

"Sergeant, move them out!"

"Yes, sir!"

The detail marched briskly down the street, lined almost solid now with spectators, laughing, waving, and cheering like it was the Fourth of July. No one believed there would actually be a shooting war. They had been on friendly terms with the Pillagers for a long time.

More and more, the situation was taking on all the aspects of a comic opera.

Morgan turned to Bradshaw, shrugged, and said, "Let's go find Chardin."

Half a dozen steps and Bradshaw stopped, pointing toward the depot. "Take a look."

Following the line of Bradshaw's finger, Morgan saw a score of men in rumpled suits and burdened with luggage hurrying across the open area between Lake and Front streets.

"Reporters?"

Bradshaw scowled. "The loudest-mouthed, hardest-drinking liars on the face of the earth. You go ahead. The Pameda's got the only wire in town. I'd better hog it while I can."

He made off down the block at a half run.

With a final glance at the horde of reporters, Morgan resumed his search for Chardin.

Emerging from Saunders' Mercantile an hour later, Jean Chardin walked rapidly toward the dock. There he boarded his fishing boat, hoisted sail, and pointed his bow across the bay for the Agency at Onigum.

The presence of troops in Walker had not surprised him. He had been expecting that. But *twenty* soldiers! Did those fools in Washington think that the Pillagers would turn tail and run from a handful of infantrymen? Or that Bog-o-nay-ge-shig would obey the orders of a two-bit Army lieutenant to come into the Agency for a council? *Chiefs sat around the council fire with chiefs!*

At first, he had refused to carry Humphrey's message to Bog-o-nay-ge-shig, and only the pleas of Gail Saunders had made him reluctantly change his mind.

"Jean, there's no one else who can get through to him," she had said. "Tell him to at least attend the council. He's been promised safe conduct and freedom from arrest while he's there. If he doesn't like what he hears, he can walk out."

"*You* tell him that," he retorted. "I will not shame him with such talk. Chiefs should only sit in council with chiefs, not with little men."

"Look, Chardin," Craig Morgan had argued. "He won't listen to her, nor to me. Maybe he won't even listen to you; I don't know. He has closed his mind to everyone."

"Then why should I try and change it? When the fighting starts, I, Jean Chardin, will be there beside him."

He felt very proud now, remembering that moment. It helped him to forget the humiliation at Sugar Point when Bog-o-nay-ge-shig had called him a half-breed and accused him of not knowing who he was, or what he was. Maybe, at the time, that had been true. But today was different. Today he had seen soldiers marching down the streets of Walker with rifles on their shoulders, ready to kill Indians who had the guts to stand up for their rights. And he had known with that certainty that comes from inner revelation that his heart was Indian; and that, if necessary, he would kill the soldiers, and die in turn.

But before that happened, he must kill Hugh Stark. It was not an obsession, as Craig Morgan believed, but a spiritual commitment to the dead, born and unborn. Until the deed was done, he would know no peace.

As Bear Island loomed up on the starboard bow, he spun the wheel and headed for the beach. Bringing the boat in to the landing, he jumped ashore. For a moment, he stood perfectly still, listening to the whisper of the wind through the treetops, the honk of wild geese flying high overhead, and the whistle of a moose somewhere in the darkness. Listened with only the quick, darting movement of his eyes to indicate that he was alive.

Then, aware that he was being watched, he slipped into the timber and padded silently toward the center of the island.

Jason Bradshaw set down his coffee cup and addressed himself to the little group just finishing dinner in Gail Saunders' home. The four of them, Morgan, Gail, Dr. Lindley, and himself, had come together in the big house on the knoll within hours after Jean Chardin's departure. Having done all they could, they had, for the moment, become spectators in the rapidly deteriorating situation.

"Do you think there's any chance Bog-o-nay-ge-shig will listen to Chardin?" he asked.

"No." It was Morgan who broke the silence. "A show of weakness now could cost him leadership of the Pillagers. Also, he's shrewd enough to realize that with the *Globe* portraying him as a hero fighting for the survival of his people, a clash with the military would work in his favor, rather than against him."

"The Army's image is also at stake," Bradshaw pointed out. "If Bog-o-nay-ge-shig defies his order to come in for a council, Lieutenant Humphrey will regard it as proof that the Pillagers mean trouble and call for reinforcements."

A slight frown drew Dr. E.C.'s heavy eyebrows together. He laid down his fork and pushed his plate aside.

"It seems to me that you're both overlooking the real issue," he said. "The Chippewas have just grievances against organized groups, as well as individuals. It's the federal government's duty to right those grievances, not to send troops in to silence those who would speak out."

"I agree with you, Doctor," Morgan replied. "But, unfortunately, we're dealing with harsh realities, not with idealistic concepts. Powerful, influential groups want the Chippewas' lands and are prepared to go to any lengths to acquire them. Justice is not the issue. Hugh Stark will tell you it's manifest destiny."

Strikingly beautiful in a rich red gown with gold piping at neck and sleeves, and with the golden robin's egg necklace accentuating her smooth olive skin, Gail Saunders lifted her eyes to Morgan across the table. "In other words, what the white man wants, he takes, whether he has any moral or legal right to it or not."

"Not just the white man," Morgan corrected her. "For hundreds of years before the last chiefs—Red Cloud, Crazy Horse, Little-Big Man, Little Hawk, He Dog, Old Hawk and Big Road —came in to surrender at Camp Robinson in 'seventy-seven, the Indians waged war among themselves. They burned villages, stole horse herds, tortured their captives, kept slaves and took over the hunting grounds of weaker and less warlike tribes. It's the history of man everywhere."

"You make it sound as though the Indian is no better than the white man!" Gail Saunders' voice rose an octave.

"Neither better nor worse," Morgan declared. "Take the Ojibways, the Chippewas. The Dakotas came to the Leech Lake country to hunt and fish; the Chippewas, more warlike, drove them out. The Sioux came in from the south and, after a lot of pitched battles, they were driven west by the Chippewas. The strong always take what they want; and they keep it until someone stronger takes it from them."

Gail Saunders colored, her chin lifting a bit higher. "You are beginning to irritate me, Mr. Morgan."

"For telling the truth?" Morgan asked. "Look, I've been studying up on your local history. Do you know how the Pillagers got their name?"

"Does it matter?"

"Yes," Morgan replied. "In the summer of seventeen hundred and eighty-one, a band of Leech Lake Ojibways, on a hunting trip, camped on a small creek which emptied into the Crow Wing River near where it meets the Mississippi. A white trader, up from the lower Mississippi, put in at the camp in a big canoe loaded with trade goods. The Ojibways hadn't seen a trader in a long time and were eager to barter. When the trader told them he was too sick to do business, they got mad. Some of them began snatching goods from the frightened crew. After they found the trader's whiskey, the pillaging became general. They ransacked the camp and took all the trade goods. The trader and his crew barely escaped in the empty canoe. Since then the Leech Lake Ojibways, Chippewas, have been known as the *Mukkundwais,* Pillagers. And the creek where it happened became known as Pillage Creek."

"So?" Gail Saunders shrugged. "What does that have to do with the powder keg we're sitting on?"

"Don't you understand?" Morgan stared at her. "Those Pillagers were strong, aggressive; the trader was too sick to fight and his men too scared. The Indians robbed him of everything he owned. If he had resisted, they would have massacred him and his crew.

"Now, it's the other way around. The white man is strong; the Indian is weak. Logging contractors, the railroads, land speculators and settlers want the Pillagers' lands and timber. If necessary, they will use the Army to kill them. It's history repeating itself. I don't defend it; I simply recognize it as an incontrovertible reality. Does that make me some kind of monster?"

For a moment, Gail Saunders searched his face, trying to understand. Slowly, the anger ebbed from her eyes. "You may recognize this law of the jungle, as you call it, but you've never accepted it. If you had, you wouldn't be here now. Craig, why *have* you fought it all these years?"

Morgan shrugged. "I don't know," he countered, not wanting to admit the truth even to himself. "Why does Dr. E.C. here fight just as hard to save the life of an Indian, a black man or a prostitute as he does a church-going white man? Why did Mr. Bailey, manager of Cole's General Store, take such good care of Bog-o-nay-ge-shig when the chief stumbled into his store? Why will a man rush into a burning house and die trying to save the life of someone he's never met, never even seen? I can't give you the answer because I don't have it."

"I understand." Gail reached across the table and laid her hand on Morgan's. "What counts is that you do it."

Observing them, Dr. E.C. smiled faintly, his face again taking on that wonderfully human expression. *So much in common,* he thought, *yet different enough to provide a constantly exciting challenge.* He wondered if they realized what was actually happening between them.

Jason Bradshaw cleared his throat. Speaking to Morgan, he asked, "What do you think Humphrey will do?"

"I think he will move his men over to the Agency tonight and have them entrenched by dawn," Morgan responded. "Some of the Chippewa chiefs are bound to show up for the council. If trouble starts, the Lieutenant's not going to be caught in a trap."

Bitter lines fanned out from Bradshaw's scarred eyes and mouth. "History repeating itself," he agreed. "Remember the Modoc War in California in eighteen seventy-two when General Canby threw a thousand troops, plus artillery, against *Keintpoos,* Captain Jack, and his seventy-five warriors holed up in the lava beds near Tule Lake? A thousand soldiers against seventy-five Indians who refused to be moved from their homes on Lost River because a bunch of land-hungry whites wanted it! Bog just might put up the same kind of fight as Captain Jack did."

"I don't think so," Morgan said. "I believe his strategy will be to strike only if attacked, and then fade back into the forest. That would put him in the role of the underdog and make him a kind of hero."

"It didn't make a hero out of Captain Jack," Bradshaw reminded him. "They hanged him when he surrendered."

"No," Morgan agreed. "But, unfortunately, Captain Jack killed General Canby in cold blood during a peace parley under a flag of truce. Reverend Elezar Thomas was also killed by Boston

Charley, and Commissioner Alfred Meecham was seriously wounded by Schonchin. That doesn't make for heroes."

"It's a matter of opinion," Bradshaw conceded. He pushed back his chair and rose. "Thank you for dinner, Miss Saunders. I don't mean to be rude, but I still haven't regained my strength. I need rest."

After Bradshaw had gone, and Dr. E.C. had retired to the parlor, Gail Saunders led Morgan into the foyer. There she paused, her hand on his arm, and looked up at him with a half grave, half gentle expression. "Someday, Craig, will you tell me the real reason, besides hating injustice?"

He did not pretend to misunderstand her; yet the fact that she had sensed the hair shirt of repentance which he wore for his father's crimes shocked him. It was the first time anyone had ever "heard" him from the other side of the glass wall.

"Someday." He bent and kissed the full ripe mouth. "Good night, Gail."

Outside, Jason Bradshaw was waiting for him, shivering in the chilly air. They made the trip back to town in silence, with Bradshaw, wrapped in the heavy woolen lap robe, breathing noisily through his swollen nose and the gap in his teeth.

Before the Pameda, Morgan reined up and let him out. "Lieutenant Humphrey will probably leave around three o'clock. I'll leave word with Pollock to wake us an hour earlier."

Bradshaw nodded. "The press will be up by then, too." On the boardwalk, he hesitated, then said with no trace of his usual cynicism, "She loves you, Morgan. Don't hurt her."

He disappeared into the hotel, a skinny figure in a shapeless suit and a Homburg hat, his shoulders hunched against the pain which Morgan knew still tore at him.

Long after Morgan returned the rig to the livery stable, he continued to think about what Jason Bradshaw had said.

She loves you, Morgan. Don't hurt her.

He knew that their relationship had gone far beyond mere friendship; yet he was not certain that he could give her the kind of love to which she was entitled. Nor whether she could fill the emptiness within him left by Anna's death. More and more, he was beginning to believe so; yet . . .

She was still on his mind when he fell asleep.

Shortly after midnight, Lieutenant Humphrey marched his detail quietly through the town to the dock. Accompanying him was Marshal O'Connor, who had arrived in Walker late the previous evening with warrants for "those aboriginal desperados." Demanding that reinforcements be called in, he had insisted upon attending the council at Onigum.

Humphrey's reaction had been blunt and to the point. "This is Army business, Marshal. If you go, keep your mouth shut. Bog-o-nay-ge-shig hates your guts. I don't want any more trouble."

O'Connor flushed. "Don't order me around, Lieutenant. You haven't got the authority."

"I'm not going to argue with you, mister," Humphrey snapped. "You disrupt this council and I'll slap you under military arrest." He walked away, leaving O'Connor no choice but to follow or be left behind.

"All right, Sergeant! Move them out!"

From the veranda of the Pameda Hotel, Morgan and Bradshaw watched the detail approach. As they stepped into the street and fell in beside Humphrey, he threw them a hard, challenging glance. Then he relented a bit.

"I'm glad to have you along, Mr. Morgan," he said. "And you, Mr. Bradshaw—I suppose you'd swim if you had to."

Bradshaw managed a lopsided grin. "If I had to, yes," he agreed. "But then the *Globe* wouldn't like that, Lieutenant. News reporters are the ones who cover battles and make heroes, idiots or cowards out of you people."

"Don't blow a loud trumpet around me, Mr. Bradshaw," Humphrey retorted. "I'm not impressed."

As they passed the Nash Hotel and, at the end of the block, the Waldorf, reporters, who had sat up playing poker, drinking and smoking foul-smelling cigars, grabbed their coats and rushed outside.

"Hey, Lieutenant!" A New York *Tribune* reporter backpedaled in front of Humphrey. "What's it going to be—a battle or a powwow?"

"Get out of my way," Humphrey said.

"Wait a minute, Lieutenant! The press has the right to—"

"Do what he says, Lassiter," Bradshaw warned, "or that sergeant of his will bash your brains out."

The *Tribune* man stepped aside and joined the pack.

At the dock, the group, Army and civilian, boarded the *Leila D.*, a small steam launch, and crossed the bay to Onigum through the Agency Narrows.

Debarking at Agency Point, Humphrey put his men to work. By dawn, he had the detail deployed in trenches, rifle pits and behind the breastwork. With their perimeter secured, the detail lit cooking fires and prepared their breakfast.

At seven o'clock, the Lieutenant, accompanied by Morgan, Bradshaw and Marshal O'Connor, walked to the Agency headquarters and introduced himself to Meir, the Indian Agent. Meir smiled at Morgan with those gunfighter's eyes and Morgan knew exactly what he was thinking. Stark had laid the trap, O'Connor had unwittingly driven the Pillagers toward it and he, Meir, had sprung the trap.

Standing beside Humphrey, O'Connor scowled. He didn't like playing second fiddle to an Army lieutenant, and Morgan's presence infuriated him. Elaine Stark still refused to see him. To add to his problems, the backlash of public opinion for his treatment of Bog-o-nay-ge-shig in Duluth had begun to sting him.

Around mid-morning, Agency Indians started to gather in front of Meir's office. They were in an ugly mood with here and there a chief voicing a bitter complaint against their enemies. Humphrey cut them off with a tough aggressiveness.

"I called for a council of the chiefs," he said. "Where is Bog-o-nay-ge-shig? Where are the Pillagers? My ears are closed until the fugitives, Pugonny-koshig and Shab-on-day-sh-king, are returned to custody."

An angry murmur rose from the half circle of Chippewas. "Look at the waves upon *Ga-sa-ga-squa-gi-mi-e-kag*, the place of the leech. The *Mukkundwais* cannot row over from Bear Island in their canoes."

Humphrey studied the white capped waves, the spindrift glittering in the autumn sun. "We'll wait until the lake calms."

"The hell we will!" O'Connor flared. "If those red niggers don't come in *now*, I'll arrest every one of them when they do!"

"You son of a bitch!" Humphrey spun around in a white heat. "You meddle in this council, I'll shoot you."

"By God," O'Connor blustered, "I've got warrants to–"

The Lieutenant stepped off the porch. "You know what you can do with those warrants," he retorted, and strode back to the detail.

"Hey, Lieutenant!" Jason Bradshaw hurried after him. "Are you going to call for reinforcements?"

"I did that last night."

The news caught Morgan, walking beside Humphrey, by surprise. "I thought you were going to give the chiefs a chance to speak in council first."

"After hearing about O'Connor's narrow escape at Sugar Point last week," the Lieutenant remarked with a faint note of irony in his voice, "I'm not going to risk having the detail wiped out."

By the time they reached the camp, reporters, sensing some new development, surrounded Humphrey, hurling a barrage of questions at him.

"You think Bog's going to come in?"

"If he doesn't, are you going after him?"

"I hear he's forted up on Bear Island."

"What about it, Lieutenant?" Jason Bradshaw was like a persistent deerfly refusing to be slapped aside. "If Bog *is* forted up on Bear Island, how would you attack the Pillagers?"

In the hope of getting rid of the reporters, Humphrey unwisely opened up and replied to Bradshaw's question.

"With a hundred men at my disposal, I would shell the southern end of the island with a howitzer to attract them in that direction. Meanwhile, I would be in another steamer carrying the majority of the command. Once the Indians were drawn south, I would land my main force and throw up entrenchments. The Gatling detail would then proceed to sweep the island, driving all the hostiles to the south where they could be captured."

Bradshaw stared at him, open-mouthed. "Are you telling me it would be that easy?"

"I didn't say it would be easy," Humphrey retorted. "I said that's the way I would do it. What General Bacon's strategy will be I've no idea."

"General Bacon's coming here to take over?" O'Connor, who had followed the group, sounded surprised and relieved.

"As Commander of the Department of Dakota," Humphrey informed him bruskly. "However, Captain Melville Wilkinson, a veteran of the Bannock War in Idaho, will be in actual command of the troops."

"Hell"—O'Connor's manner was suddenly confident—"stay here and cool your heels if you want. I'm going to bring in that bastard, Bog, and Pugonny-koshig and Shab-on-day-sh-king along with him."

"The way you did the last time on Sugar Point?" Morgan remarked cooly. "Down on your knees, whimpering like a dog."

Only the quicksilver eyes betrayed O'Connor's rage. He had learned one lesson, at least, from his confrontations with Morgan. Losing his temper accomplished nothing.

"Sheehan"—he nodded to his deputy—"as soon as the lake calms, we'll head for Bear Island."

It was a direct challenge to Humphrey's authority, and the Lieutenant snapped at it like a badger.

"Sergeant Hesbrook will go along with you to represent the Army," he said. "If you want to take on the whole War Department just get smart with him." His glance shifted shrewdly to Morgan.

"Maybe you ought to go along as an official observer," he declared. "And you, Bradshaw"—dryly—"to let the public know what happens."

With a brief nod, Morgan walked away, Bradshaw keeping pace beside him. Although Sergeant Hesbrook's presence would act as a damper on O'Connor's aggressiveness, there was the danger that Bog-o-nay-ge-shig might react to the sight of an Army uniform like a bull to a flag. Still, it was unavoidable.

At the Agency headquarters, Indians were gathered in front of Meir's office, making speeches and airing their complaints to one another. There was no one else to listen to them. Without Bog-o-nay-ge-shig, Humphrey and the reporters had no interest in what they had to say. This additional slap in the face incensed them even more.

Despite the rough water, Morgan knew that messengers were already on their way to warn Bog-o-nay-ge-shig. By the time he, Bradshaw, and Sergeant Hesbrook shoved off, the wind had laid and the waters calmed. Several hundred yards ahead of them, they spotted O'Connor and "Colonel" Sheehan in a canoe manned by Agency Indians.

Morgan made no attempt to close the distance until they raised Bear Island; then he signaled Bradshaw and Sergeant Hesbrook and the three crews dug in their paddles and hit the beach only yards behind the Marshal.

For a moment, the group stood motionless, listening, hearing nothing but the wind through the trees, the scamper of small, unseen creatures somewhere back in the thick, brushy timber.

O'Connor shifted uneasily; then, conscious of Sergeant Hesbrook's unspoken contempt, he snapped, "Let's go, Sheehan," and started inland across the sand.

One moment, the beach was deserted; the next, fifty armed Pillagers swarmed out of the timber to face the group in a curved line. Then as though the act had been rehearsed, they raised their hands high and shouted, "*Haugh!*"

It was a repeat of the fiasco of the week before.

O'Connor frozen in mid-stride, his face ashen . . . Sheehan, cool, watchful . . . Sergeant Hesbrook, Krag-Jorgensen rifle cocked, finger on the trigger . . . Bradshaw, incongruous in shapeless suit and Homburg hat, mentally writing an article on the confrontation.

In that one tense instant, the whole scene registered on Morgan's mind . . . white and Indian alike.

Bog-o-nay-ge-shig, still wearing his lumberjack waist trousers and wide red suspenders over a red, white and black checkered shirt, head and braided hair adorned with feathers, necklace of bear and panther claws, tortoiseshell rattle fastened to the French *voyageur* sash around his waist . . . Pugonnykoshig and Shab-on-day-sh-king in fringed buckskins with tomahawks thrust into their belts . . . several lesser chiefs . . . and Jean Chardin, his aquiline face more wild than Morgan had ever seen it. The half-breed's eyes met his, and then passed through and beyond him.

Jean Chardin was on the verge of "going home," as the Indians called it. At the first shot, he would revert to the total savage, killing and scalping as the Sioux had done at New Ulm thirty-six years before.

More dangerous than ever. If trouble broke out, it would be he who fired the first shot. And no way of reaching him anymore. He was beyond reason, beyond hearing.

Morgan felt a sense of real regret. He liked Jean Chardin.

"*Haaa!*" The brisk wind blowing in off the lake ruffled the feathers in Bog-o-nay-ge-shig's hair. His eyes flashed. "You were warned not to come back here, Marshal," he said harshly. "Do you think the soldier will protect you?"

His voice was so menacing that O'Connor's throat tightened, making it impossible for him to swallow. He managed a dark look and motioned toward the half circle of Pillagers.

"No." Bog-o-nay-ge-shig's voice deepened. "All those you want are here, as you can see. But, like me, they die before they are put in the white man's jail."

Somehow, O'Connor managed a false bravado. "You'll die, all right, when the soldiers come!"

"*Haaa!*" Bog-o-nay-ge-shig glanced at Sergeant Hesbrook and spat his contempt. "You think I do not know about the soldiers at the Agency? Or about the others on their way from Fort Snelling under General Bacon? *Haaa!* Let them come. Can they kill the ghosts of warriors who still live? Men will die, yes. But they will be soldiers, not Chippewas. Now, go!" His eyes, dark, somber, switched to Morgan.

"Mr. Morgan, you should not have come. You mean well, but it is too late. No"—he threw up his hand in a silencing gesture—"no more talk. It has all been said. Now we fight, if that is the way it must be."

"What about your friends, Gail Saunders and Dr. Lindley?" Morgan asked. "Have you turned your face from them, too?"

A moment's hesitation, the dark features inscrutable. "The sun is swallowed by the night; yet, each morning, it returns to warm the day. So it is with friends."

Any further attempt to reason with him would not only be futile but dangerous, Morgan realized. He had done all he could.

As he turned away, his eyes rested on Jean Chardin for what he sensed would be the last time. It was a painful moment. He liked Jean Chardin.

"Jean . . ."

The half-breed did not answer; he did not hear. The winds of the past were roaring around him, drowning out everything but the sound of the coming battle—the last battle—in which he, Jean Chardin, Cree, Yellow Knife, Ojibway, would stand and maybe die with his friends Bog-o-nay-ge-shig, Pugonny-koshig and Shab-on-day-sh-king.

For the first time in his life, he felt purified, whole. *Almost* whole. Only with Hugh Stark's death could he truly become one with his people, with the souls of all the dead warriors who had died fighting the white man . . . with All Things, All Being.

He did not see the regret on Craig Morgan's face as the Oregonian returned to the beach with Jason Bradshaw. Nor hear O'Connor's empty threats, drowned out by the jeers of the Pillagers, as the Agency canoes put out from shore and gradually faded to tiny dots in the distance.

Beaching their canoe near the dock, Morgan and Jason Bradshaw made their way wearily along Lake Street. Sergeant Hesbrook, accompanied by Marshal O'Connor and "Colonel" Sheehan, had cut away at Onigum to join Lieutenant Humphrey: Hesbrook to report, O'Connor to demand immediate retaliation against the Pillagers.

Now Morgan walked in silence, the waning sun at his back, his head bent in thought. The near-disaster at Bear Island had left him badly shaken. If pressed, there was no question but that Bog-o-nay-ge-shig would fight.

Suddenly, ahead of them and across the street, Morgan saw the troop train drawn up before the roundhouse. A crowd clustered around the depot. Smoke still rose from the stack, which meant that General Bacon had arrived within the past few hours.

For Morgan, it was a bitter moment. Despite everything he had done, Stark and Meir had accomplished their purpose. Troops were now not only in Walker, but small units were stationed at strategic points around the reservation—in the small towns, at dams and along the railroads.

Now General Bacon's arrival from Fort Snelling with reinforcements made bloodshed inevitable. Bog-o-nay-ge-shig would never yield to pressure or the threat of force. When Bacon attempted to apply it, the shooting would start.

"Craig!" Standing on the opposite corner with Dr. Lindley, Gail Saunders waved to attract Morgan's attention. "Over here!"

With Bradshaw, Morgan crossed the graded street to meet

her. "Hello, Gail." He nodded to Lindley. "What's going on? When did Bacon arrive?"

"Where have you two been all day?" Gail stared from Morgan to Bradshaw. "The General arrived with eighty soldiers more than an hour ago. He wants to see both of you as soon as possible. He's already talked with me and Dr. E.C., and"—a pause—"Hugh Stark and Frank Meir."

Morgan frowned. "What about?"

"I think he wants to get a clear picture of exactly what's going on before he takes any action."

"Gail," Morgan asked, "how did the town react to the arrival of reinforcements?"

She tossed her head in disgust. "It was just like it was when the first troops arrived, with everybody laughing, and shouting, and cheering. Captain Wilkinson told me that crowds were gathered at all the small towns en route, waving flags and having fun like it was a carnival."

"Maybe, in a way, it is," Jason Bradshaw said with a note of bitterness. "Everything's being blown up out of all proportion. Perhaps even Morgan and I have exaggerated the situation. But, mainly, it's irresponsible reporters like Lassiter of the New York *Tribune* and Horton of the Chicago *Herald* who are doing it. Also, some people here in Walker who can't seem to believe that an Indian, a *friendly* Indian, can suddenly decide that it's better to fight and die than to be treated like an animal."

It was the closest thing to a show of emotion he had ever displayed, and it took Morgan by surprise. Probably for the first time in his life, Jason Bradshaw had placed the human factor before the story.

Intuitively, Gail Saunders turned to Morgan. "You've been to see Bog-o-nay-ge-shig, haven't you?"

"Yes."

"What happened?"

Morgan told her, making no attempt to varnish the truth. Strangely, Jean Chardin's reversion to "all Indian" seemed to upset her more than anything else.

"Not Jean!" she cried. "Why, he's been like a brother to me. I can't believe it!"

"Maybe his mind has snapped," Morgan said soberly. "I don't

know. But he's whipping the young men's emotions up to a dangerous pitch. And Bog-o-nay-ge-shig's apparently doing nothing to stop him. That bothers me."

"Then you should call it to General Bacon's attention," Gail told him. "Hugh and Elaine may be in real danger."

"Stark is no concern of mine." Sharp, hostile. "However, I will inform Bacon of the fact. Doctor"—he offered his hand to the physician—"did the General say when he'd be embarking?"

"Around three in the morning," Lindley informed him.

"Then I'll see you aboard," Morgan said. As he started to move away, he smiled at Gail Saunders: a grave smile that betrayed his inner concerns. "I promise you I'll do what I can to prevent bloodshed."

"I know," she murmured, "but be careful, Craig."

Morgan nodded to Bradshaw and the two of them cut across the open ground toward the troop train.

Identifying themselves to the corporal on guard, they were taken immediately to General Bacon's private coach.

John Moss Bacon, Commander, Department of Dakota, rose to greet them. Forty-four years old, a veteran of both the Civil War and the Indian Wars, he was a professional soldier. Yet, like Lieutenant Humphrey, he saw no glory in this campaign against a couple of hundred desperate Chippewas. Motioning Morgan and Bradshaw to chairs, he came straight to the point.

"Let's talk, gentlemen."

Emerging an hour later, grim-faced and uncommunicative, Morgan and Bradshaw returned to the hotel for a few hours' sleep. The General had listened—he had had to go through the motions for the record—but he had not heard. It wouldn't have mattered anyway. The decision had already been made in Washington by the Secretary of War, listening to the Secretary of the Interior . . . and influenced by heavy political pressure from those who stood to gain, one way or the other, from the Chippewa tragedy.

3 A.M., *October 5, 1898*

Carrying General Bacon, Captain Wilkinson, Lieutenant Ross, eighty soldiers of the 3rd Infantry—plus Marshal O'Connor, Deputy Marshal "Colonel" Sheehan and two deputies, Craig

Morgan, Jason and a horde of reporters—the steam launches *Flora* and *Chief* put out from Walker on the thirty-mile journey to Sugar Point, where intelligence reports indicated Bog-o-nay-ge-shig had retreated. Following in their wake, the barge *Flora* carried the detachment's supplies, ten days' rations, a Hotchkiss revolving cannon and one Gatling gun.

Lieutenant Humphrey and his men remained at the Agency at Onigum with orders to stay there until further orders.

The news had angered Morgan, already on edge as a result of the Army's action. "Why would Bacon leave a battle-tested lieutenant and twenty sharpshooters behind?" he had demanded of Bradshaw. "That's only inviting Bog-o-nay-ge-shig to stand firm. Sergeant Kelly told me that only nineteen men of this detachment are experienced troops. The rest are raw recruits; most of them don't even know how to use the Krag-Jorgensen rifle yet. It does not make sense!"

"Never question a general's decisions," Bradshaw remarked dryly. "And since when did war *ever* make sense?"

Now, standing at the *Flora*'s starboard railing with the throb of the engine coming up to them through the deck, they listened to the low murmur of the soldiers' voices around them. Further up, near the bow, O'Connor, Sheehan and the two other deputies leaned their elbows on the railing along with the gaggle of reporters.

The night was clear, with the moon, still well up in the sky, outlining both launches and men. Save for the glint of moonlight off the barrels of the Krag-Jorgensen rifles and, aboard the barge *Flora,* off the Hotchkiss cannon and the Gatling gun, the little flotilla could have passed for simple commercial steam launches plowing across the lake.

The idea both angered and depressed Morgan. But for men like Hugh Stark, this beautiful land of forests and ten thousand lakes could have been developed gradually and without bloodshed.

"Damn!" Soft, bitter.

Bradshaw turned toward him. "What did you say?"

"Nothing."

Sunlight, spreading across the clearing, had not yet reached Bog-o-nay-ge-shig's log house, but the shadows had disappeared from the beach, the fish racks and the drying shed. A chill wind, blowing in from the lake, ruffled the tail feathers of a bluejay and sent it scolding raucously from treetop to treetop. The only other sound was the creak of the cabin door as it swung back and forth on unoiled hinges.

Assembled on the beach, the detachment shifted uneasily from one foot to the other, fingering the triggers of their Krag-Jorgensen rifles as they swept the clearing and the encircling forest, all the while conscious of the fear-sweat that dampened their armpits and trickled down their flanks.

"Jesus, but it's quiet!" a fuzzy-faced private whispered, and then tried to make himself invisible as the silence picked up his words and transformed them into a shout.

Standing beside General Bacon, Captain Wilkinson threw the private a sharp look but said nothing. He understood the boy's fear; he had known it himself many times.

Bacon also sensed the detachment's unease and it troubled him, reflecting as it did his own doubts ever since he had received his orders to march on the Chippewas. A seasoned Indian fighter, he did not, like O'Connor and Stark, underestimate Bog-o-nay-ge-shig. Two hundred well-armed Indians, taking advantage of this heavily forested country, could be a dangerous enemy. Only a fool would ignore that fact; he was no fool.

He glanced at Captain Wilkinson with a professional objectivity. Well built, five feet ten or eleven. Brown hair, parted on the right side and cresting like a breaking wave, as gray-sprinkled as the side whiskers that merged with the neatly trimmed spade beard and magnificent spiked guardsman's moustache.

A good man, he thought. *A soldier's officer, who had proved himself in the '78 Bannock Wars in Idaho, as well as during the Civil War. Breveted major during the Bannock campaigns, he should have been permanent rank in that grade. If all went well, perhaps that could be corrected.*

If all went well.

He sucked in air, let it out carefully so that the detachment would not know that their General was also apprehensive.

"Captain Wilkinson, have a couple of men check out the house. If there are women in there send them back to the Agency. We'll use the place for a hospital.

"Dr. Harris"—to the Army surgeon—"you'll set up your equipment there as soon as possible. Your corpsman will have to help you with surgery. That Walker physician—what was his name, Dr. Lindley?—didn't turn up." He swung his attention to Lieutenant Ross.

"Lieutenant, you will remain aboard the barge with twenty men as a reserve force. In the event we come under fire, you will exercise your own judgment in deploying your detail.

"As for the press . . ." Bacon's eyes chilled as they settled on the newsmen. "If there is fighting, the exaggerated stories you gentlemen send back will probably throw Minnesota into a panic. Unfortunately, since the Army tolerates you, I can't kick your butts and send you back home like I'd like to. But, by God, stay away from me and my men!"

He pivoted abruptly toward Jason Bradshaw. "Mr. Bradshaw, you're the exception. You *do* give the public facts, not fiction. I'll expect you and your paper to print the truth of what happens here."

A shadow passed over his face, settling the fine features into a somber cast. The look he gave Morgan was almost defensive, as though he were seeking justification for his presence on Sugar Point.

"Mr. Morgan, I've fought Indians much of my Army career; but I've never hated them. They were brave men. I want you to know I take no pleasure in this present assignment. If Chief Bog-o-nay-ge-shig is killed, it will be another senseless tragedy. A—"

"You Indian-loving bastard!" Marshal O'Connor shouted, his face apoplectic with rage. "You ought to be court-martialed and drummed out of the Army!"

Only the sudden flame that burned the ice out of Bacon's eyes betrayed his reaction. Without turning his head, he said, "Captain Wilkinson, if we establish peaceful contact with the Pillagers and *that* man makes any kind of hostile gesture, kill him. That is an order."

"Yes, sir." Then, "Sir, the cabin's been checked out. There's no one there. And they've taken everything with them."

Bacon grunted, his expression unhappy. "That means Bog-o-nay-ge-shig is not going to parley. All right, we go after him. We'll make a two-mile reconnaissance around the Point. Forest trails will be scouted inland. If contact is established, the scouts will withdraw and report back immediately. We move out of here in ten minutes."

"Yes, sir!" Wilkinson strode back to the detachment. "Sergeant Butler, have the men ready to move out in ten minutes."

The clearing came alive as the detachment checked rifles and ammunition, then fell in as Butler and Kelly blistered them with "Old Army" invective.

Aboard the barge *Flora,* Lieutenant Ross's recruits began breaking out supplies while the shore detail stood ready to handle them.

Observing them in silence, Morgan experienced a deep sense of personal tragedy, knowing that when the two forces met the nightmare would become a reality. He had done all he could.

With Bradshaw, he rejoined the detachment.

At the head of the column, General Bacon nodded briefly. "I'll want you with me if we make contact with Bog-o-nay-ge-shig," he said. "All right, Captain, pass the order."

"Sergeants Butler, Kelly—move them out!"

With the sun touching their faces, the detachment marched back to the beach. There, swinging south, they proceeded along the western shore of Sugar Point, rifles resting easy on their shoulders.

Behind them Marshal O'Connor, his face still dark with rage, along with Sheehan, two other deputies and the pack of reporters, brought up the rear.

The Army was on the move.

Around noon, the patrols began to work their way back to the clearing. They had little to report that Bacon, who had returned with his main force, had not already observed. Empty cabins and birchbark huts with all belongings removed. A few old men and squaws, but no warriors. Yet the scouts were convinced they had been under constant scrutiny.

Sergeant Butler, who brought in the last patrol, put it succinctly, "General, them woods are full of Indians, but they're like ghosts. You can't see 'em; you can't hear 'em; but you sure as hell know they're there. Hell, sir, they could have wiped us out if they'd wanted to."

"What do you think, Morgan?" Bacon rubbed his chin reflectively. "Will Bog-o-nay-ge-shig parley?"

For a moment, Morgan debated the question. "No," he said. "He'll force you to make the first hostile move, then fight a defensive battle. Don't try and corner him, General. In these woods, he could massacre you."

"War always involves calculated risks," Bacon replied pragmatically. "I hope to secure order here without bloodshed. But if that is not possible, then I will employ whatever force is necessary." Abruptly, he dismissed the matter from his mind. "Captain Wilkinson, have the men fall out for noon mess."

Wilkinson snapped the order. The sergeants executed it. "Fall out and stack arms!"

The detachment, still jittery, moved into a garden patch near Bog-o-nay-ge-shig's house and began to pyramid their rifles.

As Private Stalcup, a tall, skinny recruit from Wisconsin, started to lean his rifle against the last stack, Sergeant Kelly shouted, "Did you check your rifle, Stalcup? Last time, you left a cartridge in the firing chamber. By God, you do it again . . ."

Already scared, Stalcup dropped the Krag-Jorgensen, accidently discharging it.

The sharp *crack* whiplashed across the clearing, cutting up the Sergeant's words. His mouth was still open in a soundless curse when the first soldier fell.

Hidden in the timber where they had evaded Bacon's sweeping patrols, the Pillagers, believing themselves under fire, opened up with their Winchesters.

Men went down all over the clearing. Privates Lowe, Onstead, Ziebel, Swallenstocker, and Sergeant Butler died instantly; ten others fell, wounded.

With their weapons stacked and bullets screaming past their ears, the raw recruits panicked. The few veterans, under Sergeant Kelly, grabbed their rifles and dropped to the ground, seeking whatever cover they could find.

Beside Morgan, Captain Wilkinson took a bullet in the left arm but joined the fighting.

Untouched, General Bacon sought to rally the disorganized

troops. "Goddammit, take cover and fire!" Unfortunately, since for some reason he was wearing civilian clothing, few of the troops recognized him. Only Captain Wilkinson's reputation as an Indian fighter steadied them.

Running low, Morgan and Bradshaw made it to the safety of the drying shed. From there, they had a clear view of the battlefield.

Under heavy fire, Sergeant Kelly had set the troops to digging trenches on the west and north sides of the clearing, and rifle pits on the east, with Bog-o-nay-ge-shig's log house the center.

Aboard the barge *Flora,* Lieutenant Ross's detail came under attack as it sought to lay down a covering fire for the troops in the clearing and, in the process, took casualties of its own.

Ashore, Captain Wilkinson suddenly broke from the firing line and ran toward the drying shed. Dropping down beside Morgan, he leaned his head against the wall and flexed his legs. His face was pale. His tunic sleeve was blood-soaked and a crimson stream washed down over his left arm.

"Give me a hand, will you?" He fumbled with the buttons of his tunic. "I'm bleeding like a stuck pig."

Carefully, Morgan worked Wilkinson's arm out of the bloody sleeve and inspected the wound. The bullet had passed cleanly through the bicep, but the wound was still bleeding freely.

"Where's the Army surgeon?" he asked. "You need real medical care."

"He's pinned down aboard the *Flora,*" Wilkinson said. "Do the best you can. I've got to get back on the line."

He was in no shape to fight, but to tell him that would be a waste of time. Using a strip torn from his own shirt, Morgan applied a pressure bandage and a tourniquet to the arm.

"That'll do for now," he said. "But see the doctor as soon as you can."

Wilkinson eased his arm back into the tunic sleeve and got to his feet. "Thanks," he said, and zigzagged back to the entrenchments.

Moments after he reached the firing line, Morgan saw him clutch his stomach and go down—and knew instinctively that the Captain was dead. He experienced an almost painful sense of loss, for Wilkinson had symbolized a past dominated by the heroic, larger-than-life personalities to whom war had been a spiritual baptism, a test of manhood, and a search for some intangible meaning just beyond the outer perimeter of man's understanding. With Wilkinson's death, the past had dimmed a little more, the heroic image diminished; not because of his dying, but because there were so few heroes left.

"Damn!" Bradshaw swore tonelessly. "Why couldn't it have been that bungling private who—" A bullet drilled through the corner of the shed. He hugged the ground, the double-barreled derringer in his hand as useless as a toy at that range.

Morgan risked a quick look around the corner of the shed. A log butt inches above his head disintegrated in a shower of pine splinters. He stayed put, figuring out the Pillager's position. Then as sunlight bounded off the Winchester barrel, he squeezed off six shots in rapid succession. At seventy-five yards, the Colt was no match for the rifle, but it did force the marksman to switch his attention elsewhere.

Gradually, the gunfire died down to a desultory exchange, a stalemate.

Then no shots at all from the forest.

Silence fell over the clearing; a silence made all the more eerie by the whisper of the wind through the treetops. Men held their breath, bracing themselves for an all-out frontal attack.

Sergeant Kelly, who had been in the trenches, the rifle pits and behind the breastwork, shouted encouragement to the recruits.

"Don't let 'em scare you! Hold your fire! If they come at us pick a target and bring it down."

Observing Kelly's leadership, General Bacon walked over to the NCO and said, "Sergeant, take over the firing line. Captain Wilkinson is dead."

Kelly swung around, glared at the middle-aged man in civilian clothes, and snapped, "Who the hell are you to be giving orders around here?"

"General Bacon, Commander, Department of Dakota." No mistaking the crisp, authoritative manner.

Kelly paled. "Sorry, sir. I didn't recognize you." Then, "Sir, Lieutenant Ross is here, and *alive*."

"Ross is still aboard the *Flora*," Bacon snapped. "Now take charge of the right side of the line, Sergeant!"

"Yes, sir." Kelly was staring over Bacon's shoulder. "Sir, there's a white couple coming out of the timber under a truce flag."

Bacon pivoted, took one glance, and shouted, "Hold your fire! That's the Saunders woman and that Walker doctor. Sergeant, get them inside the house."

Stepping from the breastwork, Kelly walked slowly toward the two figures, the sound of his boots all but drowned in the thunder of his heart.

Behind the drying shed, Morgan heard Bacon's shouted order and risked a quick sweep of the clearing.

Sergeant Kelly, Gail Saunders and Dr. Lindley were just entering Bog-o-nay-ge-shig's cabin.

"Hey!" Bradshaw scrambled to his feet. "What's going on?"

Morgan turned, his lips compressed with anger. The shock of what he had seen showed plainly on his face. "Gail and Dr. E.C. just came in under a flag of truce. They evidently sailed over some time during the night to see Bog-o-nay-ge-shig. I should have known she was up to something. She was too quiet earlier in the evening." Suddenly, his anger exploded. "The little fool could have gotten herself killed! And Lindley—has he lost his senses? He should have stopped her."

"Stop Gail Saunders?" Bradshaw flashed his lopsided grin. "Are you serious? Lindley did the only thing he could—came along to try and protect her."

"You can't protect a willful, headstrong . . ."

Sergeant Kelly came out of the house carrying the white flag and marched back to the entrenchments.

The truce was over.

Again the silence, spreading all over the island and out across the lake.

"Come on." Morgan motioned to Bradshaw. "Let's make a run for it while we can."

"No, thanks." The reporter shook his head. "I'll stay here."

"Suit yourself."

Morgan made it to the cabin without a shot being fired. Closing the door, he stared around him. The place was empty; Bog-o-nay-ge-shig and his family had taken everything with them.

"Craig."

He set his teeth, resenting her "I've-done-nothing-wrong" innocence. When he had his temper under control, he walked to where she stood with Dr. E.C. before the fireplace at the other end of the room. For a moment, he regarded her with a frozen expression.

"That was a stupid thing to do," he said finally. "You could at least have told me what you planned."

Gail Saunders flushed, her smile fading. "I'm under no obligation to tell you anything, Craig."

"It's a matter of common courtesy," Morgan retorted. He swung his attention to Lindley. "I find it difficult to believe, Doctor, that you would become part of such a move. You both should have known Bog-o-nay-ge-shig would not talk to you."

The cool eyes rested on him without visible emotion. "It is a matter, sir, which does not concern you. I suggest you bear that in mind."

"It concerns me a great deal," Morgan corrected him. "If I had known what she was up to, I would have stopped her."

"You'd have stopped me!" Gail Saunders cried. "Mr. Morgan, I'm not one of your backwoods women. No man tells me what to do! And as for Bog-o-nay-ge-shig, he *did* listen to us. If the Army hadn't started shooting, he would have come in for a council. Now get back to your killing. Then when it's all over, go back where you belong. You're not the man I thought you were."

Her anger coiled around Morgan like a blacksnake whip. Too late, he realized that, without meaning to, he had demeaned her. She was a self-assured young woman who stood on her own feet, fought her own battles and had no need of him or any other man. By his own stupidity, he had lost her respect, admiration and anything else she might have felt for him.

"Gail"—he spread his hands in a mute gesture of apology—"you don't . . ."

Outside, gunfire erupted from all directions, the timber, the clearing and the beach.

Rushing to a window, Morgan saw the steam launch *Chief* loaded with reinforcements, heading for shore. Under constant heavy fire Lieutenant Ross's force made it to the landing without casualties. But as they fought their way toward the besieged detachment, men began to fall. A big hospital corpsman, Oscar Buckhard, led the way into the entrenchments carrying a wounded soldier in his arms.

Ross's arrival did not force a Pillager withdrawal; but the detachment, with its entrenchments now completed, at least had cover.

"Doctor"—Morgan turned away from the window—"you'd better break out your medical . . ." The cabin was empty save for Gail Saunders who stood watching him in silence.

"Where's Dr. E.C.?" he asked.

Gail lifted a frozen face to him. "With the wounded. Why aren't you out there helping him?"

Without answering, Morgan went outside. A bullet thudded into the wall chest high. The dead still lay where they had fallen in that first volley. A few of the wounded had crawled to the safety of the trenches and rifle pits. Others, badly hit, kept crying out, "Medic! Medic, help me!" or "Water, please God!"

An officer, carrying a medical kit in one hand, ran past Morgan into the cabin. Close on his heels, a big, blond-haired hospital corpsman, lugging a wounded man across his shoulder, sprinted for the "hospital" with bullets snapping spitefully around him.

Down on his knees beside a raw recruit, Dr. E.C. was applying a tourniquet to a blood-spurting thigh.

Morgan grasped him by the shoulder and pulled him to his feet. "Get back to the hospital. I'll bring this man in."

Lindley hesitated, then broke for the cabin. Even running, he lost none of his dignity.

The recruit screamed as Morgan picked him up; he kept screaming all the way to the house.

Bradshaw, you cold-blooded little bastard, Morgan thought, *why in hell aren't you here helping me?*

Private Buckhard, coming out of the cabin, held the door open for him. He staggered inside, looking for a place to put the wounded man.

"Over here!" Gail Saunders pointed to a space near the rear wall. "They're safe only when they're lying below the first two logs. Snipers keep knocking out the chinking, trying to get at us."

"What about your good friend Bog-o-nay-ge-shig?" Morgan said harshly. "He knows you're in here."

Gail's head came up. "It's our fault, not his. He pleaded with me and Dr. E.C. to go back to Walker where we would be safe. We chose to stay."

"What do you hope to accomplish?" Angry, frustrated.

"Exactly what I'm doing," Gail retorted. "Helping Dr. E.C. take care of the wounded. And, if I get another chance, to try and convince Bog-o-nay-ge-shig that the soldiers did not mean to fire upon them; that it was an accident, one man's carelessness. He might listen. I don't know. Anyway, it's none of your business."

Before Morgan could answer, she turned her attention to the wounded man, leaving Morgan standing there, aware that, for the second time, he had blundered. She was right; what she did was her own business. Certainly, she didn't need him. Maybe that was what he resented, not being needed. It was a disturbing thought. To escape it, he moved toward the door, almost colliding with the big blond corpsman, who stumbled inside with a wounded man slung over his shoulder.

As he slammed the door and cut a zigzag course across the clearing, with bullets buzzing past his head like angry hornets, Morgan spotted Jason Bradshaw, staggering toward the cabin, a soldier thirty pounds heavier than himself cradled in his arms. The familiar black Homburg was askew and the reporter's battered face was twisted with pain, but he managed a lopsided grin in passing.

Damn you, Bradshaw, Morgan thought, *just when I think I've got you figured out, why do you always prove me wrong?* and felt good that it was so.

From a rifle pit, a man called out urgently. Morgan dropped down beside him. A bullet-shattered collarbone, painful and tough to transport, alone.

While Morgan hesitated, the big hospital corpsman raced from the cabin to give him a hand. Shielding the trooper between them, they headed back, with every soldier in the trenches laying down a covering fire and the whine of Pillager bullets lashing the clearing around them.

Gail Saunders had the door open, waiting for them. Just as

Morgan stepped aside to let Buckhard and the wounded man enter, a bullet struck him in the back, passing cleanly through the fleshy part of his left side.

Seeing he was hit, Gail Saunders grabbed him by the arm and pulled him into the cabin. Already blood had begun to redden his shirt.

"How bad is it?"

"Just a flesh wound, I think."

"Thank God!" She made no attempt to hide her relief. "Come on. Lie down against the wall. Dr. E.C., Craig's been hit. Can you take a look at him?"

Turning a patient over to Buckhard, the hospital corpsman, Dr. E.C. came over, carrying his medical bag. He looked tired, haggard. Silently, he examined the wound, then nodded reassuringly to Gail Saunders.

"A clean flesh wound. Painful, but not serious. He'll be sore for a few days; that's all. I'll give him a dose of laudanum to ease the pain. Private Buckhard can do the bandaging. I'll leave the nursing to you." He rose, picked up his medical bag, and rejoined Dr. Harris on the other side of the room.

A moment later, Buckhard, the corpsman, came over and knelt down beside Morgan. Quickly and efficiently, he bandaged the wound. Then, sitting back on his heels, he nodded to the Oregonian.

"I'm Oscar Buckhard. No need to introduce yourself. I know who you are. Thanks for the help. You just may have saved a couple of lives." He stood up, flexing his knees. "I'd better get back to the firing line."

Bullets thudded into the log walls and knocked out chinking as he opened the door and ran for it.

On the other side of the room, Dr. E.C. called, "Gail, will you give me a hand here, please?"

Gail Saunders hesitated, looking down at Morgan. "Craig?" He did not answer. The laudanum had already taken effect.

"Yes, Dr. E.C.," she said. "I'm coming."

From a long way off, Morgan heard her voice and then the quick sound of her footsteps receding. Then he fell asleep.

Gail Saunders came over and stood staring down at him for a long time, seeing him, in this unguarded moment, for the fine, decent man he was. A man of strong principles and the courage to fight for them, and who, like Dr. E.C., died a little inside when he failed. An "out of time" Don Quixote tilting with the windmills of change.

Quick tears filled her eyes, remembering the way she had spoken to him earlier. He had not deserved that; yet it was too late to mend the break now. Perhaps it was better that way. At twenty-seven, the daughter of a steamboat captain turned merchant in his last years, she was too independent, too strong-willed to become seriously involved with any man. She often wondered what her mother, who had died when she was three years old, had been like. Much like herself, she suspected.

"Your mother was an extraordinary woman," her father had once told her, "with a great capacity for giving and an even greater resistance to being forced to give. She was not like other women; she was"—his face grew gentle with memory—"she was like some wild, untamed creature. I never tried to cage her. And for that she loved me."

After her mother's death, her world had been the roiling, muddy waters of the Mississippi as seen from the "Texas" deck of a stern-wheeler; the rough deckhands who had spoiled her when she was little, and who had not known quite how to treat her when her breasts began to fill out; and she, herself, had had no woman to explain to her the strange new feelings which confused and, sometimes, tormented her.

Captain Jonathan Saunders, a kind man, but totally ignorant of how to bring up a rapidly maturing young girl, had sent her to a "finishing school for young ladies" in St. Louis when she was fifteen. At nineteen, she had emerged an attractive, intelligent young woman with a natural charm, a shrewd head for business and a strong sense of justice.

Following her father's passing, she had taken over management of the general merchandise store he had left her, prospered and had devoted herself to helping the reservation Indians, especially the *Mukkundwais,* Bog-o-nay-ge-shig's Pillagers. Despite disagreements with a few townspeople, she was admired, respected and well liked.

Her personal life had been quiet, uncomplicated. A few men had interested her briefly; none had ever aroused any deep emotion within her. Incredibly, she was still a virgin, although she held no strong fundamentalist views on sex. She was simply an idealistic young woman waiting for the right man to come along and, somehow, make it all seem right and beautiful.

Until Craig Morgan had stepped between Marshal O'Connor and the wounded Chippewa Shab-on-day-sh-king, she had never met that man, although, for years, she had idealized Morgan in her dreams. Now that she had met him, she could not surrender her personal independence even for him.

Slowly, she turned and walked back to the wounded. They were quiet now, either sleeping or sedated with laudanum. She sat down beside Lindley with a rueful little smile.

"Craig's right, Dr. E.C.," she murmured. "I am a fool, but not for the reasons he believes. I've idealized that man ever since I was sixteen years old. Yet you heard how I spoke to him, as though he were some kind of monster. Oh, I really made a mess of things!"

"You're forgetting he wasn't very kind to you either," Lindley reminded her.

"That was different. He was upset because he cared for me. And he was right. I should have told him."

The fine gray eyes searched her face intently. "Morgan is a mature man, Gail," Lindley said quietly. "Be patient. He will understand."

"Which will only make it worse!" The tears flowed freely now. "Dammit, why do I have to be such a shrew, Dr. E.C.?"

Again, that transfiguring smile lighted Lindley's face. "You feel threatened, Gail. For a woman like you, that's only natural. You'll get over it. Just give yourself time."

With a little sigh, she leaned back against the wall, somehow assured. "I'll try," she said, "but it won't be easy."

After that, she lapsed into a pensive silence, watching the light stream in through the bullet-shattered window and fan out across the cabin floor.

Around four-thirty, Jason Bradshaw slipped inside, looked at Morgan, then nodded to Gail Saunders.

"How is he?"

"He's lost some blood and he'll have a sore rib for a week," Gail told him. "But nothing serious."

Bradshaw appeared relieved. "He and that hospital corpsman, Buckhard, did a fine job out there today."

"I know."

Observing her sharply, Bradshaw asked, "Did you two have a fight?"

"Not really." Gail lowered her head. "Forgive me, Mr. Bradshaw, but I'd rather not talk about it."

"Sure. I understand."

He didn't, of course, but she was grateful for his tact. To change the subject, she asked, "What's happening outside?"

The *Globe* reporter scowled. "Now that fighting has actually started, Marshal O'Connor's turned chicken. He's ordered the *Flora* to take him south to the Agency on the excuse he's going for reinforcements. But Humphrey will tell him to go to hell, and he knows it."

"Are you going along?"

Bradshaw nodded. "The General's asked me to wire in his report on the situation here to the Secretary of War. That will also give me a chance to get the story to my paper."

"What about the rest of the press?"

"They'll be leaving on the *Chief* in a couple of hours."

"Will you come back?"

"In the morning." Bradshaw addressed himself to Lindley, who was resting while he could. "Doctor, do you need anything from town, medical supplies or whatnot?"

"No, thanks," Lindley informed him. "Dr. Harris and I have all the supplies we need. However, if any of my patients ask, you can tell them I'm all right. And that if there's an emergency, they're to send for me."

Bradshaw tipped his battered Homburg to Gail Saunders and was gone.

Dusk settled over the clearing with the men crouched in the rifle pits, trenches and behind the breastwork. No cooking fires were allowed. The detachment shivered as the cold began to penetrate their uniforms.

From his command post in the center of the line, General Bacon, with Morgan beside him, had an excellent view of his perimeters. On the left, Lieutenant Ross, and on the right, Sergeant

Kelly moved quietly among the raw recruits, giving a word of praise here, a sharp criticism there.

Private Oscar Buckhard was all over the field, ready to fight, bring in the wounded or both, if the situation called for it. During the long afternoon hours, he had already saved half a dozen lives by getting the wounded to the "hospital" where Dr. Lindley and Dr. Harris could take over.

Behind the breastwork, Bacon studied the darkening forest with mounting concern. Pinned down by timber on one side and the lake on the other, his position was precarious.

"I don't like it," he grunted, hunkering down beside Morgan. "If they stage a frontal attack in force, they could overrun us. I should have ordered Humphrey up with reinforcements."

Morgan was more optimistic. "I don't think Bog-o-nay-ge-shig wants a massacre," he replied. "Right now, he's got public sympathy with him. If he keeps the Army pinned down here for another day, he will have proved his point. The Pillagers don't want bloodshed. All they want is justice."

"That may well be," Bacon conceded. "Just the same, we'll secure our perimeters tonight. If . . ." A bullet *spanged* from the treetops, the bullet smacking into the breastwork.

"Dammit!" he exploded. "Those fools in Washington don't know a bloody thing about Indian fighting! I can't corner Bog-o-nay-ge-shig with a handful of troops. It will take a full company, *if* it can be done at all."

Morgan understood his frustration. It was not a situation in which a general with a distinguished career, and on the verge of retiring, liked to be placed. Regardless of the outcome, his military image would be tarnished. Some would portray him as a ruthless opportunist striking at a small band of peaceful Indians. Others would charge that he was not the Civil and Indian wars hero he had been pictured, but an incompetent officer who could not even defeat a few militant savages.

"Everybody understands that," Morgan reassured him.

"Everybody, Mr. Morgan, doesn't write official battle reports nor record military history."

That ended the conversation.

Putting his back to the breastwork, Morgan tilted his head

and stared up at the stars, wondering why men could never seem to learn from them.

The throb of war drums booming from Sugar Point north to Five Mile Point, southwest to Ottertail Point, then southeast to Bear Island and back again to Sugar Point, awakened him.

Around him, men called back and forth to one another in quick, uneasy voices; and from the right side of the line, Sergeant Kelly shouted, "Stay calm! Keep your rifles at the ready; but don't fire until I tell you to!"

From the left flank, Lieutenant Ross echoed the order.

Outlined dimly against the sky, General Bacon knelt behind the breastwork, coordinating both flanks with the center.

Morgan got painfully to his feet, still stiff from his wound. Joining Bacon, he said, "What's going on?"

"I don't know," the General replied. "Maybe they're making medicine; maybe they're trying to scare us; maybe they just want to keep us awake."

It was an eerie feeling, the booming of those big drums coming out of the night from all directions, raising the hair at the napes of men's necks and chilling their hearts, from general to private. Even Morgan was affected.

Suddenly, a sentry posted near the shore shouted, "General, sir, the town's on fire!"

Everyone was on their feet, half out of the trenches and rifle pits, pointing across the lake to the south and calling back and forth to one another in confusion.

"The town's on fire!"

"No, it's the Agency at Onigum!"

"It's the logging camps! They've fired the logging camps!"

"The whole reservation's on the warpath!"

At first, Morgan thought that Walker was, indeed, on fire until he realized that the direction was not quite right, and then the terrible truth came to him.

Low down on the horizon, but already building rapidly to a billowing, roiling cloud of orange flame, White Pines was being reduced to ashes along, no doubt, with the man who had built it, and his daughter, Elaine, who had plotted his murder to acquire it.

Jean Chardin had had his revenge.

He was still standing there, numb with shock, when Gail Saunders joined him. As the moon slid from behind a cloud, he sensed from the look on her face that she had already guessed what he now knew.

"It's Hugh Stark's place, isn't it?"

Unconsciously, he put his arm around her. "Yes."

She twisted so that she could look up at him. "Jean?"

"He must have slipped away from the band right after dark."

"Hugh and Elaine?"

Morgan remained silent.

"What about Jean?"

"He and Stark may have killed one another. Or he may have chosen to die by his own hand rather than at the end of a white man's rope."

"Oh, no!" With a little cry, she buried her face against Morgan's shoulder. "Why did he do it? He was a kind, good natured man. *Why?*"

Morgan had assumed that she, along with Stark and Elaine, had known the reason for Chardin's driving hatred for the Pine Ring leader. That she did not meant that Jean Chardin's secret had died with him and his sworn enemy.

"We'll probably never know," he said gravely. "But whatever it was, it was too big for him to live with."

"God help him," Gail whispered, "for he's destroyed the Pillagers as well! Bog-o-nay-ge-shig will be blamed for what's happened at White Pines."

"No, Bog-o-nay-ge-shig's in the clear," Morgan assured her. "Chardin's hatred for Stark was well known, as were his threats to kill him. And I can testify that Bog-o-nay-ge-shig warned Chardin not to involve the Pillagers in his personal vendetta with Stark. Bradshaw will publish these facts in the *Globe*."

She seemed to draw some reassurance from his words, for he felt her relax within the circle of his arm.

"Thank you, Craig," she murmured, "for everything." She stepped away, ashamed of having taken advantage of his kindness, and fled back to the double safety of the cabin.

Long after the detachment had settled down to an uneasy alert, Morgan stood watching until the fiery glow on the horizon dulled and finally disappeared. Even then, he found it difficult to accept the final reality of the tragedy on Front Point.

White Pines, with its terraced lawns and splashing fountains, white patio furniture and gayly colored umbrellas, Khartoum carpets and magnificent grand piano, destroyed.

Hugh Stark and, along with him, his Great Dream, dead. Jean Chardin's tormented heart stilled. And Elaine Stark, a lovely Dresden figurine sculpted from ice and steel, her porcelain glaze acquired in the fiery kiln of a male-dominated world, only a chilling memory.

All of them gone, reduced to ashes that would soon be scattered by the wind.

Some good, of course, would come from the tragedy. With Stark's death, the power of the Pine Ring would be drastically weakened, if only for a few years. Men like Hugh Stark did not come along every day. It would take time to replace him. And time, however bought, would give the Chippewas just that much of a reprieve. Perhaps that was all they could ever expect—a reprieve.

Wearily, Morgan stretched out behind the breastwork and watched the moon wheel slowly across the sky, with now and then the sharp crack of a rifle from the treetops splintering his thoughts.

The arrival of the steam launch *Flora,* fresh from the battlefield, created a flurry of excitement in Walker. Although the boom of the war drums, carried across the lake from the eastern shore the past two nights, had kept people a little jittery, no one had really taken the situation seriously. Bog-o-nay-ge-shig was just trying to throw a scare into the soldiers.

But when a grim-faced Jason Bradshaw emerged from the Pameda Hotel after wiring his story to the *Globe* and General Bacon's report to the Secretary of War and told them the truth, that a battle was actually in progress at Sugar Point, the comic opera atmosphere changed to frantic hysteria.

Six men killed, including Captain Wilkinson and Sergeant Butler! And at least ten, maybe more, wounded!

By now, General Bacon and his whole detachment could all be massacred!

Hell, there are thousands of Chippewas on the reservation!

With the arrival of the *Chief*, loaded with a horde of reporters and grossly exaggerated accounts of the situation on Sugar Point, it got even worse.

Feeling the pain of his half-healed ribs and still-weak lungs, Jason Bradshaw left the rest of the press to fight for the single wire out of town and went upstairs to his room. Fully clothed, he fell across the bed and was asleep in moments.

"Mr. Bradshaw! Mr. Bradshaw!"

He rolled to a sitting position and then to his feet in a single motion. The frantic pounding on the door continued.

"Just a minute!"

He ran a hand through his tousled hair, crossed the room, and opened the door.

Pollock, the desk clerk, stood in the hallway, his Adam's apple bobbing nervously up and down. He tried to speak, couldn't.

"What the hell's the matter with you?" Bradshaw snapped.

"Bog's"—Pollock got his voice back—"Bog's attacked Hugh Stark's place! We'll be next! You've got to go after Lieutenant Humphrey before they wipe out the whole town! You've got to . . ."

"Shut up!" Bradshaw strode to the window, raised it, stuck his head out and looked toward Front Point.

The whole sky was aflame. White Pines was an inferno, a blazing funeral pyre.

Below him, a man shouted, "Godamighty, the Indians have burned Hugh Stark's place! They must have massacred General Bacon's whole detachment! We'll be next!"

Up and down Lake Street, people began pouring out of homes and stores, calling anxiously back and forth to one another, their voices heavy with fear and the shrill cries of the women making it hard for the men to hear.

In those first moments of terror, one sound had been forgotten. Now it hit their minds, further adding to their fear.

The booming of the war drums across the lake, vibrating throughout the town and drowning out the mad *barumph-barumph* of their hearts.

Bradshaw pulled his head back inside and slammed the window. He bolted out the door, with Pollock running after him, crying, "Mr. Bradshaw, what about Lieutenant Humphrey?"

At the head of the stairs, Bradshaw paused long enough to call back, "Humphrey can see that fire. But he's not going to move until he's ordered to. You people are on your own."

Then down the stairs, two at a time. One thought in mind. To get to that single wire out of town before Lassiter and the others beat him to it. He had another scoop. He didn't need to wait for developments to write it. Walker's reaction was as predictable as January snow in Minnesota.

Panic!

All around the shores of the reservation and reaching out to Bear Island and Ottertail Point, the increasing tempo of the war drums.

People gathered in the street, in the still open stores, in Joe Frost's saloon and in the doubtful safety of their homes to watch the glow of Hugh Stark's burning home light up the sky. Wild rumors flew everywhere. The whites at the Agency, scared out of their wits by Marshal O'Connor's account of the battle at Sugar Point, were brought over from Onigum and quartered in town.

Ignoring O'Connor's "orders" to reinforce the troops at Sugar Point, Lieutenant Humphrey remained entrenched at Onigum, awaiting direct orders from Bacon.

The small military units stationed at various points around the reservation, at dam sites and at Leech Lake Crossing, dug in, expecting the worst.

Brainerd, fearing an attack, prepared to defend itself.

In Walker, Mayor Kinkele and a few level heads met in an emergency session. An urgent appeal was sent to Brainerd for guns. Some twenty men responded with a weird assortment of weapons of various calibers, plus a lot of ammunition, much of which did not fit any of the guns.

Organized volunteer guards were stationed throughout the town. Many of them deserted their posts to boost their courage with a glass of whiskey in Joe Frost's saloon.

A train was made up to take the women and children out, but only a handful went. Most of the women chose to risk the danger with their husbands.

As the night wore on and the expected attack did not materialize, nerves grew more and more frayed and imaginations ran wild.

A woman lying awake beside her husband, listening to the weird boom of the drums, screamed at the sound of running feet and the *ki-yi-ing* of war whoops on the outside stairs leading to the apartment above. Gun in hand, her husband peered out the window, then broke into near hysterical laughter. A big collie dog, visiting the neighbor's terrier, had lost his footing on the narrow stairs and had come bouncing down, *ki-yi-ing* like an Indian all the way.

A man, on guard near his home, saw a Chippewa sneaking around the corner of his house. He put a shot squarely between the varmint's eyes and let him lay where he had fallen. Next morning, he discovered that he had shot his own pig.

Such incidents by nervous riflemen kept the town alerted all night, with few people getting any sleep.

On the reservation, logging contractors abandoned their camps in panic. Confusion struck the smaller villages. Women and children were sent to places best defended. Isolated settlers, recalling the stories about New Ulm, saw armed and painted Chippewas behind every tree.

In Walker the horde of newsmen circulated among saloons and poker parties until Mayor Kinkele ordered the places closed at 11 P.M. Many of the volunteers who had had too much to drink began to think themselves great Indian fighters.

Following the crowds from saloon to saloon, Jason Bradshaw listened to the loudmouths with lip-curled contempt. If an armed Pillager turned up in the middle of them they would break their necks running!

Not until the saloons began emptying at eleven did he find a man to take him back to Sugar Point. He was in Joe Frost's place at the time. In desperation, he jumped on a table and yelled, "Fifty dollars to anyone who'll take me across the lake!"

A stocky man with a totally bald head and a drooping gray moustache walked over to him and said, "Cash?"

Bradshaw pulled out his wallet, extracted two twenties and a ten. "Cash."

The fisherman spat a thin brown stream of tobacco juice toward a brass cuspidor, took the money and said, "Let's go."

At 5 A.M., October 6, a small boat put in at Bog's Landing. Jason Bradshaw jumped out and raced toward the trenches. The fisherman swung his tiller and headed back across the lake.

An alert sentry spotted Bradshaw coming out of the darkness and whipped up his rifle. "Halt! Or I'll fire!"

"Don't shoot!" Bradshaw cried. "I'm a reporter!"

"Hold your fire, sentry!" General Bacon shouted from his command post. "By God"—he spoke over his shoulder to Morgan—"it's Bradshaw! He made it."

A brief crackle of gunfire chased Bradshaw right up to the breastwork. Then, abruptly, it stopped. Bog-o-nay-ge-shig's strategy since the previous evening, sporadic firing intended to keep the raw recruits awake and jittery.

Fortunately, casualties during the night had been light. An Indian interpreter, fearing Pillager revenge if the troops were overrun, was shot by a sentry while trying to escape by canoe. And a soldier, digging potatoes in Bog-o-nay-ge-shig's garden patch, had been killed only minutes before. Still, even light casualties in this unreal setting were bad for morale.

Bacon dropped down behind the breastwork. "Did you send off my report?" he asked Bradshaw.

Still short of breath, the reporter nodded.

"Any reply?"

"A relief expedition of five officers and two hundred and nine soldiers is on its way from Fort Snelling," Bradshaw said. "It's due in Walker sometime today."

"Good." The General shifted his buttocks on the ground. "What's it like in town?"

Bradshaw grimaced. "Chaos! Townspeople, whites from the Agency, the Brainerd Gun Club, logging contractors and their crews who fled their camps—all jammed into homes, saloons and poker parties. And a lot of drunken fools running around pretending they're not afraid. Hell, they're scared pea green!"

Morgan, who had listened quietly, asked, "Is there any word of Hugh Stark and his daughter?"

The *Globe* reporter hesitated, looking uncomfortable. "No," he said. "The housekeeper, the maid and the groom all came into town as soon as they heard a battle was going on. The cook stayed just long enough to prepare an early dinner for three—Drew Larkin was there—and then she hot-footed into town. She said Stark refused to leave, saying there was no danger. Drew Larkin boasted that if Bog-o-nay-ge-shig and Chardin showed up, he would kill them both with one bullet.

"Elaine Stark"—Bradshaw cleared his throat—"Miss Stark appeared quite calm, but gave the impression that she was well aware of the danger and would have preferred to leave. When the cook left, they had all retired to the drawing room. She said the last thing she heard was Elaine Stark playing something 'soft and pretty on that grand piano of hers.'"

"Then they're dead."

"I'd say so."

Morgan's breath went out in a little gust of sound. "Do you think Chardin acted alone?"

"My guess is yes. Setting the fire and then shooting them as they ran out of the house would have been easy enough."

"What about Chardin?"

Bradshaw shrugged. "He knew he would hang. If Stark or Larkin didn't put a bullet in him, I figure he killed himself."

Silence, heavy with thought.

"Did you scoop the story?"

"By a couple of hours." Bradshaw tipped the Homburg over his face and promptly fell asleep.

For a moment, Morgan considered going to the cabin to inform Gail of the news from Walker. She was probably asleep.

He settled himself against the breastwork and watched as dawn spread across the clearing, lifting the shadows from the forest and changing the color of the lake from gray to blue.

Private Buckhard came out of the cabin and zigzagged to the command post, drawing only a single shot.

"General," he said, "Miss Saunders would like to know if Mr. Bradshaw brought news from town." He grinned at the reporter. "Maybe you'd like to go over and tell her yourself, Mr. Bradshaw."

"You'd love to see me get my butt shot off, wouldn't you?" Bradshaw replied sourly.

"No, sir," the corpsman declared, "but I sure do admire the way you run."

"Well, then"—Bradshaw rose—"let's run."

They could have walked.

Not a shot was fired from the forest.

Leaning his arms on the breastwork, Bacon studied the timber with a worried frown. "I don't like it. Something's wrong."

"You think they've pulled out?" Morgan asked.

"Maybe." Bacon sounded cautious. "If they've heard reinforcements are on the way. Or Bog-o-nay-ge-shig may just be playing possum. We'll play it safe.

"Lieutenant Ross, reconnoiter the timber to the east! Sergeant Kelly, probe to the north for half a mile! If you draw fire retreat immediately. We'll cover you."

The minutes dragged out. A jaybird lighted on the top of a tree and perched there, swaying in the wind and scolding noisily. A half hour, an hour passed.

Suddenly, Sergeant Kelly emerged from the forest and waved his hand. "It looks like they've pulled out, sir."

A moment later, Lieutenant Ross stepped into sight to the east. "All clear, sir."

"Post sentries," Bacon ordered. "Light cooking fires."

A cheer broke from the detachment. Soldiers piled from the trenches and rifle pits to prepare their first meal—bacon, hardtack and coffee—since the previous evening.

Carrying a couple of mess kits, Private Buckhard walked over and sat down beside Morgan. "Here," he handed the Oregonian breakfast. "Eat."

"Thanks."

A moment later, General Bacon joined them. He sat drinking his coffee and staring into the cooking fire. He looked frustrated; he had a right to be. Bog-o-nay-ge-shig had made a fool out of him.

"Private Buckhard," said Bacon without turning his head, "see that the wounded are fed. They're the ones who need it." He finished his coffee and got to his feet. "And, Private, when we return to Fort Snelling, I'm recommending you for the Medal of Honor."

He left the corpsman sitting there speechless and strode among the scattered cooking fires, a soldiers' General, causing the raw recruits to square their shoulders with pride.

Bright sunshine flooded the cabin, adding lustrous highlights to Gail Saunders' hair as she stood quietly gazing out the window.

It was the first time since her arrival that she had been alone. The wounded were fed, their dressings changed, and laudanum given to ease pain. Dr. E.C. and Dr. Harris had gone outside to eat. Private Buckhard had disappeared. Jason Bradshaw was circulating among the troops, getting on-the-spot sidelights of the battle. Craig Morgan—her mind skidded away from him.

An emotional lethargy settled over her. With the fighting broken off, she felt drained, without purpose or goal. Yet she knew that this would soon pass. For despite Stark's death, nothing had been resolved. What would be the Army's next move? Bog-o-nay-ge-shig would never surrender. In his mind, he had won the battle. If he had chosen he could have wiped out General Bacon's entire force. Bacon knew that; Jason Bradshaw would report it, giving a big boost to the Pillagers' cause.

Some of her depression lifted. Craig Morgan's investigation of the Pine Ring's illegal logging practices, Meir's fraudulent use of Chippewa activities, O'Connor's racist harassment, and Mike Davitt's moonshine activities on the reservation were certain to come under close federal scrutiny. And with Jason Bradshaw relentlessly spotlighting the investigation, some injustices would unquestionably be corrected, including, hopefully, the firing or transfer of Meir and O'Connor.

Looking out the window at the now peaceful clearing, she realized that with at least a growing light at the end of the tunnel, she should be happy. Yet she wasn't. For whatever Bradshaw had done or might do in the future, it had been Craig Morgan who had awakened the tough little reporter's sense of justice. Before that, he had been just another persistent, bulldog newsman; now he was a giant-killer. If it hadn't been for Craig . . .

"Gail."

Caught off guard, she gave herself a moment to regain her composure. Then she turned to Morgan, her mouth softening.

"I'm sorry, Craig. I didn't hear you come in."

He studied her closely for a moment, puzzled by the change in her. In many ways, she was like an open book; one could read the words, but never quite be certain as to their meaning.

"It's all right," he said. "General Bacon would like to know if you plan to return to Walker today. If so, he'll send an escort along to help you sail your boat."

"No." Gail shook her head. "I'll go back with Dr. E.C. and the wounded when the *Flora* returns. What about you?"

"I'll travel with you."

The startling blue eyes met his. "For how long, Craig, and how far?"

Her utter candor, her honesty when other women might have resorted to lowered lashes and sultry voices not only touched Morgan; it gave him a further insight into her true nature.

"I think we should both give it some thought, Gail," he said. "I would like very much for you to come back with me to Oregon for a visit."

"I just might do that." Standing on tiptoes, she kissed him, her mouth warm and sweet. "Now get back to the General. I can't afford to have my reputation ruined by Army rumors."

He left quickly, feeling an inner peace such as he had not known since Anna's death. For the first time during those long, lonely years, he felt alive, a part of humanity.

Life was suddenly good.

Walker, Minn., October 6, 1898.

Crossing an arm of Leech Lake, the relief force of 3rd Infantry, five officers and two hundred and nine soldiers, joined up with Lieutenant Humphrey's detail at Onigum.

Meanwhile, in Walker, people congregated on the streets as though finding some sense of security in numbers. For the merchants, business was good. For the saloonkeepers, it had never been better.

Armed civilians from surrounding towns and the Brainerd Gun Club, high on liquid refreshments, had turned into Indian fighters ready to put an end to the Chippewa war forthwith. Excitement, loud talk and louder boasts from men who didn't even know the meaning of manhood. A single shot from the timber along the shore and they would have broken their necks running.

Len Archer stood in front of his livery stable, chewing a straw and saying nothing. He didn't need to; the town knew how he felt.

For Pollock, the desk clerk at the Pameda Hotel, it was a Roman holiday, marred only by the absence of Craig Morgan and Jason Bradshaw. Although an inveterate gossip, he was no fool. He realized what most of Walker had not yet grasped—that, indirectly, Morgan and Bradshaw had accomplished exactly what they had intended, with more far-reaching effects to come in the weeks and months ahead. Now his nose for gossip tormented him because he didn't quite know how they had accomplished it.

From the doorway of his barber shop, Joe Pruitt watched and listened to the sounds of people up and down the street, and wondered if at last it was over, and could not understand the emptiness within himself. It didn't make sense. He still had everything—his family, his home, his shop—and yet, inexplicably, he had nothing.

He turned and went back inside to his white-enameled, silver-trimmed barber chair with its black leather upholstery and scrolled footrest. Half a dozen customers, old friends, were waiting to be clipped, shaved and tonicked. Picking up his scissors, he went to work.

He felt strangely alone.

Mike Davitt, carrying nothing but a well-filled purse, boarded the afternoon train to Duluth and more profitable points beyond. With Hugh Stark's death, he had been smart enough to read the handwriting on the wall.

At the Agency, Frank Meir sat with his booted feet propped up on the scarred desk, the bulldog pipe clenched between his teeth, watching the soldiers move past the dusty window.

Goddamn the Army, he thought bitterly. Despite its Krag-Jorgensen rifles, Hotchkiss revolving cannons and Gatling guns, it still hadn't been able to keep a mad dog half-breed from killing one of the most influential men in the country and blowing his, Meir's, future to hell and back.

He was through with the Bureau of Indian Affairs; he knew

that. For Morgan could now bring witnesses before a grand jury who would link him with Stark in a dozen criminal schemes. He still had considerable cash he'd siphoned from the Chippewas' annuity, and with Canada only hours away, he wasn't going to stay around and be sent to prison. Maybe he might even go to Mexico.

He stared morosely at the tips of his boots. Who was he kidding? What would a man trained only in the gun and the handling of Indians do in Canada or Mexico? He had grown up on a raw, untamed frontier marked by violence, quick-trigger justice and the constant challenge to simply stay alive. He had known no other life until settlers with their schools and churches and law courts had moved in and left him with nowhere to go save the reservations, where he rode herd on Indians whom he had despised through the years. Now even that was being taken from him.

Somewhere outside, a man shouted an order.

A fly buzzed noisily against the ceiling.

Frank Meir bit down on the stem of the bulldog pipe, wincing as the pressures sent exquisite pain from the bad upper molar deep into his jawbone.

Suddenly, he felt very old.

Drawn by some inner compulsion, Marshal Richard O'Connor saddled his bay and headed for White Pines. He did not want to go; he knew what he would find there. Yet he could not accept the fact that she was dead. For as she had always seemed unattainable to him, so also had she seemed indestructible. Only when he had seen the terrible proof would he believe it.

He turned off the road and rode up the curving drive with the bay's hoofs a muffled sound in the silence. Past the well-kept lawns and the tall trees with the wind whispering through their tops. Past the fountain with the water tumbling from tier to tier until it fell, a small, splashing waterfall, into the pool. Around the final curve and . . .

He reined up, his breath trapped deep in his lungs. He had known there would be damage, had been prepared for it. But that White Pines, the symbol of Hugh Stark's power, could have been totally destroyed overnight, reduced to a massive pile of charred timbers, and ashes caught up by the wind and scattered across the land . . .

Instinctively his eyes shifted toward the terrace where he had last seen Elaine Stark, her jade-green eyes flashing with anger. The lawn furniture was still there, smoke-blackened, but the umbrellas were gone. Broken glass from the French doors was strewn over the flagstones, and in the midst of it all lay the bodies of Hugh Stark, Drew Larkin and Jean Chardin.

Dismounting, O'Connor crossed the lawn. For a long time, he stared down at the three men from totally different worlds. Perspiration beaded his forehead.

Larkin must have been killed as he ran out of the house. A bullet had struck him between the eyes, knocking him back and over a wrought iron chair. His gun had skittered away from him.

Jean Chardin and Hugh Stark, still gripping a pistol, lay less than a yard apart. The half-breed had been shot through the lungs. Blood had gushed from his mouth, down his chin and over his chest. But he had lived long enough to use the razor-sharp hunting knife with ferocious dexterity. Even a Sioux, Cheyenne or Arapahoe, experts in the art, would have admired his skill, for it embodied the finer points of their tribes.

Hugh Stark had been scalped and his heart cut out while he was still alive. He had then been decapitated and his right arm severed.

The arm had not been moved. The head had rolled a couple of feet away from the body.

Jean Chardin held what was left of the partially eaten heart in his hand. The blood on his mouth, his chin . . .

"Ahhh!" Bending over, O'Connor vomited in great, heaving spasms.

When it passed, he mounted the bay and rode back to town. He had not bothered to search for Elaine Stark's body. She would not have run from any man. Whether she had died in the flames or had killed herself would remain a mystery.

O'Connor did not grieve over her death. He had not loved her; he realized that now. Just as he belatedly realized that she and Stark had used him as a pawn to bring about a Chippewa uprising. The thought that she had made a fool of him was intolerable.

Damn her! Damn her to hell and back!

By the time he reached Walker, he had already thrust her from his mind. But the memory of Hugh Stark lying there on the terrace, scalped, cut open, decapitated—and of Jean Chardin curled on his side gripping Stark's partially eaten heart in one hand—would not go away. If a half-breed could do that to a man as powerful as Hugh Stark, a full-blooded Chippewa could do it to a U.S. marshal.

With a coward's intuition, O'Connor knew that he could never again walk among the Chippewas with his old arrogance and get away with harassing them. Indians were like animals; they could smell fear in a man. They would smell it in him a mile away.

He was scared as hell.

Walker, Minn., October 7, 1898.

The steamer *Leila D.*, with a relief force of two county sheriffs and the Brainerd Gun Club, put out from the dock and laid a course across the lake for Sugar Point. The journey was anything but peaceful, what with the Brainerd "Indian fighters" getting high on red-eye whiskey and the *Chief*, towing a barge behind the steamer, running onto a rock.

Shortly after noon, the *Leila D.*, her gunwales barricaded with hay and with rifles lined on the clearing, hove to off Sugar Point, her bow to the shore.

"Hell and be damned!" a Brainerd man cried. "Look at them soldiers around Bog's house. The damned war's over and we never got to fire a shot!"

He was right.

The Pillagers had slipped away, leaving the Army holding an empty bag. The last Indian battle in which regular U. S. Army troops would ever be engaged was over.

Angrily, the Gun Club members started to swarm ashore.

"Stay where you are!" Sergeant Kelly shouted from the landing. "We'll be boarding soon and you'd only get in the way."

"To hell with you!" a man cried. "You can't tell civilians what to do!"

Kelly whipped up his pistol. "You open your mouth one more time and I'll blow your head off. Now get away from that rail."

That ended the matter.

Two hours later, General Bacon, Lieutenant Ross and Sergeant Kelly brought the detachment aboard the *Leila D.*, along with their dead and wounded. Dr. E. C. Lindley, Dr. Harris and Private Oscar Buckhard were among the last to leave Sugar Point. They looked tired and haggard; they had reason to. For two days, they had fought death on a bullet-lashed battlefield and in a crude field hospital.

Hoisting anchor, the *Leila D.*'s skipper rang for full speed ahead and pointed her bow toward Walker.

A half mile to the north, a trim sailing craft slipped out of a small cove and with Gail Saunders at the tiller and Craig Morgan handling the canvas quickly overhauled the *Leila D.* and then took position five hundred yards off her starboard beam.

"Well, what do you think?" Morgan ducked to avoid the swinging boom as she tacked to catch the wind.

A faint smile curved Gail Saunders' mouth. She understood perfectly well what he meant.

"I think it takes two to handle this boat," she said calmly. "And that, for a timber man, you're a very good sailor. But just remember"—her voice was rich with hidden laughter—"we carry no deckhands. Only captains of equal rank."

Morgan touched his forehead in mock salute.

"Nor shall either captain desert the ship during heavy seas."

Securing the boom, Morgan worked his way aft and sat down beside her. "We have a lot of storms along the Oregon coast," he said. "It's a good place to find out if your ship has a sound hull, and whether you're a good enough navigator to keep her off the rocks."

"Craig"—Gail laid her free hand over Morgan's—"I'm going back to Oregon with you for a visit. Perhaps I'm a better navigator than you think. If so, then perhaps I may stay."

Morgan searched her face with grave intentness. "I think I would like that," he said.

A freshening wind billowed the sail and sent the trim craft skimming across the lake. As it drew rapidly away from the *Leila D.*, Dr. E. C. Lindley, leaning on the railing, saw the two tiny figures in the cockpit merge, and a smile erased the deep lines from his face, making him look twenty years younger.

That was the way the "fleet" returned to Walker, with hundreds of people gathered at the dock, waving and cheering, and the soldiers grinning and waving back, but knowing in their hearts that they had not won the battle of Sugar Point. That, in fact, they were lucky to be alive.

Had Bog-o-nay-ge-shig been there, he would have agreed with them.

EPILOGUE

Walker, Minn., October 20, 1898.

After distributing a canoe load of hardtack, port, tea, coffee, sugar and other items, the Reverend Father Aloysuis, head of the Benedict Mission at White Earth, finally persuaded the Pillager chiefs and warriors to meet with the Commissioner of Indian Affairs the following day.

On October 20, at a council held on Bear Island, the Commissioner personally assured Bog-o-nay-ge-shig that neither Marshal O'Connor, "Colonel" Sheehan nor any of the deputy marshals who had given the Pillagers so much trouble would take charge of them. He further emphasized the fact that their list of grievances was now under hard federal scrutiny.

Satisfied with their victory at Sugar Point, and sensing that public opinion now favored their cause, those Chippewas for whom warrants were out surrendered. All save Bog-o-nay-ge-shig.

"I have taken the white man's oath that I will die before I go to the white man's jail," he said. "And I will keep that oath."

By the first week in November, the last of the troops were withdrawn and returned to their barracks at Fort Snelling.

The prisoners were taken to Duluth for trial. They were sentenced to from eight to ten months and fined one hundred dollars. The majority were released in thirty days with fines of twenty-five dollars, better fed and fatter than when they went in.

Although not all to their complete satisfaction, most of the Chippewas' grievances were adjusted. Injustices were righted as far as possible, and, after a thorough investigation, their logging money was set up under a new system.

Bog played it safe, remaining in the forest or on Bear Island all that winter. Finally, in late spring, he started turning up in the surrounding towns and villages. Since the whites had always liked him, and still had no quarrel with either him or the Chippewas, they left him alone.

His personal appearance was almost the same as before, except for a single change.

He now wore a new necklace—a double row of empty Krag-Jorgensen cartridges picked up in the clearing after the fight.

Max von Kreisler, who was born in 1913, lived most of his life in the state of Oklahoma. He began writing Western fiction for the magazine market in 1940, primarily for Popular Publications, using the name Max Kesler. These stories frequently were set in his native state, such as "There's War in the Cherokee Strip" in *Ace-High Western Stories* (11/41) or "Beware the Bloody Strip" in *New Western* (10/50). Oil exploitation was also a familiar theme as in "Three for the Wildcatter War" in .44 Western (10/47) or "Blood, Oil, and Bullets" in *New Western* (4/50). Later he turned to writing Western novels, beginning with *Donovan* (Zebra Books, 1975), published under the name Max Kreisler. His last novels were hardcover editions published under his full name Max von Kreisler: *Stand In The Sun* (Doubleday, 1978) and *The Pillagers* (Doubleday, 1982). The latter appeared the same year he died in Payson, Arizona. Von Kreisler was always proud of the fact that his stories and novels avoided violence and bigger-than-life characters, and in his words "concentrated more on the everyday people who gave substance and lasting character to the changing frontier both before and after the era of the trail drives."